THE BIGGEST FEMALE
IN THE WORLD

AND OTHER STORIES

THE BIGGEST FEMALE
IN THE WORLD

AND OTHER STORIES

Wendy Perriam

ROBERT HALE · LONDON

© Wendy Perriam 2007
First published in Great Britain 2007

ISBN 978-0-7090-8377-1

Robert Hale Limited
Clerkenwell House
Clerkenwell Green
London EC1R 0HT

2 4 6 8 10 9 7 5 3 1

Table for Two Words and Music © Jack Lawrence and Arthur Altman
Leeds Music 1940

Every effort has been made to contact the copyright holder but without
success. Any interested parties should contact the Publishers.

Typeset in 10/13½ pt New Century Schoolbook
Printed in Great Britain by
Biddles Limited, King's Lynn, Norfolk

For Deborah Moggach—

whose house is a paradise
and whose heart is pure gold.

Contents

Chloe

'Chloe! Your lady's here.'

Chloe, Evelyn thought? She had never heard of a Chloe. And no one had appeared in answer to Jan's shout. Jan herself was doing a trim for a raddled-looking woman with a bandage on her leg, while sturdy, solid Kathleen had just donned her rubber gloves to apply a client's colour-tint.

'Chloe!' Another yell from Jan. 'Step on it! You're needed.'

Evelyn looked up nervously as a voluptuous girl with a cascade of bleached blonde hair sauntered out from the room at the back, her jaws moving indolently as she chewed a piece of gum. She was dressed as for a party, in a low-necked glittery top that showed half her ample breasts and left a gap of naked flesh between its sequinned hem and the top of her white jeans. The jeans themselves were skin-tight, and worn with shoes so high and spindly they surely constituted a risk to life and limb.

'Hi!' she pouted, teetering over and, with no sign of embarrassment, transferring the gum from her glossy, full-lipped mouth to the back pocket of her jeans. 'Are you the perm?'

'No,' said Evelyn. 'Just a shampoo and set.' No way could she afford a perm, even at the cut-price rates they offered for the over-65s. A pity, she'd been thinking since her birthday last July, there wasn't a still cheaper rate for the over-85s.

'Mrs Andrews, isn't it?'

No, Miss Bellingham, she stopped herself from saying, suddenly experiencing a tiny twinge of doubt. *Could* she be Mrs Andrews, booked in for a perm? No, the thought was quite absurd. She hadn't

9

lost her wits. In fact, just this morning she had finished an extremely challenging book on the concept of atonement in Coleridge's early poetry, before completing *The Times* crossword – the latter in record time. At her age, it was vital to keep her brain alert. The slightest sign of confusion and she might be whisked off to a care-home and stuck in the dementia wing. Thus, to circumvent such horrors, she had embarked on a formal programme of reading and memory-training.

'Right, let me take your coat.'

She unbuttoned it with some reluctance. It was freezing outside, and none too warm in here. Though the salon did look cheery with the Christmas decorations still in place: blue and silver streamers looped across the mirrors, and matching ribbons and rosettes tied on all the cupboard doors. She had deliberately made her appointment for this first week in January. Not only was the salon far less crowded than in the pre-Christmas rush, but she wouldn't be expected to leave a lavish tip or buy an expensive present for the stylist. Some clients went to inordinate lengths, lugging in great bottles of champagne, or five-pound boxes of chocolates, complete with fancy bows. But she simply couldn't run to such extravagance and, anyway, was it really wise to encourage greed in these young girls?

As Chloe stepped towards her with the gown, Evelyn noticed the girl's ear-rings: large gold hoops, with the name 'Chloe' spelled out in gold italic letters, dangling from a bar across each hoop. Hardly very practical wear for a hairdresser, but striking none the less.

'What you starin' at?'

'Oh, I do apologize. I didn't mean to stare. It's just your ear-rings....'

'Yeah, smashin', aren't they? A present from my boyfriend. Right, take a seat at the basin.'

Evelyn was still struggling with the gown, which didn't seem to fasten and had a strange brownish stain down the front. But no point in complaining when she was paying the cut rate.

'The ordinary shampoo?'

'Yes, please.' She had learned long ago not to ask for extras. It could mean a substantial addition to the bill, just for a dab of something that came in a luxurious bottle, with an ostentatious name, but was still basically detergent. She eased herself into the chair –

an extraordinary contraption with a rigid metal frame, made with no concern whatever for comfort or old bones.

'Could you put your head back, please. I can't get at you like that.'

Evelyn did her best to oblige, though her stiff arthritic neck permitted little movement. She hoped Chloe might say more about the ear-rings, or even about the boyfriend. After ten days on her own, she felt starved of conversation. She had even planned an answer if Jan or Kathleen were to enquire about her Christmas. 'Yes, very quiet, but I prefer it that way.' Best to give the impression that she'd turned down invitations by the score, rather than been stuck indoors alone. 'You're new here, aren't you?' she asked, deciding to make the overtures herself.

'Yeah.'

'And where were you working before?'

Chloe shrugged. 'I wasn't.'

Well, they weren't exactly getting very far. Perhaps she'd try a different tack. 'Did you have a lovely time on New Year's— Goodness *gracious!*' she broke off, jumping in alarm. 'The water's frightfully hot.'

'Why didn't you say?'

'I am saying.'

'Is it OK now?'

'Not really. It feels as if it's burning my scalp.'

Another shrug. 'There's probably somethin' wrong with the mixer-tap.'

'I see.' Evelyn gritted her teeth and put up with it – and also with the stream of water now trickling down her neck, seeping under her blouse and wetting half her back. Perhaps Chloe was so new, she hadn't mastered the art of shampooing. And it *was* an art – no doubt about that. Kathleen did it beautifully – *and* she was kind, *and* chatty – but she'd recently been promoted, so she no longer did the pensioners' hair. And Jan cost almost double, because she owned the salon; had set it up ten years ago, after her divorce.

Her head was hurting from Chloe's assault. The girl was even using her nails: long, lethal, scarlet talons digging into her scalp. Still, she was extremely lucky to have her hair shampooed at all. Doing it herself, at home, was now well nigh impossible.

'Conditioner?' Chloe asked, pausing for a moment in the drub-bing.

'No, thank you.'

'Your hair could do with it. It's very dry, you know.'

'No, I prefer it without.'

'Please yourself.'

As if in punishment, the ferocity continued, although now the water was freezing cold rather than scalding hot. Evelyn hoped she wouldn't go down with pneumonia, as she'd done this time last year. Already, her blouse was soaking wet, along with her so-called Chilprufe vest.

At last, the ordeal was over. Chloe wrapped her head in a towel and escorted her to another chair, equally uncomfortable. Evelyn kept her gaze on the blue and silver streamers, to avoid having to face her reflection in the mirror. The age-spots on her skin were definitely getting worse, so best simply to ignore them. Nor did she wish to be confronted, when Chloe removed the towel, with the drab colour of her hair: a dirty cinder-grey, yellowing at the ends, as if stained with nicotine. Kathleen had once suggested a special salon treatment to transform it into lustrous white, but the price was astronomical.

'What style did you have in mind, Mrs Andrews?'

Miss Bellingham, she corrected silently, still harbouring a prickle of doubt. One of the books on her reading programme was a scientific study of the brain. Apparently, delusion was frighten-ingly common, especially in the elderly, and even a conviction about one's sanity could actually be an illusion in itself. Yet if she were truly Mrs Andrews, she must have been married at some point, and she was hardly likely to have forgotten her own wedding. She allowed herself to fantasize a moment, picturing the distinguished priest, robed in white and gold, the thunder of the organ as she sauntered down the aisle towards her bridegroom. 'I *will*', she heard him say, her mind tingling at the prospect of someone committing to her utterly – loving and protecting her, as long as they both should live. What devotion it would prove, what total trust, total dedication – qualities so magical they surely belonged in the realm of dream.

'Did you hear me, Mrs Andrews? I asked what style you want.'

'Oh, I'm sorry.' Evelyn forced herself out of the church, still hearing that miraculous 'I will'. 'Well, Kathleen always said that looser curls looked better on me than those little sausagey ones.'

'Yes, but that means using bigger rollers and, frankly, your hair's too sparse to take them.'

'Sparse' was blunt (and hurtful), although true, in fact, not only of her hair but of her present way of life. 'Whatever you think best,' she said, having long since learned that submission prevented discord. She winced in anticipation as Chloe picked up a large, sharp-toothed comb, more suitable for a shaggy-coated dog. 'So where did your boyfriend get them?' she asked.

'Get what?'

'Your ear-rings.'

'Oh, I see. He had them made special. You can order any name you want. It costs, though. These are real eighteen-carat gold.'

Evelyn studied them with increased respect, her eyes lingering on the fancy italic letters. Such a poetic name, and so rich in connotations! She remembered studying *Daphnis and Chloe* long, long ago, at Cambridge, and thrilling to the story of the goatherd and the shepherdess falling ecstatically in love. As far as she could recall, Chloe had been barely more than a child – younger even than *this* Chloe, who looked about seventeen, although her dress and her demeanour made her seem much older and extremely worldly-wise. When *she* was seventeen, she had been a shrinking violet: bashful, tongue-tied and distinctly apprehensive in the company of men. Even after Cambridge, and right on through her years and years of working for the Civil Service, sex for her had remained safely within the confines of Art. Books, paintings, opera, ballet, could all express her own deep longing for passion and romance, without the risks of real entanglements. And, according to her mother, those risks were truly frightening: pregnancy, dishonour, making oneself cheap. Yet now, at eighty-five, some small and secret part of her wished she *hadn't* been so strict and chaste, so dutifully subservient.

'I'll use these smaller rollers, OK?'

'Yes, fine.' Evelyn flinched as a strand of her hair was tugged out at an angle from the scalp and wound tightly round a bristly purple contraption. Daphnis's Chloe would have had long, flowing, golden tresses, crowned with a circlet of wild flowers. Even after all these decades, she remembered much of the tale – one part in particular, when, on a sweltering summer's day, a grasshopper, fleeing from a hungry bird, found sanctuary in Chloe's bosom, hopping down between her breasts, and chirping in relief from this strange but sensuous haven. Daphnis, also hungry, though for passion rather than food, could not forbear to reach down his hand and pluck the creature out.

When she'd read that passage in her tutor's panelled room, she had experienced the sensations in her *own* breast: the tickle of the insect's legs and wings, followed by the pressure of Daphnis's warm, deft fingers, lingering on her skin. And she had felt the heat of summer kindling her whole body, as if she herself were Chloe, burning with desire. 'Who chose your name?' she asked, a shaming flush seeping into her cheeks once more, from the memory alone.

'Pardon?'

'Your name – Chloe. Did it have some special meaning for your mother or ...?'

'No idea. All I know is it's bloody murder to spell! I sometimes wish I was just plain Jane or Jill.'

'But Chloe's a beautiful name. It comes from a Greek word meaning "green shoot", so it's associated with youth and spring. And it's immortalized in a wonderful Greek romance called *Daphnis and—*'

'Look, could you keep still, Mrs Andrews. You keep movin' your head around.'

'I'm sorry.' That must be the third time she'd apologized. Her mind still on the poem, she began thinking about *another* wedding: that of Daphnis and Chloe themselves. It had taken place outdoors, as befitted a pastoral tale, under arbours of green boughs and clusters of ripe purple grapes. All the villagers assembled on that perfect autumn day, along with nymphs and shepherds, to join in the celebrations: singing, dancing, feasting, until the sun itself grew sated and was replaced by moon and stars. Even the goats were awarded special rations, fed to them by Daphnis's own fair hand.

'And on their wedding night,' the poet added in the closing lines, 'the two lovers slept as little as owls.' That phrase had always struck her as exquisitely erotic: so little said; so much suggested. Did *this* Chloe 'sleep as little as an owl' when spending the night with her boyfriend? And had he ever plucked a grasshopper from her all too prominent bosom?

She examined the girl in the mirror, riveted by the expanse of naked flesh – pale creamy flesh, repeated further down around her midriff. Her navel was on public display and, still more remarkable, pierced with a tiny gold ring. Another present from the boyfriend, perhaps. She tried to picture herself with a ring in her navel, but the imaginative leap was too great. When *she* was young, clothes had been designed for modesty and warmth – the exact opposite of present trends. She had actually developed very early, much to her embarrassment, but far from flaunting her pubescent breasts, she had done her best to disguise them. Borrowing her younger sister's liberty bodice, she had buttoned it as tightly as she could, hoping to flatten her new shameful curves. A strange name, 'liberty', for something that constricted.

'Are you going out tonight?'

'Er, no,' said Evelyn, roused from her reflections.

'I was asking Debra, actually.'

'Oh, I'm sorry.' Apology number four. She turned her head to look at Debra, who had just appeared from the private room at the back: another shapely little madam, her pouting lips emphasized by peculiar blackish lipstick.

'Yeah, we're goin' clubbin'.'

'*We*? You mean, with Gary?'

'Yeah. And you?'

As the girls continued to discuss the evening's pleasures, Evelyn studied Chloe with increasing fascination. Her jeans were so low-slung, she must be wearing the very briefest of pants – the sort of thing one saw in all the shops now, which contained less fabric than a handkerchief. In her mind, she garbed Chloe in the capacious bloomers *she* had worn at that age: elasticated drawers that came right up over the waist and down almost to the knees. She couldn't recall a time in her girlhood when she hadn't been swathed in layers of restricting undergarments, including prickly petticoats that rustled as she moved. Even today, in addition to the Chilprufe vest, she was wearing interlock knickers, a panty-girdle attached to thick lisle stockings and a full-length thermal under-slip.

Chloe fastened the last roller with a pin, then covered her head in a garish purple hairnet. 'Right, that's *you* done. Come over to the drier, will you?'

As Evelyn tried to manoeuvre herself into a third uncomfortable chair, while inserting her head into the deep hood of the drier, she wished she were made of India rubber instead of stiff arthritic bone.

'I'll put it on "high", to start. Just give me a shout if you want it turned down, OK?'

She nodded, tensing herself in readiness for the roaring in her ears, the blast of hot air, the feeling of confinement.

'Cup o' tea?'

'No thank you.' The tea cost £1.50, and that wasn't for a proper pot, but just a doll-sized cup. Though it *did* come with a chocolate biscuit, wrapped in scarlet foil – a cut above the plain digestives she allowed herself at home. If she cancelled her standing order to UNICEF's Emergency Fund (which siphoned off her entire Civil Service pension), there would be money enough for a *ton* of chocolate biscuits. But she couldn't live with such a mean, uncaring self. Compared with those poor souls – starving children, earthquake victims, lepers, orphans, amputees – her life was one long luxury.

'Want a book to read?' Chloe mouthed, stooping down to Evelyn's level and putting her face up close.

'No, thank you,' she repeated. Here, 'books' meant magazines, mostly tatty and always meretricious. She should have brought her Coleridge, but it was impossible to concentrate with all the distractions of the salon. Besides, Samuel Taylor might strongly disapprove of these frivolous surroundings. The wall opposite was enough to make him blush: posters of pouting models displaying not just their hairstyles, but much of their anatomy as well. One little minx was naked from the waist up, save for a black leather jacket, blatantly unbuttoned, which she was trying (vainly) to pull across her bosom. Another had bare shoulders and was gazing up suggestively at a tall, foreign-looking man, who also appeared to be unclothed, though his lower half was conveniently lost in shadow. She kept looking at that shadow, wondering what it hid, ashamed of her own innocence, yet somehow still alarmed.

Everything around her only served to emphasize how little she had lived herself. Even the magazines, as she knew from past experience, would be full of yet more pictures of scantily clad girls, and contain extraordinarily detailed articles on sexual techniques that left her literally shaking with envy, amazement and disgust. Yet too easy to blame the modern world. When *Daphnis and Chloe* was written, way back in the second century, the two lovers had seemed inordinately keen to experience fleshly delights. Admittedly they were naïve in the extreme, ignorant of the mechanics of actually making love, but that hadn't stopped them trying. In fact, as far as she could recall, they had been kissing and embracing more or less continuously throughout the tingling, budding spring and on into sultry, shameless summer. *Her* season had been perpetual winter: cold, closed, bleak and barren.

'Hi there, Miss Bellingham! Haven't seen you for a while.'

Evelyn smiled in recognition, not only pleased that Kathleen still remembered her, but glad to have her surname officially confirmed.

'How was your Christmas?' Kathleen shouted above the noise of the drier.

'Very quiet, but I prefer it that—' The words died on her lips. Kathleen had already turned away. Well, the girls were exceptionally busy and couldn't be expected to find time to stop and chat. A pity, though, she hadn't asked for the drier to be turned down. It really was unbearably hot, and her ears in particular felt as if they were burning. She glanced around the salon, wondering whom she could call for help. There was no sign of Chloe or Debra, and she wouldn't dream of disturbing Jan on such a minor matter. Never mind. If she viewed it in a positive light, the higher the heat, the quicker her hair would dry.

She sat imprisoned in her own small world, the voices in the salon silenced by the self-important salvo of the drier. With that huge metal dome extending from her head, she must resemble some ageing spacewoman, about to lift off with a thunderous zoom. To distract herself from the noise, she started counting the hair-products shelved beyond the dryers: twelve shelves in all, each crammed with tubes and bottles. Could any woman really need such an array of voluminizers, protein rinses, colour enhancers, glossers, masques, defrizzers? In *her* day, it had been basic shampoo, with perhaps a little lemon juice or vinegar added to the final rinse, for blondes and brunettes respectively. Yet these products seemed to symbolize once more the very narrowness of her existence. Work apart, her entire life had lacked body, colour, gloss and shine, remaining dry and parched and meagre through each successive decade.

When Chloe came to release her from the drier, the girl seemed still more radiant in comparison; her hair shiny-thick, her lips plumped up, her whole body full of health and verve and zest. And, as she set to work removing all the rollers, her ear-rings jounced and jangled, as if they too were vibrantly alive. Evelyn tried to picture her lying naked in the boyfriend's flat, although again her imagination proved unequal to the task, until she added scenes from *Daphnis and Chloe* to help fill in the gaps. The resultant images were admittedly confusing: pirates, nymphs and grazing goats cavorting on a modern double bed.

'Right, that's the comb-out finished. D'you want a bit o' lacquer?'

'No thank you,' Evelyn murmured, the sound of Pan-pipes fading, along with the creaking of the bedsprings.

Chloe went to fetch the hand-mirror and stood holding it up, so that Evelyn could see the back view. 'Well, do you like it?' she asked, a touch of impatience in her voice, as if she had lost interest in her handiwork already.

Evelyn bit her lip. No, she *didn't* like it. As she'd feared, the curls were far too tight. Kathleen had always achieved a softer, more attractive style, not this crimped and formal look. But at her age, did it matter? There was no one to see her anyway, except the milkman and the paperboy. 'Very nice,' she said.

Chloe helped her out of the gown, suddenly more solicitous – in the hope of a tip, no doubt. Evelyn gave her a large one – far more than she could properly afford – but the girl was young, with the whole of her life ahead of her, and probably badly paid. She would learn in time to be less brusque, more gentle with the elderly.

As she stepped out of the salon and trudged towards the bus stop, it started pelting down with rain. The furious, spiteful downpour seemed to be taking vengeance on roofs, cars, pavements and hapless pedestrians alike, slamming against car windows, cascading along the gutters, turning flimsy umbrellas inside out. She scuttled into the covered shopping precinct, grateful for some shelter, and wandering idly from store to store, in an effort to kill time. However much she disliked her hair-do, she didn't want to reduce it to a mass of sopping rats' tails.

Ambling past the café, her attention was attracted by the jeweller's shop just opposite, and she paused a moment to look in at the window-display: ear-rings, pendants, bracelets, rings, arranged tastefully between slender silvered twigs. Then she meandered on again, only to stop dead, suddenly double back and steal into the shop.

'Do you make ear-rings to order?' she asked the man behind the counter: a wiry little fellow, with thinning sandy hair.

'We can do, madam, yes. It depends on what you want.'

'Well, I was thinking of a pair of hoops in eighteen-carat gold.'

'We have plenty of hoops in stock, madam. Would you like me to show you a few?'

'No, I want something very particular.' Gesturing emphatically, she described the small gold bar across each hoop, the gold italic letters dangling from those bars.

'That shouldn't be a problem, madam. Though, as you say, they'll have to be made to order, which means we're looking at a price of at least nine hundred pounds.'

Her mouth dropped open. 'Nine *hundred*?' she repeated, tempted to bolt straight out of the shop.

'Yes, madam. Maybe more.'

She remained rooted to the spot, torn between unselfishness and longing. Over the years, she had given literally thousands to the UNICEF Emergency Fund. Would it really hurt to cancel the standing order, just for a short while?

Yes, it would. More children would die of malnutrition, or be mutilated by landmines, suffer drought and famine, fail to reach their natural—

'And they'll take a good six weeks to make.'

Was the salesman trying to put her off, refusing to take her seriously, refusing to believe that such a shabby, undistinguished-looking spinster could actually raise the money, or even *last* another six weeks, without collapsing in a heap of skin and bone? In fact, she would need that long, just to make up her mind, let alone rearrange her finances.

'Would you like to reconsider?' The man was clearly puzzled by her silence.

Silence not for her. There was a roaring in her ears, as if she were still sitting under the drier, the dials turned up dangerously high. Still saying, doing nothing, she continued to wrestle with herself.

'I'm sorry, madam, I don't quite understand. Do you want to go ahead, or not?'

She glanced around the shop, relieved that it was empty. No one else must hear this statement of betrayal: betrayal of her principles, betrayal of the vital work UNICEF was doing. 'Yes,' she whispered. 'I do.'

'Right, I'll need to take some details. Please take a seat, while I fetch the order pad.'

A *normal* chair, with arms, and a nicely padded seat. Guiltily she sank into it, trying to avoid the heaving throng of amputees and lepers, starving babies, victims of child rape, now pouring into the shop, stretching out their arms to her in silent supplication, each more desperate, needy, ravaged than the last.

The man returned with his order pad, and half-a-dozen pairs of ear-rings, arranged on a blue velvet cushion. 'I've brought some basic hoops for you to look at, so that you can let me know what size you want. And whether you'd prefer them in plain gold, or with a slight patterning, like this.'

All at once, an extraordinary sense of elation began bubbling in her chest – so strong and overwhelming, it suppressed her guilt and shame; even drove the hordes of victims clean out of the shop. Trying to seem businesslike, she scrutinized the hoops, although there was no doubt about her choice. She had to have the ear-rings closest in size and style to Chloe's. 'This large pair, please,' she said, 'but with a bar across each hoop, and the name spelled out in letters hanging from the bar.'

'And what name would that be, madam?'

The tingly, bubbly feeling was spreading through her body, electrifying her bloodstream, enlivening every cell. She didn't hesitate. '*Chloe*,' she breathed, closing her eyes a moment, so she could concentrate on Daphnis: the rugged, foreign-looking man from the poster in the hair-salon. Both he and she were naked; his deft, bewitching fingers sliding up across her breasts, up further to her earlobes, as he fastened the gold ear-rings: his token of undying love, his precious wedding gift.

His voice was trembling with emotion, his breath warm and deliriously thrilling in her ear, and every shepherd, nymph and goatherd from every pastoral romance began showering down confetti, as he whispered that incredible 'I *will*'.

Table For Two

'Table for two, madam?'

'Er, no,' she murmured, shrinking from the *maitre d'*, an overbearing figure, who had fixed her with his cold grey eye. 'For... one.' Was that *pity* on his face – pity, with a trace of contempt – or was she just imagining it? She rushed to justify herself. 'It *was* for two. I mean, we booked for two a week ago. Name of Spencer-Scott. But my friend ...' Ditched me, she refrained from saying; broke off the relationship three days before this anniversary dinner. 'He, er, couldn't make it in the end. Something came up at his work, you see, and ...' She was babbling now, not making any sense. Why should he be working on a Saturday night?

The man consulted the list of bookings, glancing up impatiently. 'But, madam, that table was booked for seven-thirty, and it's now almost ten to nine.'

'Yes, I'm sorry.' She should have rung and cancelled, but for the last three days she'd been in a state of near-paralysis, lying on the sofa, staring at the wall. And, of course, she'd never had the slightest intention of coming on her own. The very thought was repellent. But just half an hour ago, she'd suddenly leapt up from the couch, changed her clothes, grabbed her coat, and come rushing out to Anatole's, in the desperate but ridiculous hope that he might be here, after all. Yet a glance around the restaurant showed every table occupied by a couple or a cheery group. Dining as a single was social suicide, especially on a Saturday, and in a ritzy joint like this.

'And I'm afraid it's taken now, madam. We held it for an hour, but ...' He completed the sentence with a dismissive shrug.

He hoped she'd leave – that was clear enough – but she'd be damned if she'd creep out, now she had made the effort to get up and get dressed. Why *shouldn't* she have a decent meal, instead of dining on regrets and tears? Anyway, Neville might still come. Her email had been playing up, so he could have left her a message that simply hadn't come through, telling her he'd changed his mind and would join her rather later than arranged. 'Isn't there another table?'

The *maitre d'* perused the list again, raising just one eyebrow: another wordless gesture calculated to reduce her to a pulp. Then, reluctantly, he led her to a table – the worst table in the place, of course, stuck in a dark corner, and close to the swing doors, where a bevy of mostly foreign waiters were dashing in and out.

The table was laid for two, thank God. With any luck, the other diners would assume she was waiting for someone – as, actually, she *was*. Neville might be on his way by now; even feeling remorse. She tried to assume an expression of calm expectancy, but at that very moment, a tall, snooty-looking waiter glided over and started clearing away the second set of cutlery and glasses. The action seemed to dash her hopes, as if fate were saying, 'Who d'you think you're kidding? Of course he won't turn up.' But it was too late to make an exit. She'd die of shame if she had to face that *maitre d'* again and tell him she wasn't dining after all. Yet her humiliation was now on public view – everyone aware that she was abandoned and alone. Indeed, the couple at the adjoining table were already glancing her way. She met the woman's eyes – a raddled blonde with a plunging neckline, exposing too much freckled flesh, sitting opposite an attractive guy who seemed too young for her. They were clearly celebrating. A bottle of champagne stood cooling in an ice bucket, and the woman was flamboyantly dressed in a flounced silk frock, with flashy ear-rings, diamond rings and an ostentatious orchid spray pinned to her *décolleté*. As she watched, the man groped his hand across the table and began stroking the ringed fingers, lovingly and sensuously.

Lizzie looked away. The waiter was still bustling around, fetching her the menu and the wine-list, lighting the small scarlet candle that stood beside a silver vase containing one red rose. Both rose and candle seemed totally inappropriate to her present jilted state, as did the presence of a pianist, dressed in full-fig tie and tails, trilling out romantic tunes from a heart-shaped white piano in the corner.

'Can I get you a drink, madam?' the waiter asked, with an obsequious bow. At least he was polite, not treating her as a loser or pariah. The trouble was, she didn't drink – well, rarely more than half a glass of wine. And it was always *Neville* who chose the wine and drank the rest of the bottle. He was something of a wine buff, who liked to indulge in long discussions about vintages and regions before making any decision, whereas for her the stuff was simply red or white. 'I'll just have some wine with my meal, if that's all right.'

'Of course, madam. Would you like to order now?'

'Er, I'm not quite ready yet.' Why did everything she say sound so apologetic? She had every right to be here. Didn't she?

'I'll be back in just a moment,' he said, unfolding her damask napkin with a flourish, and laying it on her lap.

'Fine.' Nervously she opened the menu, which, with its leather cover and old-fashioned italic script, looked as self-important as a Bible. Not only was it cumbersome to hold, but all the dishes seemed extremely rich and complicated, when her stomach yearned for simple comfort food. And the prices were exorbitant. How on earth could she afford it, without taking out a loan?

She studied the list of starters, each more pricey and elaborate than the last: escargot and wild mushroom pie; oysters grilled with ginger chilli and coriander; carpaccio of sea bream, with crab fritters and red onion marmalade. What in God's name was carpaccio? Not that she could touch it. The very thought of crab or oysters, let alone escargots, brought a surge of nausea rising to her throat. And the main courses sounded equally florid, if not downright gimmicky: parmesan-crusted veal on sesame spinach, with roasted garlic gnocchi; pan-fried fillet of black dorade, with char-grilled fennel, saffron tagliatelle and roast red pepper salsa. What she really fancied was a soft-boiled egg with Marmite 'soldiers', or a bowlful of her mother's chicken soup. She closed her eyes a moment, to see her mother in the kitchen, chopping onions for the soup. She could hear her soft, consoling voice, murmuring as she worked, 'There, there, little Lizzie, everything will be all right.' The picture paled and faded. Her mother was just ashes now – ashes and a rosebush in Mortlake crematorium.

She glanced at the couple beside her, to see what *they* were eating. It was difficult to tell because the food was exuberantly garnished with sauces, salsas, coulis and even fruits and flowers, which concealed any meat or fish or fowl lurking underneath. Besides, the pair of them were gazing into each other's eyes, clearly more concerned with billing and cooing than with what was on their plates. Odd, she mused, that Neville never looked at her like that. In fact, he always seemed embarrassed by any sort of eye contact, and certainly wouldn't feast on her face, as this man was devotedly doing. Yet the guy's partner was not only older than him but distinctly less good-looking. The blonde hair was demonstrably false, and the freckles were so numerous, they could be regarded as a blemish, rather than simply cute. So what on earth was her secret? Claiming a man's complete attention was definitely an art – one she'd failed to master herself, despite the fact she wasn't unattractive: slim (though it took effort), with greenish eyes, decent teeth and a reasonable complexion. And she was much younger than Neville, not older. None the less, he had thrown her over, discarded her like a broken shoe.

She dragged her attention back to the menu, concentrating more now on the prices than the food. Even if she picked out all the cheapest items, she'd still be forced to work overtime in order to meet her other bills. Though, with Neville gone, at least she'd have more time for her job, which had been sorely neglected of late.

She decided on the poussin, not only because it cost the least, but because it didn't come with a whole raft of embellishments. And salad to start, though, of course, it wasn't billed as salad, but as 'a medley of lime-dressed Kentish lettuce, radicchio and dande-lion leaves.' The price was daylight robbery, especially as dandelions were free for the picking in any patch of waste ground. As a child, she had gathered them by the armful for her rabbits and her guinea pigs. And as for Kentish lettuce, was it really any different from any other sort of lettuce? And even radicchio was now distinctly *passé* – according to Neville, anyway.

Still, at least she'd made a decision, not that anyone seemed interested in actually taking her order. Waiters were bustling to and fro, in and out of the swing doors – she could feel the draught on her back as the doors opened and shut, opened and shut – but there was no sign at all of *her* waiter. Perhaps he'd gone off shift, forgotten all about her. She should have brought a book or, better still, her knitting. She might have finished Neville's sweater – though, of course, now he'd never see it. *Why* had he ended the relationship, she asked herself for the thousandth time, when they'd been together a whole year? All he'd offered as an explanation was the enigmatic statement that it was 'time for him to move on'. She suspected that she bored him, or was too passive and submissive, but then it wasn't easy with Neville to take a more dominant role. He liked to be in charge, to dictate all the moves.

There was a sudden plangent cadence from the pianist, as he finished playing 'A Fine Romance', before launching into 'Some Enchanted Evening'. Every love song seemed bitterly ironical to someone who'd been dumped; their very titles a mockery. Yet she felt a certain bond with the fellow – a youngish, fairish, plumpish guy, who seemed, like her, essentially alone. No one was paying him the slightest attention, as he sat marooned in his corner, pouring a veritable flood of emotion into the music, while people chattered heedlessly above it.

Her waiter had not yet reappeared, and she was becoming even more self-conscious, envying the amorous couple, whose every action only served to emphasize her plight. The man was feeding his partner, spearing tasty little morsels on to his fork and sliding them between her lips. Neville wouldn't do that in a million years. He didn't believe in sharing food – although he was always more than willing to finish hers, if he assumed she'd had enough. It had never actually struck her before, but now she came to think about it, wasn't he a trifle mean? On the few occasions he'd taken her out to dinner, he somehow seemed to order himself the most luxurious dishes, whilst talking her into humbler fare – always for her good, of course. The first time they'd been out together, to a restaurant in the City, he had opted for a huge, sizzling T-bone steak, and sat devouring it in front of her, bite by juicy bite, while *she* was eating quiche. In fact, she had wanted steak herself, but he'd said T-bones were a 'male thing' and she'd be better off with something less substantial and easier to digest. And he never asked her if she'd like a pudding, although he knew she had a sweet tooth. The special for that particular day had been pear and almond tart, which she'd been eyeing with some interest, but when he called the waitress over, it was 'Coffee and the bill, please', not 'How about dessert?'

Yet with his high-powered job in banking, he certainly wasn't short of money. And she was punctilious about paying him back – in kind, if not in cash; cooking all his favourite foods in her cramped and stuffy kitchen, then taking them round to his airy mansion-flat.

On impulse, she waved her hand at a passing waiter. 'I'm sorry, but could you take my order, please? I've been waiting for some time.' She flushed at her temerity, but it had the desired effect – within seconds her own waiter appeared, order-pad at the ready

'So what would madam like?'

'Er, the poussin. No – wait a minute ...' The blush deepened, seemed to spread, even to her toes. It was as if Neville were actually standing there, daring her to challenge him. 'Do you have, er, T-bone steak?' she asked, her voice shaky as she spoke.

'I'm afraid not, madam. But I do recommend the entrecôte. It's one of our signature dishes, served with Béarnaise sauce, wild mushroom duxelles and grilled asparagus spears.'

He was pointing to the item on the menu, but she saw only the price – flagrant, unbelievable. Was she out of her mind? She could buy a pair of shoes for that. Yet her nausea had now completely vanished and she actually felt ravenous.

'You'll find it exceptionally tender, madam, with a most distinctive flavour. All our beef is certified organic, and comes from a small private herd in Gloucestershire that has won dozens of awards. In fact, I think I can safely say it's the finest meat in the country.'

In that case, bugger the price! The finest meat in the country was *bound* to be expensive. 'Yes, I'll have it, please. And the pâté de foie to start with.' The foie gras cost almost twice as much as boring Kentish dandelions; more even than the oysters, but suddenly she didn't care.

'Certainly, madam,' the waiter purred, already looking at her with new respect. Money *bought* respect – as Neville knew, of course. 'How would you like the steak cooked?'

'Medium rare.'

'And have you chosen your wine?'

She panicked for a moment, now completely out of her depth. He handed her the wine list, which only confused her further. There appeared to be no half bottles, nor even wines by the glass. And she dared not *ask* for just a glass, for fear of looking cheap. If she was taking up a table for two, she had to make it worth their while to have her there at all. In any case, it was only Neville who had encouraged her to eat and drink so sparingly, for fear she might get fat. Well – that was what he said, but it could be for a different reason: it left more for *him* to guzzle. Again her eyes strayed to the adjoining table and the bottle of champagne. Only the best was good enough for that adored and pampered woman. They were now toasting each other, clinking glasses, entwining little fingers.

'Er, what would you suggest?' she asked the waiter.

'Well, the *Chevalier de Lascombes* is seriously good, madam – a ripe, rich, plummy wine, with real finesse.'

She fought an urge to giggle. He sounded just like Neville, who claimed to identify all sorts of tastes in wine: not just plums, but cherries, raspberries, redcurrants, even irises, for heaven's sake, and violets.

'And you'll find it an excellent partner to the steak.'

If even steak had a partner, that made her own predicament all the more reprehensible. She sat dithering a moment more. Any wine this waiter recommended was bound to be the priciest, maybe even the equivalent of half her weekly rent. But she longed to indulge herself, for once – in fact, go completely wild. Did Neville really have the right to lay down what she could eat or drink; dictate her shape and size? 'Thank you. It sounds perfect.'

'Shall I bring it straight away?'

'Yes, please.' While she waited, she continued watching the couple, who were fortunately so absorbed in one another, they seemed oblivious of her scrutiny. Had they just got engaged, she wondered, or was this some adulterous affair? The man put down his glass, kissed his palm, closed his fingers round the kiss, then transferred it to the woman's hand. How enchanting, how demonstrative! Neville would never dream of doing such a thing, let alone in public. She had always tried to understand his emotional detachment – in fact, blamed it on his public school: a strict, no-nonsense establishment, bound to leave its pupils repressed, if not deeply scarred. Her attempts to bring him out even appeared to be succeeding, at least in minor matters – until this week's body blow.

The waiter was back in minutes, carrying an impressive-looking bottle, with a picture of a château on the label, surmounted by a swanky coat of arms. He poured the wine for her to taste. She knew the protocol. She must roll it round her mouth, frown in concentration for a moment, then pronounce it drinkable. 'Yes, fine,' she said, feigning Neville's air of expertise, which seemed to convince the waiter, who now filled her glass with a deferential bow. She sat up straighter, refusing to slump hunched-shouldered any longer, as if she were only here on sufferance. If she couldn't celebrate her and Neville's first-year anniversary, she'd celebrate her birthday instead. It had actually been a fortnight ago, and Neville had forgotten it. Not that she could blame him, when he'd been going through such a hectic time at work. 'To *me*,' she whispered, taking a long draught of wine. 'Many happy returns, Lizzie!'

The waiter returned with the pâté and a plateful of hot toast. The portion was extremely large, but she intended to finish every morsel, to make up for the many times she'd rationed herself for the sake of her figure. Neville detested chubby women; damned them all as 'gross'. Well, that freckled blonde was 'gross', yet her partner didn't appear to mind – in fact, couldn't get enough of her. His hand was now caressing her neck, making teasing little forays up towards her earlobe and down between her breasts. They'd be undressing any moment, having it away, right there on the white tablecloth. And it would be quite a sight, she guessed. Neville was so *serious* in bed. Though she couldn't fault his performance, he never let his hair down, never giggled or played lovers' games, and had frowned in disapproval the one time she'd used a nickname for his cock.

While she ate her pâté, she imagined the couple tonguing it from one another's bodies, or passing wine from mouth to mouth, or hanging fronds of parsley over each other's nipples and giggling as they nibbled it. And what would they do with *butter*, she wondered with a grin, as she spread it thickly on the toast, before digging into the pâté again, with unaccustomed greed. Since Neville's cruel announcement, she had barely touched her food, but now she had to fill that hole – the hole not only in her stomach, but in her heart, her life. The wine was helping, certainly. She was drinking far too fast, gulping rather than sipping, but she needed it to soften her raw edges, heal the painful wounds. 'For heaven's sake, slow *down*, Lizzie,' she could hear Neville reprimanding. 'And you don't need butter – that pâté's rich enough.' Larding still more butter on her final piece of toast, defiantly she crammed it into her mouth.

The waiter removed the dirty plates, brought her a steak knife, refilled her glass (again), and finally presented her with the entrecôte – the biggest steak she had ever seen, preening on an oval platter, crowned with tomato flowers and fresh green herbs, and covered in a thick, creamy sauce. The accompaniments were equally impressive: tiny, tender asparagus spears; dark, rich, buttery mushrooms and, as decoration, deep-fried parsley sprigs. All at once, the food seemed worth the money. Indeed, she even felt relieved that it was she who was paying the bill. Only now did she realize that being subsidized by Neville came at a high price, since, in return, he assumed the right to tell her how to live. She was also beginning to see advantages in eating on her own: no one to reprove her, or contradict her views, or make her feel she should leave some food, even if she were hungry enough to finish every scrap. All she needed was confidence – confidence to do as she liked – and that was growing steadily, courtesy of the *Chevalier de Lascombes*. A connoisseur she might not be, but even an ignoramus could tell this wine was special.

The pianist was playing 'You're Nobody's Sweetheart Now', which, though apt, was hardly tactful. '*Damn!*' she said out loud, annoyed with herself for letting grief creep back, instead of booting Neville out of the restaurant and giving her full attention to the meal. Normally, she didn't have the chance. She had to concentrate on *him* – his opinions and his needs – often barely noticing what she was putting into her mouth. But, this evening, as a singleton, she could surrender herself to all the different sensations: the dark, exotic flavour of the mushrooms, the silky-soft asparagus tips, the velvety yellow sauce. This was, no question, the most delicious food she had eaten in her life. She even forgot to watch the couple as she focused on each mouthful, registering the various tastes and textures – eggy sauce, exquisitely juicy steak, soft, translucent onions, the zizz and kick of herbs – only noticing the pair again when a waiter bustled up to clear their table.

'If you can't decide, have both,' she overheard the man say, as his partner studied the dessert menu. 'And I will, too, which'll give us four to share.'

Lizzie listened, fascinated, as he ordered, yes, four desserts, along with coffee and liqueurs. No restrictions *there*; no attempt to tell the blonde she should be aiming for a dress-size ten, rather than settling for a 'gross' sixteen.

She continued watching as the waiter brought their puddings: a tart, a gateau, a plateful of ice-creams, and a foamy cream confection, served in a tall glass The man picked up his spoon and fork, but instead of tucking in himself, began feeding his mate with mouthfuls of each one in turn, keen to gratify her sweet tooth. Of course, Neville didn't *like* sweet things, but did that mean no one else should, either?

It was hard to tear her eyes away from the wodge of chocolate gateau, with its swirls of cream and shoals of nuts on top, and surrounded by a darker chocolate sauce. And that strawberry-studded tart, topped with miniature meringues and more whipped cream, of course. And the ice-creams looked amazing, obviously home-made, and in colours that she didn't know existed: palest green, deep purple, burnt almond, tangerine. As for the foamy thing, it could be zabaglione, or some sort of mousse or soufflé, and was also richly decorated, with tiny berries, star fruits and a shower of toasted almonds.

She could hardly wait to finish her steak, so *she* could choose a pudding. 'The problem is,' she told the waiter, 'I don't know which to have. The mascarpone and lemon pepper sorbet definitely sounds intriguing.' (Pepper in a sorbet – how outlandish!) 'On the other hand, I'm tempted by the pomegranate vacherin, with aromatic rose cream.' She had no idea what a vacherin *was*, but by now she was game for anything.

'We could make you up a tasting plate, madam, comprising a portion each of all of our desserts.'

She almost heard Neville choke, but there was a real pleasure in ignoring his objections. 'Yes, that would be quite brilliant.' Sheer stupefying gluttony, in short.

'And a liqueur for you, madam?'

That couple were sipping liqueurs, so why shouldn't *she* indulge? Again she asked the waiter's advice, no longer caring if he thought her ignorant. He was there to serve her, wasn't he?

'And I'd like to buy a drink for the pianist, if you'd kindly give it to him, with my compliments. Do you happen to know what he likes?' Her self-assurance was incredible! Neville wouldn't recognize her. She barely recognized herself. In fact, the way she was feeling at present, she might even succeed in going home with that youngish, fairish, plumpish guy, who was really rather gorgeous, and must be exceptionally emotional, judging by the passion he lavished on his music.

The waiter returned with her Grand Marnier, the tasting plate (enormous) and a message from the pianist, who was delighted by her offer of a drink and happy to play a number of her choice.

'Ask *him* to choose,' she murmured, eying the feast of desserts – everything from cranberry crème brulée to brandied truffle cake – and noting with a sense of shock that she actually felt relaxed, the first time in a year. It had always been an effort, she realized only now, trying to keep up with Neville, without being judged as 'crass'. His interests and his conversation were so pedantic and sophisticated, usually she failed to make the grade. On her own, however, she could simply sit and smile, or bat her lashes flirtatiously as the pianist caught her eye. She suddenly imagined the fellow in bed. Yes, he was tearing off his tie and tails, to reveal tight black underpants, which he yanked down in a trice. And, before she knew it, he was running his hands across her keys, coaxing deep, ecstatic sounds from her. He had thrown away the score and began thrillingly to improvize; she responding to his rhythm, melting at his touch.

All at once, she was aware of being watched – and by the *maitre d'*, of all people. Giggling, she tried to get a grip on herself; dispel the riotous fantasies. Yet when she glanced across at the object of her lust, he was still gazing at her intently – in reality, in truth. Then, with a teasing smile, he launched into 'her' tune, playing with his usual panache and even breaking into song. His voice was wonderfully powerful, and he seemed to be singing just for her, as if she were the only person in the room; the one woman he desired.

'All or nothing at all', he crooned, his eyes riveted on hers still.

> 'Half a love never appealed to me.
> If your heart never could yield to me,
> Then I'd rather have nothing at all.'

How extraordinarily apt the words were, as if he knew her situation. Wasn't it patently true that Neville had tried to fob her off with half a love, half a heart, half a glass of wine?

'If it's love,' the song continued, with a thunderous accompani-
ment that made her whole frame tingle, 'there *is* no in-between.'

Absolutely, she agreed, startled that the pianist should understand so well. Love was a sacred bond, demanding total
commitment, unreserved devotion.

> 'Why cry for something
> That might have been?'

Why indeed? She had cried quite long enough.

> 'So, you see, I've got to say
> No, no ...'

As he reprised the word 'no', with new, determined emphasis,
she was mouthing it to Neville. '*No*, Neville, you can't hurt me any
more. *No*, Neville, it was never right – I just let you bully me. *No*,
Neville I shan't change my mind, even if you come crawling back
on your knees.'

> 'All, or nothing at all ...'

Picking up her spoon, she plunged it into the centre of the plate,
sampling all of the desserts in turn – yes, each and every one. She
wanted *everything*: the works, the world, the full length and
breadth. Why settle for less, when one day she'd meet the kind of
man who could give her his whole heart? It might even happen
tonight. When the pianist had finished his stint, might he not come
over and ask if he could join her?

Join her at a table for two.

'If it's taken away, you feel not just deprived, but actually bereft. A vital part of you has been cut off and ...'

Catching the words as she walked into the kitchen, Helen darted towards the radio and turned the volume up. A fellow sufferer, obviously.

'It's such an essential thing – absolutely central to you, so if you lose it, you lose your whole identity.'

Exactly how she felt herself. Although about to go out and already in her coat, she remained hovering by the set. This was too important to miss – the shops would have to wait.

'There's a sense of dislocation. Suddenly everything's changed, and you're not prepared for it.'

Could one *ever* be prepared? It came as such a shock: a meteorite falling from a clear and cloudless sky.

'And there's nothing you can do. It's beyond your control. You're informed of the situation and that's it – end of story.'

Perhaps she could get in touch with the caller: email the programme, or phone the producer. *Woman's Hour* was unfamiliar territory – she was normally in the office at this hour of the morning, meeting clients, working on reports. But it would be good to have someone to talk to: someone in the same situation, who would understand, commiserate.

'Actually I blame the manufacturers. Don't they ever consider their customers when they discontinue brands?'

Helen frowned in bewilderment. Customers? Brands?

'I mean, there's such a thing as loyalty. I've been using *Magique* for the last fifteen years or more. It's become my signature perfume, an essential part of my psyche, you could say. I can't just switch to another brand, any more than I'd walk down the street in a ra-ra skirt. *Magique* is – well, *me*. It took me long enough to find it, for goodness sake. I'd experimented with other scents, but never felt they were right. So, when I discovered *Magique*, it was like the perfect match – a marriage made in heaven. And now that I can't buy it any more, it's as if I've been divorced.'

Helen snorted in contempt as she switched off the querulous voice. How *dare* the woman complain about something so ludicrously trivial. Snatching up her bag and keys, she strode out of the house. She had better things to do than listen to some pampered bitch mourn the loss of her favourite scent.

The coffee was exceptionally good at Francesca's. Although it meant taking the lift right up to the fifth floor, it was worth it for the atmosphere alone. The bustle of the store seemed left behind in this oasis of a café, with its soothing blue-grey walls, its prints of Victorian London on the walls, and the romantic music playing softly in the background. Sitting with her expresso and a slice of almond gateau, she checked her shopping list, ticking off the items she'd just bought: ready-meals for Philip, so he wouldn't have to cook; pyjamas for herself, and a stack of greetings cards, to thank the friends who might send flowers; presents for Sue and Sarah, to divert them while she was *hors de combat*, and a silk scarf for her mother, who would be looking after them. Should she have bought *more* presents for the girls – to last them through the decades, if she died before her fortieth? That crucial birthday was only eighteen months away, but she couldn't actually count on being around for it.

She gulped her coffee scalding hot, almost welcoming the pain. A lesser form of trauma sometimes cancelled out a greater, she had learned in the past few weeks. But she must stop being so damned negative and remember the statistics she'd looked up on the web: approximately 41,000 new cases diagnosed every year, and only 13,000 deaths. And, on top of that, at least seven out of ten women survived five years or more. She forked in a piece of comfort-cake. Five years seemed frighteningly short. Children needed a mother until they could manage on their own, or had even flown the nest.

And, anyway, the chances of survival were actually *worse* for younger women, like her. Paradoxical as it might sound, if she were fifty-nine instead of thirty-nine, she'd be statistically more likely to beat this dread disease.

Back to the list. It was important to keep control, focus one's mind on practicalities, instead of giving way to constant apprehension. She had already cleaned the house from top to bottom, and typed out all the phone numbers Philip might require: Sue's school and Sarah's nursery, their ballet teacher and best friends' mothers, the hospital ward, her personal nurse, the plumber and electrician, in case of emergencies. And the funeral director – just her little joke.

Forking up the last morsel of cake, she glanced around at the people in the café, longing to change places with them – yes, even with the old crone in the corner, dribbling tea and butter down her coat. Just at this moment, she would swap lives with anyone, however old and raddled, so long as she was spared tomorrow's ordeal. And, as she glided down the escalator, past Women's Fashions and the Designer Boutique, she was seized again with envy – envy for those shopping purely for pleasure: here to revamp their winter wardrobe or buy a new exotic party dress. Yet 'Why me?' was a pointless question. Half the world could ask it, with good reason: torture victims in Darfur, beggars in Calcutta, AIDS orphans in Botswana, or just ordinary folk in England, born poor, sick or disadvantaged. 'Why *not* me?' was a better line. Self-pity was quite loathsome – a cancer in itself.

As she made for the main exit, she passed the perfume counters: Chanel, Dior, Givenchy, Lancôme and half a dozen others. On impulse, she approached a salesgirl – a tall, languorous creature, with bleached blonde hair and scarlet nail extensions. 'Do you sell *Magique?*' she enquired.

'*We* don't. But see that counter on the left and the girl in the black trouser-suit? They should have it there.'

Black trouser-suit apart, the girl was almost a carbon copy of the first – bottle-blonde, skinny as a drinking straw, and with long, red, lethal talons. 'I hear it's about to be discontinued,' Helen added, having repeated her original question.

'Yes, I'm afraid that's true, madam. We do have a few bottles left, but only the *eau de toilette* – nothing in the full-strength perfume.

But you'll be pleased to know it's reduced to less than half-price. Did you want the small size or the large?'

'Neither,' she was about to say, when she was struck by an idea – a completely crazy notion and ridiculously extravagant, even at half-price – yet appealing none the less. She would buy up all the stocks of *Magique* and dispatch them to that woman on the radio, if only to heap coals of fire on her head. She changed the 'Neither' into 'Both, please.'

'Right, let me show you what we have. This is the little spray bottle, which is perfect for the handbag. Pretty, isn't it?'

'Yes, gorgeous.' *Woman's Hour* would probably agree to forward a small package, if she enclosed a covering note.

'There are just three of these, at a knockdown price.' The girl laid them on the counter, then rummaged in the drawer again. 'And this is the larger size. We only have the one left, but again it's a genuine bargain. And there *is* a matching body lotion, if I can interest you in that.'

'I'm grateful to have anything. In fact, when this lot runs out, I don't know how I'm going to manage.' Helen suppressed a smile. She had wanted a change of role and here she was enacting one.

The salesgirl gave a sympathetic nod. 'I know exactly how you feel, madam. Several other customers are extremely disappointed. And, of course, it *is* a lovely fragrance – magical, like its name.'

'It's the *only* fragrance as far as I'm concerned.' Helen maintained her new persona. It felt better being someone else: a lady of leisure, who spent her mornings phoning *Woman's Hour*. Arabella, she would christen her. Yes, she was coming into view: a wealthy fashionista, lying on a day-bed, snuggled up to a couple of Chihuahuas, and sipping chilled champagne 'It's become part of my identity,' Arabella whimpered. 'And I feel completely adrift without it.'

'I can understand that, madam. Perfume is so individual, isn't it? And extremely powerful, too. I've been reading this new research study, which shows it works directly on the brain, to lift our mood and increase our sense of well-being. Apparently it activates the limbic system, and that's the seat of emotion, you see. Which is probably why you've been feeling so low without your usual stimulus. But if you're looking for a replacement, madam, let me recommend *Pizzazz*. You'll find it has the same floral note, with undertones of musk, and just a hint of—'

'No!' Arabella snapped, handing over her credit card. 'Nothing can replace *Magique*. It's my signature scent, an essential part of my psyche. I'm just praying that the manufacturers will reconsider their decision.'

'Well, that's always possible, madam.'

'We'd better live in hope then.' Her mantra for the next few weeks.

Once back home, she wrapped the scarf in pale pink tissue, with a silver bow on top, then used brightly coloured paper for all the children's presents. She hoped her mother would remember the instructions: just one gift apiece each day, and not the whole lot all at once. Of late, her mother's memory was giving cause for concern. If it were to develop into dementia, there would be no one to look after the children, should anything happen to *her*.

'It *won't*,' she said aloud. 'I *will* survive. I must.' It wasn't just the children who needed her, but poor old Philip, too. Talented he might be, but domesticated, no. He could boil an egg – just about – but the new complicated washing machine left him both baffled and indignant, and if he tried to plait Sue's hair, it would have come undone by lunchtime. And how would he deal with periods and boyfriends, once the girls got older? He'd probably remarry, on the pretext of providing them with a stepmother – a convenient excuse for ensuring that he got his oats. He might remarry anyway; unable to cope with her disfigurement. The scar on each of her breasts would be at least seven inches long and, if the surgeon made a mess of the job, the end result could be quite horrendous. She had seen pictures on the Internet: hideous gashes, with stitch-marks like barbed wire.

She gave herself a sharp slap on the wrist; her wrist still stinging as she went upstairs to pack. Since her diagnosis, everything took longer, as if the continual worry was beginning to wear her down. It seemed extraordinary now that she had ever done a full-time job, run a home, cared for two daughters, and still had energy to spare for a weekly aerobics class.

She hauled the suitcase down from the top of the wardrobe, and stood looking at the double bed. When she came home from hospital, she would be lying there, next to Philip, with two raw, red wounds instead of two pale breasts. Would it make him physically sick, drive him into the spare room – or even out of her life? If she *had* a life, that is. Her future remained uncertain until after the operation. Only when they'd removed her breasts and the lymph nodes in her armpits, could they study them under the microscope, to check the size of the tumours and how far the cancer had spread. There would be another endless wait for the results – every day dragging like a month until her appointment with the oncologist. She loathed his dispassionate voice. When he'd told her she had cancer in the first place, the word had reduced her universe to ruins, yet he'd pronounced it almost casually.

She suddenly caught Philip's eye. He was smiling from their wedding photo, in his slightly-too-tight morning-suit, with his arm around her waist. *She* looked almost shocked, as if amazed to be doing something so conventional as getting married in church. If only he were here with her, to distract her from her worries. He might be totally impractical, but he could always make her laugh. She had assumed he would take the day off, but that had proved impossible because some loathsome guy – a director of the company – was flying in from New York. At least he'd promised to be home by four, to drive her to the hospital, and she was literally counting the minutes: only fifty-eight now. And nineteen and a quarter hours before the operation. She doubted if she would sleep tonight, in a noisy, overheated ward, with all her terrors escalating, and images of scalpels slashing through her mind.

She laid her new pyjamas in the case. Philip would abhor them. He liked her black lace nightie, slit up to the thigh, or the frilly baby-doll with matching thong. It was the hospital that had specified pyjamas – something that unbuttoned down the front, to give access to the wounds. The only pair she had managed to find looked totally unfeminine, in blue-checked winceyette. Already she seemed to have changed; become a sexless, neutered invalid, a reject on the 'seconds' pile.

'Just *stop* it!' she reproved herself, trying to concentrate on the packing. Having fetched her slippers and spongebag, she trekked downstairs again to choose a book for the hospital – something easy and upbeat, with a happy-ever-after ending.

She brought up the bottles of scent, as well as a shamefully frothy novel. If she could find a shoebox to put the bottles in, it would make posting easier. The idea still appealed, despite its extravagance – restoring a stranger's identity with a present out of the blue. If only *hers* could be restored with so little effort.

She removed her evening shoes from their smart gold cardboard box – the perfect receptacle, in style as well as size. The five bottles fitted snugly, and once she had showered and washed her hair, she would parcel up the box and phone the BBC, to get the correct address. She was actually quite grateful to have something to distract her; something else to think about. For the last few weeks, her mind had barely moved from scans, biopsies, mammograms, blood tests, implants, prostheses ... One advantage of this whole ghastly saga was that her vocabulary had increased. Two months ago, she simply hadn't heard of phrases such as keloid scarring, lymphoedema, axillary clearance, tissue-flap reconstruction. And she would be learning more each day. When she came home from hospital, she might be damaged beyond repair, but she would have gained a stock of new impressive words.

She stood, still dripping from the shower, staring at her reflection in the full-length bathroom mirror. This was the last occasion she would see herself with breasts, and it seemed crucial to remember what they looked like. She had a sneaking suspicion that Philip had actually married her for her breasts. Even at school, they'd been large – a source of deep embarrassment in those days but, bit by bit, Philip's admiration had changed her attitude.

Yes, she had to admit, they were still reasonably full and firm, despite having fed two infants. They looked completely healthy, in fact – the skin smooth and glowing, with no sign of any tumours. Were she to touch her breasts, she could *feel* the lumps, of course, but she had no intention of doing so. Every time her fingers made contact with those evil little growths, a wave of panic jolted through her, as she pictured the ruthless cancer cells silently spreading through the body – out-of-control bully-boys invading normal tissue.

But *how* could it be going on, when everything seemed so normal on the surface? Her nipples, for example, were not only pink and plump, but actually erect – which she couldn't understand, unless they were cruelly trying to emphasize exactly what she'd lose.

Certainly Philip would have legitimate grounds for complaint, faced as he'd be with a grotesquely different woman from the one he'd originally married. And worse was to come. Once she had recovered from the surgery, there would be at least six months' chemotherapy, which was bound to make her hair fall out. Could she really blame him if he decided not to stay with a bald and breastless freak?

There was always reconstruction, of course, but it sounded almost worse than the mastectomy itself, and would leave another extensive scar, either all along her back, or underneath her stomach, depending on the site they used to remove the fat and muscle needed to rebuild the breasts. And the procedure was so complicated (not to mention painful) that things frequently went wrong, necessitating still more operations. One girl she'd met at the Breast Clinic had spent the last two years in and out of hospital, in an effort to replace her breasts, including reconstruction of the nipples – an extremely tricky procedure in itself. And, judging by what she'd heard, implants weren't much better. They could rupture, leak, infect, or even cause further cancers, some authorities believed. With all these obstacles ahead, there wasn't a chance in hell now of getting promotion at work – in fact, she'd be fortunate to keep her job at all. Worse, all the pain and trauma could prove so much wasted effort, if the cancer were to spread to, say, her liver or her bones, and she was given only months to live.

That was another facet of the illness – never knowing when it might recur. After the initial diagnosis, every tiny lump that subsequently developed might prove to be your death knell.

'*Stop* it,' she repeated, towelling her hair so vigorously it hurt. She was lucky to have a decent surgeon – one unlikely to mess up. *And* a lovely husband and two healthy, lively children. *And* her own personal breast-care nurse, whom she could phone at any time. *And* all her treatment free on the National Health. She could even get a wig free – a choice of wigs, in fact: blonde or auburn, poker-straight or curly – any style she chose. OK, wigs felt hot and uncomfortable, and they could itch, or slip, or even come right off, but they were a definite advance on …

The phone interrupted the counting of her blessings. Still naked, she darted into the bedroom and picked up the extension. 'Oh, Philip – good! Are you on your way, darling? … What, you haven't even left? … He *can't*! I don't believe it! Didn't you *tell* him that...?' She sank down on the bed, feeling completely crushed. Yet she mustn't make things worse for Philip, who already sounded distraught. 'It's OK, darling. I understand. No, honestly, I'll be all right. See you about eight, then. Victoria Ward, remember.'

She crept into bed and pulled the duvet over her, as if trying to escape this latest blow. The one thing she'd been dreading was going to the hospital alone. If she took the car, she wouldn't find a parking space, yet cabs were unreliable and, anyway, she needed moral support.

She *wasn't* going – she'd changed her mind. In fact, there wasn't any hospital to go to. She was Arabella, wasn't she, and Arabella enjoyed perfect, radiant health? She had never been ill in her entire pampered life, and nothing would deprive her of her glamorous looks, her luscious femininity or her rock-hard confidence. And her husband was so wealthy he didn't need to work, so he was with her all the time – yes, even at this moment, hovering by her side, popping grapes into her pouting mouth. And she would never, ever lose her mane of hair – hair so long and thick and shining, she employed a team of hairdressers just to brush it every day. And a beautician and a masseuse were on twenty-four-hour call, to primp and knead and titivate. She never had to work, of course. Meeting clients, meeting deadlines – all unknown territory. And as for juggling family and career, the concept was utterly foreign. She didn't *have* any children, so she would never stay up half the night making costumes for school plays, or fairy cakes for end-of-term bazaars. Nor did she have an odious boss, who made her feel constantly guilty having to ask for sick leave when he'd just lost two of his staff.

'You don't know you're *born!*' she shouted suddenly, springing out of bed. 'Your life's one long endless holiday, sitting on your arse all day, with your doting husband in attendance. Mine's hardly ever *here*. He's stressed out of his mind. He works fifty hours a week, and some weekends as well. And the girls are in a dreadful state because an idiotic child at their school told them that everyone with cancer always dies. And my mother's losing her marbles, so I'm worried sick about leaving her in charge. Yet there's no one else, for heaven's sake. You think *you* have problems, do you? Oh, yes, of course, I'd forgotten – you've lost your favourite perfume, so you're absolutely devastated!'

Snatching the largest bottle from the shoe-box, she wrested it from its carton, unscrewed the cap and poured the entire contents over her naked breasts. Hardly pausing to think, she grabbed the second bottle, opened that and sloshed it across her stomach. The reek of musk and frangipani filled the room. Why should useless Arabella enjoy this luxurious scent? If the stuff was meant to be magic, let it work its spell on *her*, not on some idle parasite.

She seized the first of the spray-bottles, aimed it at her head and kept pumping it and pumping, until her hair was drenched with scent. Maybe she *wouldn't* lose her crowning glory if the magic actually worked. She picked up the second spray-bottle and squirted the contents down her shoulders and back – a difficult manoeuvre, but essential none the less. If they took the skin and muscle from there to make the substitute breasts, then it, too, needed a miracle, to prevent too deep a scar.

Rivulets of perfume were streaming down her body, trickling on to the floor. The smell was so exotic, she paused a moment, simply to breathe it in. Then all at once she laughed – a peculiar sound, half squawk, half shout of triumph. The sound was truly startling. It was *weeks* since she had laughed; months since she'd experienced the slightest sense of triumph. So what on earth had happened? Could the scent itself have changed her mood, as that salesgirl had explained, worked on her limbic system – whatever that might be – affected some subtle region of her brain?

She had no idea. All she knew was that a mysterious sort of magic had, in fact, occurred. She did feel vastly better: reanimated, cleansed, ready to face the surgery with new courage and composure. All fear had gone, all racking thoughts and prophecies of doom. More than that – she was now convinced, at a deep instinctive level, that things would be all right. She wouldn't die. And Philip wouldn't leave her. Bald and breastless she might be, but somehow he'd put up with it, and somehow she'd survive – survive way beyond her fortieth, to see her children's children.

'I'm sorry, Julie,' Megan mumbled in embarrassment, 'but I can't eat anything with parents.'

'With *what*?' Julie froze, her ladle poised above the serving dish.

Megan cleared her throat. 'Mothers and fathers.'

'I'm sorry. I don't follow.'

'Well, you've just told us this is fricassee of lamb, and lambs have parents – you know, ewes and rams.'

'I don't think rams are involved these days.' Fiona gave a vulgar laugh. 'It's all artificial insemination, isn't it?'

'That's not the point,' Megan tried to say. Her voice always seemed to shrivel to a strangulated whisper when the other two ganged up on her. Last night, they'd attacked her taste in clothes; the evening before they'd expressed their amused astonishment that anyone could actually *listen* to Céline Dion. What she *wanted* to articulate was that, however the lamb had been conceived, those small brown chunks in the casserole had once been a beloved child.

'Well, you've had meat before,' Julie countered irritably, 'and never said a thing. It's a bit peculiar, isn't it, suddenly becoming a vegetarian just as I'm dishing up?'

'I'm sorry, Julie, honestly, but it only dawned on me this after-noon, after I'd read a piece about something called the Life Force. And I'm not *quite* a vegetarian. This is rather different.'

'You're telling me!' Fiona chortled. 'I've heard people say they won't eat anything with *eyes*, but parents is a new one.'

Megan looked nervously at the second dish, which was full of boiled potatoes. *Potatoes* had eyes – at least before they were peeled. She was suddenly aware of several brown potato-eyes watching her in horror and regret.

'Actually,' Julie reflected, scooping up two potatoes and plonking them on Megan's plate, 'you could argue that *everything* has parents. Take these spuds, for instance. They're grown from seed-potatoes, and surely seed-potatoes are sort of single parents – and extremely fertile ones at that. My father used to grow them and he'd always get a bumper crop from just one or two small tubers.'

'And what about *this*,' Fiona added, thrusting the wooden salad bowl in front of Megan's nose. 'Tomatoes, lettuce, cucumber – all grown from seed, as well. So, as far as I can see, my love, it's starvation rations for you tonight.'

'That's OK.' Megan put her fork down and sat fiddling with her hair. She could fill up on dessert. 'So how was your meeting?' she asked Fiona, determined to change the subject.

'Unspeakable! Bruce hogged the limelight, as usual, so none of us poor lesser mortals could get a word in edgeways.'

Fiona was hardly 'lesser', Megan thought – not in any sense of the word. Even a surreptitious glance at her flatmate's ample figure showed whole slabs and hunks of animal trapped and festering inside her, and bulging out in rolls of surplus flesh. Fiona was an enthusiastic meat-eater – pig for breakfast (sausages and bacon), cows for lunch (beefburgers, lasagne, spaghetti Bolognaise) and hen, or lamb, or even calf for dinner. Yesterday she had actually eaten a tongue sandwich – yes, without the slightest trace of guilt. That sensitive, extraordinary organ, which allowed a cow to moo, munched to a pulp by her own unthinking tongue.

'I had a shitty day as well,' Julie put in, heaping her plate with stew. 'My computer crashed and I lost my entire morning's work. Rupert went ballistic, of course, so I had to cancel my lunch with Kay and do the sodding thing all over again.'

'Gosh, how awful,' Megan said. She was lucky in her own work: no megalomaniac boss or terrifying deadlines. Admittedly, librarians were often seen as dull – and she hadn't even *become* one yet; was still a mere assistant, who hoped, one day, to train – but, with a hundred-thousand books as friends, there was constant stimulation. And books were much more merciful than people; didn't judge, didn't scoff, didn't let you down. Yet all of them had distinctive personalities; some passionate, tempestuous, others calmly comforting, a few quirky or rebellious, several downright strange. She also got involved with many of the borrowers, trying to tell their characters by the sort of books they chose – often a source of some surprise. A quiet, kindly-seeming matron would shuffle out with a gruesome tome about the world's most heinous murderers, or a hunky macho-man, with a nose-stud and tattoos, spend a full hour in the baby-care section, poring over books on bottle-feeding and nappy-rash. She was also intrigued by the sorts of things that people used as bookmarks and left behind in the pages: lottery tickets, shopping lists, love letters, hairpins, bits of string, old shoelaces, and even once (she shuddered at the thought) an uncooked bacon rasher.

'Hey,' said Fiona, forking in more lamb. 'Everyone's raving about that remake of *Cape Fear* – the one with Clive Owen as the ex-con. Shall we go this Sunday?'

'Good idea,' said Julie. 'It's on at the Renoir, so we could have lunch at Lone Star first. Megan, are *you* free?'

'Er, no.' Lone Star was a steakhouse, but it wasn't only that. There was enough cause for fear in her own life, without sitting through a movie with Fear in its actual title. Besides, Sunday was the day she saw her grandma, although she wouldn't dream of mentioning it again. When she'd brought it up a week ago, the other two had derided her. Apparently, trekking all the way to Lewisham to visit a confused and elderly widow was desperately uncool. 'I'm ... busy, I'm afraid.'

'You're not much fun, you know,' Fiona observed, removing a piece of gristle from her mouth.

Yes, she *did* know. They were severely disappointed in her – that was increasingly obvious – just as it was becoming more apparent by the day that it had been a grave mistake on her part ever to have joined this flat-share. The advertisement had sounded so appealing – 'Friendly, fun-loving third girl required for spacious Fulham flat' – but, of course, she hadn't realized then how treacherous the word 'fun' was. She had assumed in her naivete that it meant someone bright and cheerful, ready with a laugh or joke, but for Julie and Fiona it was a different thing entirely, and involved getting drunk, smoking pot, staying up all hours, watching movies about rape or murder, and devouring things that could see and feel and speak. And 'spacious', too, was totally misleading. All the rooms were tiny, and her bedroom in particular was barely more than a cupboard. True, she paid less rent than the others, but it was still extremely inconvenient to have to keep her clothes in a blanket-box underneath the bed. Every time she dressed, it meant pulling out the bed, shaking out the creases.

She shifted her chair back from the table, risking the others' derision, if not wrath. But she was finding it impossible to sit so close to the casserole dish. She could actually hear the dismembered lamb bleating in distress; its mother howling frantically, its father inconsolable. Fiona, though, had no such qualms, and was biting into glistening lumps of living, breathing animal, while Julie smacked her lips with equal satisfaction.

Thank God she was on a one-month trial and two weeks of that had passed. In another fortnight she'd be free to leave, and the prospect cheered her hugely. Of course she couldn't afford a place of her own, not in central London, but her grandma had offered her a room for free in Lewisham. And the fantastic thing about her grandma was that she ate nothing but ginger biscuits and blancmange.

'Gran,' she said, putting a hand on the old lady's bony shoulder, 'would you mind terribly if I made a jelly this evening instead of blancmange?'

Her grandma's face creased in consternation. 'But I *always* have blancmange, dear, and I don't like change at my age. In any case, Dr Crawford told me I had to drink more milk. It's my bones, you see. They're crumbling. Unless you made a *milk* jelly – I suppose that would be all right.'

'But ...' The objection petered out. This afternoon it had suddenly occurred to her that it was deeply immoral to drink milk. Milk belonged to calves and, in depriving them, she was perpetuating the cycle of gross, unthinking cruelty. On the other hand, wasn't it equally cruel to allow a woman of eighty-six to run the risk of developing osteoporosis? 'Don't worry,' she said, determined to put her grandma first, whatever her pangs of conscience. 'We'll have blancmange, as usual. Just let me take my coat off and I'll get cracking in the kitchen.'

'Thank you, dear. I bless the day you came.'

Megan allowed herself a smile. She, too, was feeling better –

apart from the matter of the milk. And, in a way, she was grateful for the strict regime, the lack of change, the lack of choice. She had long since been aware that she needed regulation in her life, just as she had at work. All the books were catalogued according to some system she hadn't fully grasped yet, but which meant that everything was in its proper place. And, even though she was new to the job, she would never dream of filing a novel by, say, Catherine Cookson among the Ps to Qs, or – worse – in the cookery or science section. Order was essential, as she had learned early on in life, when her parents died in a car-crash the very day she'd started secondary school. She had been forced to develop strategies for staying in control – all the more essential when she was sent to live with with an elderly aunt who had never had (and never wanted) children. It had taken her a while, of course, to work out ways of keeping safe, but she had gradually succeeded by limiting her crying sessions to exactly seven minutes by the clock, touching every lamp-post on her way to school, never treading on cracks in the pavement, and never, ever getting into a car.

Now, faced with the upheaval of moving out of Fulham (which had deeply angered Julie and Fiona, who were landed with the expense and trouble of advertising again), she felt the same deep longing for a survival plan that would heal the scars and soothe the shock. And it *had* been a shock – that was not in doubt. All her life she had wanted friends and siblings, craved to live with people her own age, and, once she'd become an adult, the thought of sharing everything – a sitting-room, a kitchen, shampoo and clothes and hand-cream, recipes and even thoughts – seemed totally enchanting. But now it was back to social isolation. Much as she loved her, Gran wasn't exactly company, since she spent half the day asleep. Still, at least they met at mealtimes, and could comment on the weather (which Gran experienced only second-hand, as she had stopped going out some time ago), or chat about the Old Days, when you washed in water poured from a jug instead of running the taps, and cleaned the knives with silver-polish, and boiled puddings in a cloth. And, as far as she could make out, you were continually answering the door – to the coalman and the knife-grinder, the man who lent you money, the rag-and-bone-man, the baker, with a tray of loaves and buns.

'Yes, it was threepence for a cottage loaf in them days,' her grandma said, transferring a spoonful of blancmange to her mouth. 'This is really nice, dear.'

'I'm afraid it's not quite set.'

'I like it warm and runny. It makes a change from normal.'

'You just said you hated change.'

'No, I didn't. That was someone else.'

Megan shrugged. Her grandma's memory was fading, like most things in the house: the wallpaper, the carpet, the once-fuchsia-patterned curtains.

'I'll tell you what I'd really like – rice pudding! I haven't had it in an age. They sell it in tins, but I can't be doing with tin-openers. And, anyway, you don't get that nice brown skin on top.'

Megan was suddenly transported to her parents' sunny kitchen; a dish of rice pudding steaming on the table. 'Give *me* the skin! Give *me* the skin!' she'd cry. And her parents always did, of course. She was the only child, the spoiled child, invariably indulged – until that pile-up on the motorway had wrecked their car and bodies, along with her own life. 'OK, Gran,' she said. 'We'll have rice tomorrow evening, with lots and lots of brown skin.'

She stood just inside the supermarket doors, appalled at the uproar bellowing and yowling from the cabinets and shelves: chicken clucking hysterically, trout and plaice blowing bubbles of distress, crabs and prawns, flushed deep pink from trauma, screeching out in pain. Why had she never noticed it before? And why enter this vile abattoir for a mere packet of pudding rice, when she could get it at the health shop, ten minutes' walk away?

Once she reached Nature's Bounty, her heartbeat calmed and her breathing slowed to normal. No gills or scales or fins here; no claws or feet or beaks; no bloody juices, mottled flesh, no carcasses, no skeletons. Only boxes of blithe cereals, bags of good-natured prunes, jars of contented peanut butter, merciful packets of nuts. And there, facing her on the shelf, was the answer to her anguish over calves: soya milk and rice milk, oat milk, almond milk – not one of them produced by penalizing her fellow creatures. With a sense of huge relief, she piled half a dozen cartons into her basket, along with a packet of rice and a bag of organic sugar. She wasn't exactly sure how to make rice pudding, having never learned to cook, but Grandma had a shelf-ful of tattered cookery books, which she had already used when tackling the blancmange. She, too, was looking forward to the rice, not just as a treat, but as a rich, sweet, creamy memory of her loving, longed-for mother.

She hurried home, entering to the familiar smell of stale pee, mouldering walls and Fox's Embrocation. She must really give the place a thorough spring-clean: scour the toilet floor, scrub the greenish growths off the damp patches on the wallpaper. As she crossed the dingy hall, she experienced a pang of loss for the clean, bright Fulham flat. Small and cramped it might have been, but never filthy dirty. Neither Julie nor Fiona had ever got in touch. She'd been hoping they might ring, if only to ask her how she was, but presumably they were still smouldering with resentment. And could she really blame them? When it had been *her* turn to cook, she had invariably made a mess of it, producing plain spaghetti one day (which had prompted cries of 'Where's the sauce, for Christ's sake?'), then trying her hand at salad (damned by Fiona as 'not a proper meal'– in fact, 'not enough to keep a measly rabbit alive'), and finally resorting to the chip shop, which was apparently against the rules and so provoked another outburst.

At least Gran was never angry. In fact, Megan could hear her cheerful voice rising from the sitting-room, singing one of the few hymns she knew by heart.

> *O Jesus, I have promised*
> *To serve thee to the end;*
> *Be thou for ever near me,*
> *My Master and my Friend …*

'Is that you?' she called, breaking off.

No, it's Jesus, Megan wished she could reply, just to make her grandma's day. Gran and Jesus had a very close relationship – one she couldn't share. Jesus was the tyrant who had snatched her parents in their prime, to live in Heaven with Him, leaving her with a deaf, cantankerous aunt.

'Did you have a good day?' Gran asked, as Megan bent over her chair and gave her a welcoming kiss.

'A rather weird one, actually.' A small, weasly man had shuffled in, claiming he could only read authors whose names began with M. Although he hadn't given any reason for this quirk, it was probably another sort of system for keeping things under control. Anyway, as the only person on the desk, she had done her best to help, recommending Iris Murdoch, John Mortimer, Alice Munro and Deborah Moggach. 'Gran, I may be a while in the kitchen. I'm making your rice pudding.'

'That's all right, dear. I'm watching this thing about surgeons cutting off young women's breasts, to prevent them getting cancer later on.'

Megan glanced down at her own breasts, imagining malignant cells already rampaging around, and even feeling for the mastectomy scars as she removed her coat and scarf. Alarmed, she sought distraction in reading the labels on the milk cartons, trying to decide between the different brands. Finally she opted for the soya, since not only was it calcium-enriched, but also contained the highest percentage of protein, lacking in their usual diet. Next she hunted through the cupboards to find a shallow baking dish, which would give a large amount of skin, before consulting one of the cookery books. 'Bake in the oven for four hours,' she read. Four *hours*, for heaven's sake! That would take them to ten o'clock, way past her grandma's bedtime. Perhaps the book was wrong. In fact, she distinctly remembered both Julie and Fiona cooking rice in a saucepan on the hob, in less than twenty minutes. She would do the same, then transfer it to the baking dish just for the last five minutes, in order to form the skin.

While she worked, she listened to the radio: a phone-in programme about problems in relationships. Her problem was she didn't *have* a relationship; hadn't been out with anyone for close on eighteen months. Of course, working in the library didn't help. All the librarians were female, except Leo who was way past forty, and Terence who was gay.

'He's completely unemotional,' a woman was complaining. 'He's never said he loves me, not once in three whole years.'

'I love you,' Megan mouthed, wondering what it would feel like if someone said it to *her*; how she'd respond, what might happen next – and next, and next. She was so intent on the fantasy, she didn't notice that the rice was boiling over, until she was brought abruptly back to earth by having to clean the spattered hob.

She poured the rice into the baking dish, and added sugar and a pinch of spice (which she'd found at the back of the largely empty cupboard, beside a packet of clothes pegs and a mysterious can of dog food – Gran had never owned a dog). There was a certain sense of achievement in producing something from scratch, instead of relying on tins and packets. If she carried on at this rate, she might even manage to bake a cake – her mother's Victoria sponge, maybe, which she could still recall in its moistly golden glory. Those childhood sponges had been filled with jam and cream, which oozed out in a glorious gunge as she bit into the cake. Then Mum would reach across and gently wipe her mouth, and Dad would plant a doting kiss on the top of her dark head. By the time she was ten, she had as many kisses on her head as actual hairs. They stayed in place for years, sticking up from her scalp like little shiny hair-ornaments – until they perished with her parents, clearly losing heart. (In any case, her aunt soon chopped her hair off, in an attempt to 'tidy her up'.)

She began flicking through the recipes, each one bringing forth new memories of her mother in the kitchen, making magical meringues, all air and crunch and sweetness, or chewy brandy-snaps that left lovely, treacly fragments on your teeth, or slabs of sticky gingerbread, so dark and rich and soft she'd imagined curling up and sleeping on it, like a mattress with an in-built midnight feast.

Regretfully, she closed the book and peeked into the oven, relieved to see that a good brown skin had formed. 'It's ready, Gran,' she called, putting the dish on a tray and carrying it into the sitting-room. This clean and simple supper was a definite advance on lumps of mangled meat, repulsive bacon rinds, obscenely sizzling sausages, or eyes forlornly staring from decapitated fish-heads.

'It tastes funny, dear,' Grandma said, having swallowed the first spoonful.

'That's just the milk. I used a different sort.'

'No, it's the rice that's odd – all gritty.'

Megan sampled it herself. 'Oh, Lord! It's still half-raw. I'm sorry, Gran, you'll have to wait a bit longer while I put it back in the oven. But I'll make you a nice cup of tea and you can fill up on ginger biscuits.'

As she returned to the kitchen and re-lit the ancient oven, she was suddenly struck by an appalling thought. She had completely overlooked the possibility that both soya beans and rice might well have sensitivities, and, indeed, parents. Wouldn't they be much the same as potatoes and tomatoes? Yet here she was abusing them, subjecting them to blistering heat – even *eating* them, for God's sake. Horrified, she ran a sinkful of cold water and submerged the baking dish, leaving it there to recover, while she went to fetch the biscuits. But just as she was arranging them on one of Gran's chipped plates, she was assailed by further doubts. Biscuits were made from wheat, and wheat was undeniably a plant. And hadn't she read in this morning's *Daily Mail* (though obviously not taken in) that it was now scientifically proven that plants could and did feel pain? More than that, the article had said, they actually responded to love and kindness, growing taller and more luxuriant than those maltreated or ignored. So how could she allow her grandmother to dunk ginger biscuits in scalding tea, then chew them to extinction? She stood undecided, agonized, her eye falling on the sugar packet. Yet more cause for alarm. Biscuits were full of sugar, and she had poured sugar into the rice, despite the obvious fact that both sugar cane and sugar beet were also living, feeling plants.

Wretchedly she sank onto the kitchen stool, running through various categories of food. Not one seemed safe to eat. Oil? No, cruel to olives. Cereals and bread? No, wheat again, or oats. Fruit and vegetables? She'd already ruled out plants. Chocolate, perhaps? No, cocoa beans had parents, and were also susceptible to pain. Jelly? That was mainly water and ought to be safe enough, except gelatine was derived from cows, and even the vegetarian kind was made from some sort of moss. One day, science might invent a new, miraculous foodstuff, fashioned solely out of chemicals and swallowed in pill form. But Grandma couldn't wait that long. Her health was bad already, and her weight had dropped to barely seven stone.

Glancing up, she caught sight of her reflection in the grimy windowpane. She, too, looked thin and gaunt, and her hair was straggling round her shoulders in so limp and lank a fashion, it would have had her aunt reaching for the shears. She had never been much to look at, with her boyish figure, sallow skin and insipid grey-blue eyes. Fiona might be overweight, but she had gorgeous auburn curls, and Julie's Cornish-cream complexion was the sort you saw in beauty magazines. Compared with them, she was a complete and utter failure, prone to eczema and spots, with no taste in music or clothes, no proper job, no savings, and unable even to cook. And, on top of everything else, she had spent her life to date inflicting mindless cruelty on other living things.

She stole back to the sitting-room, longing to share her pain with Gran. But the poor soul was fast asleep, her open mouth trailing a long spittle-chain across her shabby cardigan. However, she did look truly peaceful as she lay dozing in the old armchair; hands loosely clasped, wrinkled face serene. Perhaps, if she explained things, went through all the arguments carefully and slowly, even showed her the piece in the *Daily Mail*, Gran would understand. It would mean they would have to die, of course, and death by slow starvation was a terrifying prospect. On the other hand, Gran was highly principled and had always hated cruelty, so once she grasped the harm they were doing, she would want to take some action. Indeed, Gran herself had given up meat, several years ago and, although they'd never discussed the issue, it might indicate she was already prey to scruples and misgivings. Besides, she was nearing the end of her life. Life expectancy for women was somewhere around eighty-two, and not only had Gran passed that figure, she was ready and willing to go. She had admitted as much just recently; saying she hoped she wouldn't linger on to become a vegetable.

A vegetable! The wrong word entirely. Why did every line of thought lead back to the same dilemma? Yet a solution was now in sight, which, although frightening in the extreme, would also solve a host of problems for them both. If her grandma lived much longer, she might have to face such horrors as dementia or deafness, arthritis or incontinence, stroke, angina, macular degeneration – the list was grim and endless. And her own future seemed composed of haunting questions with no answers: how she would find the time and money to train as a librarian; how and where she would live once her grandma passed away; how she'd face the loneliness (not to mention shame) if no boyfriend ever materialized? A slow extinction, even at *her* age, would bring merciful release from her terror of a car-crash, her dread of ending up alone, her fear of crowds, of people. If she and Gran were simply to fade and fray, like the once-claret-coloured carpet, the once-brilliant fuchsia curtains, wouldn't that constitute a natural, peaceful end? And they could die with a clear conscience, knowing they would never harm a fellow sufferer in this sad and brutish world; never add to the tide of cruelty raging all around.

Decisive at last – even calm – she seated herself beside Gran's slumbering form, taking the small, claw-like hand and warming it in her own. The vigil would be painful and protracted, but help would be on hand. In fact, even as she closed her eyes, she felt her parents' never-quite-extinguished love beaming down from Heaven, giving her the courage to face the long, dark, hungry, empty, weary end-time.

'Happy, darling?'

'Mm.'

'More wine?'

'No, thanks.'

'Hey, are you *OK*?'

'Yes, fine.' Amy slumped back irritably against the slab of rock. Everywhere she looked was barren, dehydrated – parched and rugged ground panting for some rain. The brochures from the travel agent were totally misleading. Where were the lush green pastures, studded with wild flowers? The sparkling sapphire skies? Despite the malevolent heat, the sky *here* was more the colour of a bruise.

'Want to finish up the *keftepes*?'

She shook her head. Two were more than enough. A peculiar country, this, in which all the sap and juice had been leeched out of the landscape, while the food was clogged with grease. Everything they had eaten for their picnic seemed to be oozing fat through its pores; globules of yellow gunge pooling on the aubergines, salad leaves slippery with oil, even the blubbery cheese leaving a greasy after-taste.

Removing her gaze from the leftovers, she stared up at the mountain range, its row upon row of craggy peaks like the back teeth of a giant. Teeth with no saliva. The whole area was arid. Though who was she to criticize, when her insides were much the same? Her vagina was no longer soft and plushy but dried up and inhospitable; her womb a shrivelled husk. Rob hadn't seemed to notice yet, but that was the trouble with marriage. You became one flesh, and remained more separate than ever. She flashed him a guilty smile. It was *she* who was at fault. Sterile. Damaged goods.

'Where would you like to go tomorrow?' he asked, reaching out to squeeze her hand.

Home, she longed to say: back to a rainy English summer and their overgrown back lawn. 'How about that church you wanted to see?' A church would be cool, at least, and, anyway, she ought to try to please him. *He'd* done nothing wrong. 'St Nicholas's, wasn't it?'

'*Aghios Nikolaos,*' he corrected her, proud of his basic Greek.

She hadn't even bothered trying to learn. The language seemed too alien, and the words all felt like pebbles in her mouth.

'Yes, we could take the bus.' He fired half a dozen olives into his mouth, spitting out the stones in quick succession. 'And another picnic, if you like.'

'Great.' Rob's love of picnics had less to do with buying food and more to do with extending his vocabulary and improving his pronunciation by chatting with the natives in the warren of local shops. And she'd stand silent, perversely missing *English* shops. She couldn't understand why she felt so low, so homesick. This was a holiday, for heaven's sake, a second honeymoon, not a spell in gaol.

'Pudding time!' Rob announced, unwrapping a package of Greek pastries. He held out a baklava, offering her a bite. The pastry was literally dripping oil and honey and, since oil and honey were symbols of fertility, she ought to devour the lot – eat every baklava in every shop in every town in Greece.

'More?' he asked, sucking a drool of syrup from his thumb.

'Yes, please.' She took another bite, mechanically chewing and swallowing. The sweetness was so intense it hurt her teeth, but perhaps it would transform her, change her bitter mood.

'I love you, Amy,' he whispered, kissing her on the lips.

'Love you, too.' The kiss tasted of olives, with an overlay of aubergines. She wondered what *she* tasted of – honey-tinged despair?

'Hey, watch out – a wasp!' He sprang to his feet to drive off the intruder.

'Don't, Rob! They're usually quite harmless if you just leave them be and don't react.' She stared, entranced, at the creature. As it sucked frantically at the syrup, its whole body and being were throbbing with desire: black eyes bulging, transparent wings vibrating in a paroxysm of pleasure. And the powerful, throaty buzzing sounded majestically loud in proportion to its modest size. 'It's really rather beautiful, you know. I wouldn't mind a dress like that – black and yellow stripes.'

'Well, it's your birthday next month ...'

She had no desire to think about her birthday. With every year, her egg supply declined. 'No need to worry at your age,' the GP had reassured her, but she had a strange, uneasy feeling that her ovaries were twice as old as *she* was: already in their forties and shrivelling by the second.

'Oh, God! More wasps.' Rob let out an exasperated sigh. 'I know you say they're harmless, but I think we ought to decamp.'

'OK.' She made no move, however, but continued to gaze with fascination at the half-dozen new arrivals, all equally enraptured by the feast. Their tiny bodies were quivering and pulsing, their wings whirring in near-ecstasy. If only *she* could be that focused when she and Rob made love, instead of trapped inside the counting-house of her head, checking days and dates, trying to pinpoint the exact time of ovulation.

As if reading her mind, he came to sit beside her on the rock and stroked his fingers teasingly along the length of her bare arm. 'Why don't we go back for a siesta?'

A siesta meant more sex, of course. And sex meant disappointment. Would it happen *this* time? Almost certainly not. And, on top of that, she just couldn't seem to relax; forever watching herself like a harsh, judgemental critic. Even now, while Rob was kissing the inside of her elbow, she was sitting tense and wary, rather than enjoying the sensation and surrendering to his touch. She felt a genuine envy for the wasps. *They* didn't agonize about how to suck up honey, but just literally got stuck into it.

One of their small band, however, was staggering about, clearly having difficulties, as it lurched towards the pastries, only to blunder back again. 'Hey, Rob, see that wasp? It looks completely drunk!'

'Well, sometimes they *do* get drunk, if they've been eating fermented fruit.'

She laughed, despite herself, as the creature continued to zigzag back and forth, buzzing louder than the rest, as if crying out for help. 'It needs to lie down in a darkened room, with a couple of Alka-Seltzer!'

Far from lying down, the wasp suddenly zoomed up from the picnic cloth and dive-bombed straight towards her, landing on her hand. Alarmed, she tried to shake it off – too late. A tiny, thread-like sting shot out from its body and jabbed into her finger. 'Ouch!' she yelled, as a jolt of pain shocked through her whole arm.

'Shit! I *knew* that would happen!' Rob frowned in dismay as he inspected her hand. 'It's already swelling badly. We'd better go straight back to the hotel and ask them for some ice. Is it hurting much?'

She nodded. The pain was so acute it was as if an entire swarm of wasps was stinging her at once, and with a sort of manic glee. She hardly recognized her hand, which had swollen to the thickness of a boxing glove. There was also the pain of betrayal. She had trusted and admired those little beasts. She sat nursing her hand, letting Rob do all the clearing up. Finally he heaved the knapsack on to his back, and helped her to her feet.

'I wonder if you've had some sort of allergic reaction? I mean, *I've* been stung in the past, but the swelling was nothing like as bad as that. Look how red your knuckles are! And your whole hand's incredibly hot.'

Then it's a punishment, she thought, for being moody and morose, and about as sexy as a bowl of congealing porridge.

They trudged back along the steep and rocky path, occasionally tripping on loose stones, which rattled down in front of them in a rush of indignation, as if annoyed at being disturbed. The whole terrain was sun-scorched; not a blade of grass in sight, not a single bush or tree; the only colours stagnant-brown and sluggish-grey. It was as if some giant had come here with a blowtorch and cauterized the landscape, leaving it seared and charred. And the sun was like another sort of blowtorch, carbonizing everything it touched. She found it quite a struggle to keep going and was tempted simply to sink down where she was. The blistering heat of the sun and the burning in her hand had somehow fused together into vicious, flaring spasms. The sting had also started to itch – an itching so intense it was all she could do not to rip the skin off; even rip her fingers off. A wasp's venom must be incredibly potent to wreak such damage in so short a time.

It was a relief to reach the town and see signs of life, normal cheerful bustle, splashes of rich colour: the russet-red of roof-tiles, the green of succulent shrubs. She paused beside a fig tree, its overhanging branches bursting with ripe fruit – each lush, fat, purple globe a brimming womb.

'I'd pick you some,' said Rob, 'but I don't think we should stop. Your hand's looking really nasty. It's puffed up even more.'

She tried to keep her mind off it as they traversed the maze of streets that led to their hotel. There was no one in Reception but, in answer to Rob's shout, the grandmother came shuffling out – one of the large family that owned and ran the place. She had greeted them when they first arrived with a series of wide, tooth-less grins, while her surly son registered their details. Unlike the son, the woman spoke no English, but Rob addressed her now in Greek and, after a long and somewhat halting exchange, gave a reassuring smile.

'Darling, this lady will look after you. Her name's Demetra and she tells me she's had thirteen children and knows something about wasp-stings! She's also given me the name of a pharmacist, so I'll trot off and get some antihistamine, while you stay here, OK?'

'OK,' she muttered nervously, as she stood watching Rob depart. The old crone took her arm and led her through a door marked 'Private' into a gloomy, cluttered room that seemed to combine the functions of snuggery and storehouse. Piles of cardboard boxes full of toilet rolls and paper towels jostled against a shabby, battered sofa and a couple of past-their-prime armchairs. Stale cooking smells lingered in the air, maybe from a nearby kitchen, although there was no one else around save a mangy cat dozing on the windowsill: a skinny creature with matted, off-white fur.

Demetra sat her down on the sofa, plumped a couple of cushions behind her, then examined the injured hand, all the while letting out a stream of soothing words. Despite the grim surroundings, Amy gradually felt herself relax. Although she couldn't under-stand a single syllable, she *did* grasp the obvious sympathy in the woman's kindly tone. And she appeared to know exactly what to do. First, she fetched a bottle of vinegar and swabbed some on to the sting, which helped reduce the itching. Then she made a compress by wrapping several ice-cubes in a towel and holding it against the swelling – the shock of the cold assuaging at least the worst pangs of the pain.

Trickles of cold water were dripping on to the woman's lap, though, to Amy's surprise, she didn't seem the slightest bit concerned. Her own English grandma, Nadine, would have jumped up in alarm, worried about her expensive clothes being spoiled by watermarks. Demetra's old black frock, however, looked as if it had already taken centuries' worth of punishment and was expecting plenty more. Nadine and Demetra must be roughly the same age, though the fact was hard to credit. The former, with her make-up and her Botox and her sessions in the gym, looked twenty-odd years younger, whereas Demetra was a shapeless sack, with an undefined though massive bosom drooping down onto her belly, and veiny, pockmarked legs. And what on earth had happened to her teeth? Nadine spent a fortune at the dentist, opting for every cosmetic enhancement from whitening to veneers, and her hair was professionally blonded, then larded with conditioner to give it shine and body. Demetra's hair, in contrast, was scanty and lack-lustre; the iron-grey locks scraped into an unflattering bun. Her face was a mass of wrinkles, and her bulging calves were clad in woolly pink socks, which looked utterly incongruous with her scuffed black lace-up shoes. Yet this total lack of concern about her appearance was somehow very comforting. What freedom it must bring, not to give a toss if you put on weight or your clothes were decades out of date or – dare one even think it? – not to care if you were sexy. Demetra *didn't* care. She was at ease in her own body, and in her role as respected matriarch. And since she had given birth thirteen times, she must *once* have been desired.

Amy was suddenly aware of tears pricking at her eyelids. Horrified, she tried to blink them away, but they began streaming down her face, unchecked.

'Ssshhh, sshhh,' the woman clucked, putting her arms around her and rocking her to and fro.

'I'm not crying because of the sting,' Amy sobbed, her voice muffled in the pillowy folds of flesh. 'I'm crying because we can't have children. We've been trying for over a year, but nothing ever …happens. Rob wants them even more than me. Not thirteen, of course, but three or four. And I've let him down, you see. I know it's all my fault because …'

Although Demetra couldn't understand, it was a relief just telling someone what she'd kept secret for the last eighteen months. No way could she confide in her mother, let alone in Nadine. How could you admit that you'd faked every single orgasm since your wedding day, including those on honeymoon; that you'd almost come to *dread* sex, mired as it was in worry and deception? Which is why she hadn't conceived. It was down to stress – she was sure of it – and the more she lied to Rob, the more the stress increased. If he didn't know how she felt, then they were strangers rather than lovers; she acting the part of the sensuous, responsive wife, who actually often longed for single beds.

'Making love's become like an exam. Will I pass or fail? Will I fall pregnant or won't I? And I'm so keyed up each time, I simply can't let go, let alone enjoy it. I'm no good in bed, in any case. I know it's meant to be a natural thing and you just trust to instinct and stuff, but it doesn't seem to work – not for me, in any case. My *friends* can come – they discuss it all the time. In fact, I'm sick to death of hearing about their orgasms. It's just *me* that's weird or frigid or something. I can't blame Rob. He's great in bed – never rushes me or anything. But instead of feeling close to him, or grateful, it's as if we're in two separate worlds, especially afterwards, when we're lying there together and he's all out of breath and sort of smug. I don't say a word, of course, but underneath I'm really mad because he can't *see* I'm putting on an act, and assumes I'm just as starry-eyed as *he* is. Yet if he ever got to know I've been pretending all this time, he'd be bitterly upset.'

Scarcely pausing for breath, she continued pouring out her dilemma: being forced to lie to the person she adored. A great weight was lifting from her chest simply by this process of confessing to a stranger who couldn't grasp a single word and therefore couldn't judge. 'I'm scared I'll lose him anyway, because if we never have a baby, he might – you know, piss off. He was adopted, you see, and his adoptive parents weren't exactly loving, so he's always longed for a proper happy family. In fact, that's probably why we married in the first place. I wasn't like the other girls he'd been with, who mostly wanted money and careers, and refused to be tied down. It's ironic in a way – me the only one who wanted kids, and I turn out to be infertile. Oh, I know we haven't been trying all that long, and the doctor says there's heaps of time.

They won't even let me have the tests for another year at least, but suppose they're wrong and I end up as … as …'

The words stuttered to a halt, at last. She could barely breathe, in any case, pressed as she was against Demetra's bosom, and hoarse from the long outburst. Finally forced to lift her head, she saw the woman nodding emphatically, as if she had, in fact, understood the gist of it. Oh, *no*, thought Amy, blushing in confusion. This stuff was highly intimate, and she had never told another living soul.

Then, all at once, Demetra lumbered to her feet and shuffled out of the room. Amy watched in consternation. She must have walked out in disgust, sick of listening to the spiel. After all, most hotel guests didn't demand first aid, then, instead of saying thank you, start sobbing, sounding off. And, anyway, she must be really busy, involved as she was in running the hotel, so why should she waste her precious time comforting a cry-baby?

Amy wiped her eyes on her sleeve. Without the relief of the ice, the sting was nagging and throbbing as fiercely as before. She had better make a quick retreat, sneak up to her room and wait till Rob got back. But, just as she moved towards the door, Demetra bustled through it, holding something on her palm: a small, highly polished stone, deep glossy black in colour and perfectly round in shape. She slid it into Amy's hand – the left, uninjured one – speaking very solemnly. What on earth could she be saying? A stone was no damned use. Yet, as she closed her fingers round it, she felt a peculiar sense of peace suddenly flooding through her body. Could it be some lucky charm or talisman, like the miraculous medals she had believed in as a child? Intrigued, she glanced at Demetra, but the wrinkled face gave nothing away as she led her to the sofa and sat her down once more. However, she was still talking with that same high-flown intensity; the words sounding like a religious rite or mantra. And Amy could certainly sense a difference in her *own* mood. She felt purged, revived, in some way; even the frantic pain beginning to dull down. It was as if she'd become a chrysalis, safe in some dark, meditative place, encased in a protective sheath that nurtured and cocooned her, until she could emerge again in different guise.

The spell was broken by a tap-tap on the door, and Rob's voice calling from outside.

Jolted back to reality, her first emotion was embarrassment. Suppose Demetra told him that she had broken down and cried? As the woman went to greet him, Amy, too, sprang up and tried to catch his eye. 'What's she *saying*, Rob?' she demanded.

'That you're beautiful and I'm a lucky man!'

She flushed. Demetra was still addressing him, wagging her finger vehemently, even tugging at his arm. 'Rob, what's she telling you now?'

'That these pills I've got from the pharmacy could make you rather dozy, so you ought to go to bed and rest. In fact, she wants you to have a good long sleep and not do a single thing.'

'OK,' she said, nodding in relief. Clearly Demetra hadn't said a word about the tears. She gave the woman a grateful hug, but Demetra took her arm and linked it solemnly through Rob's, as if joining them symbolically. Then, ushering them out into the foyer, she stood gesturing to the staircase, as if saying, 'Up to bed.'

Amy opened her eyes with a start. Some furious, vengeful presence was lodged in her right hand, spitting at her, letting fly. The sting! She stared down at her fingers, now as thick as small bananas, despite the antihistamine. Had Rob's Greek let him down and he'd brought back the wrong pills? No – she had actually managed to get to sleep, which itself was a minor miracle.

She fumbled for her watch to check the time. Half past four. Brilliant light was streaming through the gap in the curtains and the room was stifling hot. She had gone to bed with nothing on, yet her whole body was flushed and feverish, the skin covered with a film of sweat. So much for Demetra's magic stone. She had put it under her pillow with a sense of total trust, yet her hand was worse than ever.

'Hey, darling, are you awake?'

She jumped, not knowing Rob was there. He was sitting in the corner, on the floor, studying one of his Greek books. The hotel was so basic it provided only a bed and a row of hooks for clothes, not any sort of chair. 'Oh, Rob!' she said. 'You look terribly uncomfortable.'

'Well, I didn't want to wake you.'

'You should have gone out for a walk or something.'

'No, I felt I ought to be here, in case … How's the pain?'

'Vile!' she snapped, suddenly furious with herself and her stupid, swollen fingers, furious even with *him*: his kindness and concern, his constant maddening decency.

Scrambling to his feet, he came to sit beside her on the bed. 'Let me see.'

'No.' She held her hand behind her back, deliberately out of reach. 'I'm sick and tired of the bloody thing.'

'I don't blame you. I only wish it was *me* that was stung, so—'

'Kiss me!' she demanded, cutting off his words. He looked surprised and hurt – with reason. Never before had she ordered him about or used that peremptory tone, let alone when he was offering sympathy.

He kissed her very gingerly, as if she were an invalid but, seized by a wild impetuousness, she forced her tongue inside his mouth, ran it round the sharp edges of his teeth, bit his lips, then thrust her tongue still deeper. 'Take off your clothes.'

'But surely you don't want to …?'

'Yes,' she said, 'I *do*.' It wasn't a question of 'wanting'. She was being driven by the venom in her body – the venom left by the wasp, which was now throbbing through her with a seething sort of rage: rage at her own barrenness, her failure to conceive.

And her fury had affected Rob, roused him in the best sense. Excited by her dominance and by her edgy, febrile mood, he began tearing off his T-shirt, tugging at his belt, trying to kiss her breasts while still dragging down his jeans. She knocked his hand away, too het up for preliminaries, then rolled on top of him, legs astride his hips.

'Amy we *can't* do this!' he faltered, suddenly catching sight of her red and swollen hand. 'Just look at you! You're probably running a fever.'

'I'm not, I'm not. We *must*!' She grasped his penis and tried to stroke it stiff again – not easy, with one hand out of action. Frantically, she used her mouth instead. Her usual passive, bashful self had vanished, and she was now forcing the pace, bearing down on top of him the minute he was erect, and ramming him inside her, then moving in long rhythmic strokes. And he, too, started thrusting with a wildness and abandon she had never seen before. Of *course* her hand was hurting – the pain was near unbearable – but pain was simply part of it. Only now, with that wasp venom inside her, did she understand that making love was really making war; that she had to forego all tenderness, had to heave and wrestle, bite and scratch. This was the only way to conceive – not to hope and plead and piss about, as she'd been doing for so long, but to *demand* a child, force one from the fates above, insist on her God-given right to it. And at last she'd got the knack. All distracting thoughts had gone; all pointless, paltry head-talk. She was as sharply, intently focused as the wasps; her body burning with anger, pain, desire.

'Wait!' she cried, pausing for a second to reach beneath the pillow for the stone. She clasped it in her fingers, desperate to release its magic. It was Demetra's stone and it had worked for that old crone, thirteen times, for God's sake, so let it work once more. It *would* – it bloody must.

Then, all at once, even thoughts of the stone were stifled and engulfed, as she was swept into a rhythm – some essential, ancient rhythm, in tune with the very movement of the earth, the circling of the planets, the ebb and tug of tides. The rhythm was taking her over, carrying her along, building up, building up, with a force and sheer fanaticism that couldn't be resisted, couldn't be denied, until suddenly she was arching her body, screwing up her eyes, screaming out, 'I'm coming, Rob! I'm *coming*!'; nails clawing at his shoulders, the injured hand erupting in a maddened lash of pain. Who cared? After eighteen months of faking, this was the real, amazing thing. Her whole body was exploding in a sort of fizzing, spitting triumph: stupefying, savage, outlandish, gross, exquisite.

And he was coming, too – the most powerful come of his life, because any second, any second, his sperm would shoot out into her, with the same force and fury as the sting – make her swell and swell.

Yes, their child would be born in blessed nine months' time.

Happy Ending

'Thank you for calling "Happy Endings". We are delighted to welcome you as a customer—'

'Cut the cackle,' she muttered under her breath.

'And we wish you a pleasant shopping experience with our—'

Couldn't they just get *on* with it? Most people were far too busy for such vacuous pleasantries.

'To contact our call centre, please press the star key on your phone.'

She jabbed it irritably, using her other hand to wipe a trail of dust from the bookshelf.

'Hello. Welcome to "Happy Endings!"'

They had welcomed her already. Once was more than enough. 'Happy Endings' was a peculiar name, in any case – maybe suitable for maternity wear, but not for general mail order. On the whole, she mistrusted happy endings – in films and books, at least. They seemed not only contrived, but often a form of self-delusion.

'In order to continuously monitor services, your call may be recorded for quality or training purposes.'

She noted the split infinitive. At the end of last term, there'd been a heated discussion in the Staff Room about split infinitives, Geoff maintaining that if Shakespeare split them, so could he. But then Geoff taught Physics, not English.

'To reduce waiting time for services, choose one of the following options. To place an order, please press "one". For queries regarding—'

Quickly she pressed 'one', in order to interrupt the second recorded voice, which sounded even more inanely cheery than the first.

A third voice then piped up – recorded again, of course. A person actually addressing her would be too much to expect. *'You would like to place an order?'*

'Yes,' she said to empty air. 'I've just pressed "one", for heaven's sake!'

'Please hold the line. An operator will be with you shortly.'

Thank God, she thought, continuing her impromptu dusting. Now that she had broken up, she must get down to some serious cleaning. She had been too busy marking essays to bother about the state of the flat. It was the state of the essays that gave real cause for concern: misspellings, execrable grammar, cribbings from the Internet.

'All our operators are currently busy. Please hold, and your call will be answered as soon as possible.'

'Currently', she repeated, reflecting on its etymology: from the Latin *currere*, no doubt. Though wouldn't it be simpler to say 'at present'?

The inevitable music came next. Why was it always Vivaldi? Though perhaps, on reflection, *The Four Seasons* was wonderfully apt. If she held on long enough, summer would fade into autumn, autumn freeze to winter, winter fanfare into spring, and spring laze into summer again – and all before she'd specified the first line of her order.

'All our operators are still busy, but your call is important to us, so please continue to hold.'

Patience had never been her strong point. She remembered as a child, working herself into a frenzy waiting for Christmas or her birthday, or for her father to come back (which he never did, of course), or waiting to be old enough to have ice-skates or a dog.

'When *I* was a child,' her mother used to say, 'there were more serious things to worry about – when meat would come off ration, or the street-lights be turned back on.'

The war had been her mother's favourite subject – the bombings, the privations, the danger, the adrenaline – but to a kid of eight or nine, it seemed as long ago as the Battle of Hastings, and every bit as boring.

Even now, her mother took a perverse delight in living in the past. 'And, of course, we didn't have supermarkets, with all that bewildering choice. There'd be Cheddar – mild or strong – not hundreds of fancy cheeses from all over the world. "Like it or lump it" was the attitude in *those* days. And we had to wait for fruit and vegetables to come into season – things like strawberries or runner beans. Whereas today you can buy anything at any time of the year.'

'And what's wrong with that?' she'd countered

'It makes everyone too greedy and demanding. They expect too much and expect it instantly. And it's getting worse and worse, what with mobile phones and email. When *I* was little, we didn't even *have* a phone.'

A blessing, perhaps, she mused, as the same recorded message was repeated for the seventh time. '*All our operators are still …*'

All their operators could well be in a call-centre in Delhi or Calcutta, enjoying an extended lunch-break, eating chapattis or stretched out on their prayer-mats.

More music. Well, at least she was getting a free concert, although, given a choice, she would have opted for Bach in preference to Vivaldi. But she ought to count her blessings. She had six whole weeks ahead of her until school restarted in September, so a little wasted time was of no real consequence. Besides, waiting was simply part of life, and there were many grimmer aspects of it than merely waiting to order a few items from a catalogue. She might be waiting for an operation (up to two years on the National Health), or waiting for the results of a biopsy (was the tumour cancerous?), or waiting for the AA to arrive (having broken down in a blizzard in the wilds), or waiting by a hospice bed for some beloved friend to slip away, or waiting to hear news of a missing child or kidnapped relative, or waiting for the rescue team to arrive, stranded on Mount Everest with a collapsed lung or broken leg.

'*All our operators are still ….*'

She sat down heavily, the receiver still clamped to her ear. Although she'd been fortunate enough to avoid all such catastrophes, she had still spent much of her life waiting for things that hadn't yet materialized. A partner, for example. Of course, when it came to marriage and relationships, you had to be willing to compromise, but not to the extent of a total (fatal) mismatch. She reviewed the past contenders, wondering if she'd been too hasty in dismissing them. Barry? No. She couldn't live with a man who read the *Daily Express*. Daniel? No, again. His devotion to the gym bordered on the obsessive. Three hours each day pumping iron would leave little excess energy for pumping *her*, in bed. Michael? Yes, a possible. Indeed, more than that – much more. They had truly been in love, even started planning a future together, then all at once he'd changed his mind and ended the whole thing. And, most recently, Francisco, who was Spanish, hunky, cultured and amusing, but wedded to his (female) therapist.

A total of four men wasn't exactly impressive. In fact, just last week she'd read a survey claiming that in the ten-year period between the ages of sixteen and twenty-six, women had, on average, seven different sexual partners. And *she* was pushing forty. Still, she always tried to spin the line that she was perfectly happy with her current single state. Any hint of bitterness would only drive a man away. And as for loneliness – the very word was taboo. 'There's no risk of being lonely in a school the size of yours,' her mother once remarked. Which was patently untrue. Besides, working with a thousand children and fifty other staff was a completely different matter from finding your one own special someone.

'*We are sorry to keep you waiting, but we are experiencing an unusually high volume of calls …*'

Ah, a change of message now – a fourth recorded voice, still maddeningly upbeat. She was tempted to ring off, but she did desperately want that scarlet dress in the catalogue. It was dramatic, different and perfect for her fortieth. She was planning a little party and wanted to make it clear that although she'd reached a significant birthday – the start of middle age, no less – she had no intention of greying into pathetic anonymity. Anyway, although the chores were piling up, and she ought to start the lengthy process of preparing next year's lessons, she had no actual engagements today – nor any day this week – so she might as well continue with the call.

Most of her friends and colleagues had already gone away: Geoff camping with his children in St Ives; Ella and her husband touring Tuscany; Claire and John caravanning in Wales. Easy for *them*, of course, with company built in. Holidays for singles were a contradiction in terms. Who would choose to eat alone each night, or wander round churches and museums with a crowd of uncongenial strangers, all eyeing up each other with suspicion and distaste? And there was also the little matter of paying a single supplement to get a room to oneself. Easier and cheaper to dispense with a proper holiday and simply spend a long weekend with Great-Aunt Kate. OK, the shabby Shropshire cottage didn't have quite the ambience of Bali or Barbados, but at least her aunt was extremely hospitable, and even the old spaniel always barked a croaky welcome. Which was another reason to continue hanging on. She had found the perfect present in the 'pets' section of the catalogue: a very superior dog basket – actually styled a 'designer sofa' – in burgundy leather, with velvet-covered cushions. Although horrendously expensive, it was particularly recommended for older and less agile dogs and, since Rex was even more decrepit than his owner, would make a very suitable gift.

The Vivaldi had come round again – although she didn't much care for the recording, which was lush and over-romantic. *The Four Seasons* sounded better on authentic baroque instruments, which gave it more astringency and bite. Not that she played it overmuch. However, Vivaldi had his uses, if only in her frequent father-fantasies. Vivaldi had been taught music as a child by his violinist-father, and she enjoyed swapping places with the favoured little boy. Several times each week, the loving, caring father would be sitting at the harpsichord playing her a lullaby before she went to bed, or tenderly restringing her child-size violin, so they could perform duets together.

'*All our operators are still ...*'

So it was back to the old message. She ought to keep a tally of how many times it was repeated, so she could complain to the managing director, giving facts and figures. It wouldn't make the slightest difference, though. He'd merely pass on her complaint to some minion, who would respond with a bland letter – probably full of the same grammatical errors she found herself correcting every year. Mind you, she could mark the letter and send it back: 'C-minus. Must try harder.'

'Must try harder' had always been her own motto – not that it had got her anywhere. It was a scandal really that Rory should have been appointed Head of Department, when *she* was better qualified. And it wasn't just a matter of qualifications. Rory always shot off home the minute he'd finished teaching, whereas she stayed on, evening after evening, typing up new handouts, photocopying books, or giving extra tuition to any needy pupils. And even when she *did* get home, she found herself still worrying about Angela's dyslexia or Abdul's lack of social skills, and wishing she could divide herself into a thousand different pieces, so she could help every member of every class with all their different problems all at once.

'... *please hold, and one of our operators will be with you as soon as possible.*'

She winced at that final phrase. 'As soon as possible', like 'do one's best', was far too vague to be meaningful. When people said, 'I did my best', she was invariably tempted to challenge them. 'You *really* did your best? You spared no effort, toiled night and day, sweated blood, strained every nerve and muscle?' Unlikely in the extreme. The words were so much guff – indeed sometimes spoken defensively to disguise actual negligence.

Appalled by her own idleness, she sprang up from the chair and, using her free hand, tried to tidy the top-heavy pile of *Times Educational Supplement*s. Would she ever get promotion? And how long could she afford to wait, without considering a move else-where? But, if she moved, who would bother about Angela or Abdul, or the difficult children from dreadful homes, or those, like her, who'd had no father in their lives?

She had always longed to have children of her own – another type of waiting, and one almost at an end if she didn't meet the right man fairly soon. Her ovaries must be flagging by now; her egg-supply decreasing daily in both quantity and quality. And even if modern technology developed to the point that allowed her to give birth in her fifties, she'd be too old to deal with her offspring's teenage tantrums and too poor to pay their college fees. Though, once again, she never said a word in public about broodiness or biological clocks, but let it be assumed that her job was so fulfilling, she simply didn't have the incentive (let alone the time) to start a family. Fortunately, many of her contemporaries did truly feel that way, so at least she was in tune with the *Zeitgeist*, rather than pitied as a childless spinster, as her great-aunt would have been. Yet although she kidded all and sundry, it was much harder to deceive herself. The sad, stark truth was beginning to hit home: without a husband and a family, she *wasn't* fulfilled and never would be.

'Thank you for calling "Happy Endings". We ...'

Lord, back to the beginning again! Perhaps she'd held on for so long, the whole sequence of recorded messages was about to be replayed. Or maybe her luck had changed for once and a real-life person would come on to the line. A happy ending from 'Happy Endings' would definitely be welcome: a helpful, willing operator who'd dispatch her order this very afternoon.

'*... please hold, and ...'*

No, foiled again.

Still chained to the receiver, she wandered to the window and stared out at the communal garden. Well, hardly communal. On the rare occasions she'd sat there, she hadn't spoken to a single soul. Still, it was a bonus to have a decent view rather than look out at a bare brick wall and, with the roses in full bloom and the fuchsias cascading pink and purple, the flowerbeds looked magnificent.

The Vivaldi had restarted – the same short section repeated *ad infinitum* between the recorded announcements. She'd been wrong about the seasons. It was still the beginning of *Spring* and, at this rate, would continue to be, long after the roses had shrivelled and the fuchsias were covered in snow.

Well, she'd better use the time to learn some patience – probably a more important virtue than fortitude or temperance. After all, the whole of life could well be regarded as just a series of different periods of waiting: waiting to be born, waiting to grow up, waiting to leave school, or college, waiting for the right job, waiting to get married, waiting to conceive, waiting for your children to become grown-ups in their turn, waiting for retirement, waiting to enter a geriatric home, waiting for decay – and death.

She remained standing at the window, watching a pair of blackbirds peck around the lawn. The sun was actually shining today, in contrast to the recent drizzly showers. In fact, she was tempted to sneak out there, if only for five minutes, just to feel the warmth on her face. But it would be madness to ring off when her call was being held in a queue and must, if there was any justice, be almost at the head of it by now.

'*... please hold, and ...'*

For heaven's *sake*! Was the queue a million-strong? – hordes of thwarted customers glued to the phone in their offices or sitting-rooms in every town and village in the land, trying desperately, heroically, to get through before they expired from sheer frustration.

'*All our operators are still busy, but your call is important to us ...*'

'Rubbish!' she retorted, her newly developed patience suddenly snapping at a stroke. If her call were truly important, they would hire a load more operators, or overhaul the entire ordering system. Anyway, since they hadn't a clue who she was, or what her call was about, how the hell could they claim it was important? It reminded her of those people in her life who had told her that she mattered, then disappeared without a backward glance. Oh, yes, she'd been desperately important to her father – his cherub, his pet lamb, his favourite little girl in all the world – but that hadn't stopped him walking out. In fact, he hadn't so much as penned her a brief letter in the ensuing thirty-five years, to find out how she was. And what about her friend, Suzanne, who had never stopped enthusing about how precious their relationship was, and how much she'd always treasure it – until she found a husband. Now she couldn't even be bothered to send a Christmas card. And Michael, of course, swearing eternal love, even planning all the details of their wedding, before getting cold feet and fleeing back to Mother.

She slumped onto the sofa with the phone. Why was she still hanging on? Did she *really* want that dress? Wasn't it too blatant and seductive, when her normal style tended towards the sober and the safe? Besides, the things you bought on mail order were often disappointing – the colour or style quite different from the illustration, the quality less good. Then you had to go to all the trouble of packing the stuff up again and trekking down to the post office (often waiting in a lengthy queue again) just to send it back.

Come to think of it, did she even want the party? Why go to all that trouble and expense for friends who might not bother to turn up? And she certainly *didn't* want the dog-basket because she wasn't going to stay in Shropshire with an ailing aunt and an arthritic dog. The welcome might be warm, but the cottage itself was invariably cold, not to mention damp, and her great-aunt's cooking centred mainly on potatoes.

In fact, the longer you waited for something, the less its appeal. You could look forward to a holiday all year, only to find yourself beside the Seine or Danube, feeling homesick for the Thames. And birthdays were a letdown – just another day, no different from the one before, except you had to grapple harder with self-pity. And even promotion would probably end in tears. Any Head of Department job was bound to bring extra stress and strain, with few advantages to compensate. As for finding a man, there was no guarantee that he would actually be congenial, and you could hardly package up a husband, like a party-dress or dog-basket, and send him back for a refund. The same with giving birth. Your longed-for child might turn out to be delinquent or just plain diffi- cult. Far better to have nothing and thus no chance of disillusionment. And far better to stop waiting, in order to free yourself to live.

'... *your call is important to us ...*'

'Bugger off!' she yelled, and banged down the receiver, though with relief instead of fury. She *had* her happy ending – at no cost whatsoever and without ordering a thing: she would no longer hope, or wait, or wish, or even keep pretending – there wasn't any need. From this day forth, she would be perfectly content with what she had and who she was.

And today she would spend in the gloriously sunny garden, not preparing next year's lessons or catching up on reading, but doing nothing more demanding than making daisy-chains – and revel- ling in her new self-satisfaction.

Robin

Reaching out in panic, she pushed at the coffin lid. It was pressing down, pressing down, enclosing her in darkness. Cramped and claustrophobic. She could hear clods of earth thudding on the wood. The gravediggers must be filling in the hole.

'Help!' she screamed, but no sound came out. Her voice had gone. Her eyes had gone. Even the gravediggers had left now. She was all alone, alone for all eternity.

Her hand snapped on the bedside light. Its beam dispersed the darkness, replacing the coffin with the marital bed, the graveyard with the bedroom. She opened her eyes to large pink cabbage-roses blooming on the walls, neatly drawn pink curtains, mahogany chest of drawers. For a moment she lay still, just listening to her heartbeat. Then she groped for Robin's pyjamas, which she kept folded on his pillow, and buried her face in the stripy cotton fabric, trying to gather strength from him before she dared to look at the clock. If it was only 2 or 3 a.m., she would be plunged back into nightmare. In the early hours the normal world mutated; became a grotesque, deformed, hallucinatory void.

Fumbling for her spectacles, she finally forced herself to check. Ten to blessed five. It would be light in less than an hour, and light was like a kindly mother, soothing away the terrors. It was time to get up, in any case. The alarm-bell would be shrilling any moment.

Turning it to mute, she eased herself out of bed, trying to remember what day it was. Tuesday? Wednesday? Not that it really mattered, since all days were much the same now. She buttoned her thickest woolie over her long white nightgown, deciding to stay that way till bedtime. No point getting properly dressed when there was nobody to see her. Besides, it was becoming increasingly difficult to do up her bra or fasten her suspenders. She was as stiff as one of Robin's wooden coat hangers.

Having washed her face and cleaned her teeth, she went downstairs to make the tea, setting out the usual two cups, and opening the big, square tin with the picture of the Queen on, in her coronation robes. She doled out Robin's three biscuits: one ginger nut, two custard creams. They had gone very stale and crumbly, but she refused to throw the packets away when Robin's hand had touched them. Yet food was now the enemy – all those hundredweights of meals she had cooked over fifty-seven years: Cornish pasties, chicken pies, apple dumplings, steamed jam rolls. She had made them in her innocence, producing all his favourite things – and killing him in the process. But then how could she have known? In *her* day, sugar gave you energy and fat helped to oil the joints. You rarely made a sponge cake without filling it with jam; never served up mashed potatoes without a generous dollop of butter. Those were simple little luxuries, not poisons that clogged arteries or led to heart attacks.

She drank her tea – and Robin's – spooning the half-melted sugar from the bottom of the cup, the way he did himself. Then, putting on his anorak, she unlocked the back door. She had taken to wearing his jackets, even indoors in the warm. Being enveloped in his faint, intimate smell made him feel much closer, and she liked finding his small treasures in the pockets: lengths of string, old stained and faded handkerchiefs, the odd nail or screw, even, once, a dead beetle in a matchbox. The beetle was now precious, since presumably it had been alive when *he* had. Maybe he had spoken to it, as he often did to creepy-crawlies. ('Not so fast, old boy. Where d'you think you're off to?' 'Look, I don't mind sharing the bath, but ...')

As she ventured into the garden, the chilly darkness pounced on her like a cat; its dense, clotted fur cold against her face. She detested cats – murderers, the lot of them. There was no sign yet of daylight, though a plump half-moon hung above the conifers; a ripe chunk of Edam, Robin's favourite cheese.

She stepped on to the lawn, the frosted grass crunching slightly under her bedroom slippers, and her spirits lifting, as always, when she heard the birds singing through the darkness. Their life was so precarious, faced with hunger, cold – and cats – yet every morning they were up before dawn, pouring forth that symphony of sound: twitterings and chirpings, throaty coo-coo-cooings, triumphant caws and squawks.

As she stood listening in the shadows, the sky slowly began to lighten; its deep indigo blue paling to a mysterious slatey-grey. The moon was fading, too, as if an invisible hand were slowly rubbing it out. And the yellows in the garden started shining through the gloom: daffodils, forsythia, bright stars of winter jasmine. Moving very quietly, so as not to frighten any living thing, she unscrewed the jar of seed and poured some onto the bird-table. She knew who'd be the first. Like his namesake, the robin was an early riser.

As yet, though, no birds at all were visible and, as far as human beings were concerned, she appeared to be the only one awake. The houses on either side were plunged in total darkness, and the bungalow at the back had only its porch-light shining. But she liked that sense of a fresh, new-minted morning rising from the shroud of night just for her alone. And certainly night was losing ground; the slate-grey sky now pearling into silvery-white, like the inside of an oyster shell. And colours other than yellow were coming into focus: the exotic, waxy pink of the magnolia, the scarlet shout of camellias.

Suddenly she tensed. There he was, on the bird-table, head jauntily cocked as he surveyed the pile of seed, then sharp beak jab-jab-jabbing as he began to peck it up. She smiled in recognition. Size apart, they were so alike: both avid for their food (and consequently both plump around the midriff); both with dark, bright eyes; both friendly, cheery souls, eager and alert. The day she'd first met Robin, over sixty years ago, he had been wearing a red sweater, which immediately attracted her amidst the dirge of drab grey suits. The red had set off his dark hair and seemed to promise passion – a promise duly kept. And the bird's own cheerful splash of red had somehow kept her going throughout the recent winter: the first winter on her own. Indeed, there were robins indoors, too. Any Christmas card that featured the birds she refused to throw away, but had kept strung above the mantelpiece for the last three months and more. Some of the cards she could hardly bear to read: those from odd acquaintances who hadn't known about the death and had simply written automatically, 'To Robin and Joanna …'

Jab and gulp, jab and gulp. The bird ate with Robin's famished concentration, and with the same immoderate interest. Her husband had rarely missed a meal in all their years of marriage, and usually seated himself at the table long before the pie had browned or the carrots been dished up. And he invariably asked for seconds and, even then, would scrape out all the serving dishes, as if loath to leave a single morsel. It had been a sort of tribute, a homage to her role as provider – now repeated by the bird, which had already reduced the pile of seed to the merest scattering. There was little left for the wood pigeon that lumbered heavily down, with a slightly drunken demeanour, as if suffering from a hangover. Robin had always referred to wood pigeons as 'Arthurs' – *why*, she couldn't tell – but she regarded this particular Arthur with a certain indignation, since it had frightened off her favourite little bird.

'Don't worry, darling,' she whispered as it sought refuge in the shrubbery. 'I'll be back later with your lunch, and then with tea, of course.'

On 22 March she got up even earlier, needing extra time to make herself look presentable. She couldn't slop around in her nightie all day on her wedding anniversary. When she finally slipped out into the garden, she was wearing Robin's favourite dress: the greeny-blue shantung, with his camel-coloured car coat buttoned snugly over it. The sky was scattered with stars, as if he had bought her diamonds and flung them down in handfuls from on high. She stretched up to try to touch one, wishing she had his height. He had always been the one who got things down from the top cupboards in the bedroom, or from the highest kitchen shelf. Now anything she couldn't reach she had to do without.

As well as the diamonds, he had laid on a full orchestra; every bird singing its small heart out, to celebrate their fifty-eighth. And she could hear the robin's confident voice amidst all the other chirrupings – that clear, melodious, jubilant sound, challenging the darkness to disperse. Obediently, a few white cloudlets began massing in the east, pale against the inky sky, and the dense murk in the garden gradually thinned to gauzy mist. As she moved away from the shelter of the fence, the robin appeared, as if from nowhere, a blurred shape in the gloom. He normally stayed hidden in the shrubbery till ten to six at the earliest. Yet here he was, alighting on the table at only half past five. But then Robin, too, would always get up earlier on the day of their anniversary, to bring her breakfast in bed, putting a red rose on the breakfast tray and an exciting little package. And she, in turn, had a present for the robin: a box of writhing mealworms.

'Happy anniversary,' she murmured, tipping three worms on to the table and watching as they were gobbled in delight. Mealworms for a robin were the equivalent of Dundee cake for her husband – the food loved best of all. And between each luscious mouthful, the bird cocked its head and gazed at her in gratitude, as Robin had so often done.

Intent as she was on the spectacle, she almost failed to notice the activity on the lawn. Two blackbirds were scouting for breakfast and a posse of hopeful pigeons strutting self-importantly. She had brought food for them, as well, wanting everyone to feast today. Breaking the bread into pieces, she threw the scraps on to the grass, and was immediately rewarded with a flurry of wings and beaks. There seemed to be far more birds than usual, even a couple of jays on the bird-table, which was definitely unprecedented. Such shy, retiring creatures rarely ventured so close to the house, let alone when people were around. In fact, she had never seen a jay at such close range, and stood admiring the pinkish-brown plumage, with its contrasting patch of electric-blue, gleaming iridescent on the wings. Could this be Robin's doing – her husband laying on more anniversary treats?

She suddenly knew that, lonely or no, the day could and would be happy. Warm spring weather was forecast, so she could take herself out to the park, maybe even buy an ice. If Robin was watching over her, then she owed it to him to rejoice.

A week later, she was totally confused. She had put the clocks back, in error, then, hearing the time on the radio, realized it was quarter to six, not quarter to four, as she'd thought. Every year, in late October and late March, she had trouble working out whether the clocks went forward or back. It was Robin who had put her right – along with the clocks and watches – and without him she was lost.

Disoriented, she hurried into the garden, where the sky was still funereal-dark; the natural world following its normal pattern, regardless of British Summertime. At least the robin hadn't missed his breakfast – in fact, there was no sign of him at all – but she quickly tipped his seed onto the table, along with a couple of mealworms.

Despite so-called official summer, a spiteful wind was blowing, and seemed to pierce right through to her naked flesh, as if a nightdress and a cardigan and even Robin's anorak were trivial defences, easily assailed. The last few days had been so bright and sunny, this unexpected cold was like a brutal tyrant displacing a kindly altruist. Shivering, she looked up at the sky, which, instead of paling to its usual slatey-grey, had become a threatening reddish colour, as if reflecting fire, or war. Even the birds seemed cowed. The deep melancholy cawing of the crows drowned out all other sounds.

There was a sudden rush of wings – three pigeons flapping down, closely followed by an 'Arthur', a portly fellow, with its feathers all fluffed up against the cold. She prayed the robin would be next, but a magpie came instead, its black and white livery so shiny-smart and dapper it could have been a waiter at the Ritz. The crows had stopped their cawing now, so she strained her ears to listen for the robin. But all she could make out was the faint, insistent drumming of a woodpecker in next-door's blighted beech, and the croaking cough of a jay.

Increasingly anxious, she went to fetch some mealworms. The robin would no more ignore his favourite food than her husband would turn his back on a fresh-baked Dundee cake. Laying the worms on the table, she stepped back into the shadows, so as not to scare him off, keeping a constant lookout all the while. Two tits swooped down, pouncing on the treasure, then a chaffinch braved the table, in search of the remaining seed. Still no robin, though. He had appeared every single morning since the day of Robin's death – indeed *sent* by him, she believed, to help her through those empty, aching months.

She stamped her feet to try to warm them up. The flimsy, unlined slippers afforded no protection from the cold. Her eyes were watering in the wind, and her fingers almost numb, yet she couldn't bring herself to go inside. If she waited long enough, the robin *would* arrive.

Prising the lid off the plastic box, she tipped the last of the meal-worms on to the table, but it was a squirrel that arrived to claim the booty. 'How dare you!' she reproved, as it began tucking in with relish. 'That's Robin's food, not yours.' But the creature simply ignored her, eating with jerky, darting movements, as he watched constantly for predators. The *cat*, she thought with horror – that sleek, black, sly assassin who slunk into the garden without a by-your-leave, trampled down her daffodils, did its smelly business in the middle of the flowerbed, scrabbling up the earth with no concern for the poor plants. Had it killed her robin, on top of all its other crimes, left nothing but a pathetic pile of feathers? Those angry streaks of red, still daubed across the sky, now seemed like bloody paw-prints.

Miserably she crouched down by the fence, but her knees objected to the unnatural, painful posture and immediately gave way. She sank on to the ground, hardly caring if she rotted where she was. Without her robin, there was no point going on; nothing to look after, nothing to get up for, nothing to give meaning to her day. Perhaps he'd gone to a new territory to try to find a mate. It was strange he hadn't paired up several weeks ago (along with most of the other birds, who'd been busy wooing and courting), but she had seen it as a mark of his devotion, refusing to share her with a stranger.

Now, though, all was changed. Even the dawn chorus seemed less a celebration than a mockery – the jeering laugh of the wood-pecker ringing out in contempt. Her joints were complaining bitterly as she lay slumped on the cold earth, yet she couldn't face returning to the empty, silent house. If only she were a bedding plant: a petunia or zinnia, which, after a few months' flowering, would be consigned to the compost heap. As a human being, she might soldier on for years yet, like all those clacking widows at the Day Centre; widows with no purpose in their life.

Suddenly a plane roared overhead, and, as if it were an alarm clock, summoning her from bed, she somehow found the strength to struggle to her feet, clinging to the fence-posts for support. As she straightened up, she gazed, startled, at the sky. The plane had left a vapour-trail so frothy-white and billowing, it reminded her of a wedding veil. And the blood-red streaks had vanished, replaced now by an expanse of blue, with glints of gold and benign white fluffy clouds. The whole garden seemed transformed, all the colours brighter, as if they'd been enamelled, and the golden trumpets of the daffodils blazing a proud fanfare, as they had done on her wedding day. That perfect day was printed on her memory, like a film she could rewind at will, whenever she felt low. Yes, there she was again, walking proudly up the aisle, supported on her father's arm; the swoony scent of lilies perfuming the church, and arrow-shafts of excitement pricking at her skin as she glided towards her husband-to-be.

Then all at once she realized, with a jolt of mingled shock and joy, that Robin was actually waiting for her still. All she had to do was float towards him along that shining vapour-path which led from earth to heaven. But did she have the courage? It would require a terrifying leap to reach the path at all – a leap of faith in her present ailing state. And she would have to do it quickly, before the trail dissolved.

Closing her eyes, she sprang recklessly, and desperately, towards the vapour-path, hearing only the wild pounding of her heart. She lost her footing and began plunging back to earth, a mere clod of pain and panic. But, even as she fell, some kindly power seemed to snatch her from the unfathomable depths and bear her up again, sustaining and supporting her until she was safely on the path. Dazed, she looked around. Everything was shimmering, tremulous, ethereal, as if made of gossamer. The foamy path beneath her feet felt pillowy and soft, and the air from this high vantage point was purer altogether, easier to breathe, Buoyed by hope, she ventured step by groping step along the gauzy track, climbing even higher until she was above the hills, above the clouds, advancing ever onwards to her mate. All earthly noise was dwindling and, in the expectant hush, she could gradually make out the faint rustle of her wedding dress and the soft swishing of her silken train. She was young again, a bride again, her whole weight of years erased, and all pain and anguish fading to the merest, thinnest mist. The vapour-trail, in contrast, was still distinct, still curving high beyond her, pointing out the way. All she had to do was follow its bright arc, guiding her to the realm of Eternal Summer.

And, as she took her final step, the majestic organ started pealing out the wedding march as Robin swooped triumphantly to claim her.

Sugar Plum

'Can I help you, dear?'

'No, just looking, thanks.' Not exactly true. She was, in fact, desperate to find something to wear for tonight, but the process would hardly be helped by some old biddy fussing around. The advantage of this shop was that the two ancient sisters who ran it usually left you to browse in peace, rather than hovering or pouncing the minute you took a hanger off the rail. Fortunately, the wrinklie shuffled off, vanishing into the storeroom at the back.

Karen riffled through the rail again, finally lighting on a leopard-print top, which she held up against her body to study the effect in the mirror. 'Tarty,' her mother snorted, but her mother was in Jedburgh, 500 miles away and, in any case, 'tarty' was precisely what she wanted. Anthony liked her to look vampish, as he called it. A wave of fear flurried through her gut. If only he wasn't married, or so *old*. It made it really awkward when he started discussing things that had happened before she was born. Yet boys her own age now all seemed immature – though admittedly less intimidating.

She squinted at the price-tag on the garment: £4.99 – which she could just about afford. It would have cost double in the Princess Alice, but that, of course, was the Bond Street of charity shops, whereas this place was bargain basement. No arty window-displays or upmarket mannequins; just a heap of assorted tat jostling for space in the window and, inside, a faint smell of cat and damp.

Wrinklie Two was serving behind the counter – the image of her sister: both with tight grey perms, bulging calves and grotesque lace-up shoes, and both wearing poncy twinsets, one primrose, one pale blue. On previous occasions, she'd heard them both called 'Mrs', which meant they must have both had sex. She tried to picture them naked and in bed with Anthony, but immediately felt another surge of panic. He liked playing these weird games – games his wife disliked, he said. No wonder. They would make any woman feel a fool, if not downright gross. But *she* pretended to like them, and now he actually believed that she was into all that porn stuff. You had to pretend, in order to keep men happy – to keep them at all, come to that.

Yes, she'd take the top – he'd like it – and now she had settled the vital matter of what to wear tonight, she'd better try to find a lampshade for her room. It was bare bulbs at the moment – and bare boards underfoot. However, the only lampshade on display was a monstrosity in purple, with a hideous matching fringe, and thus unlikely to improve her already grotty pad. Most of the stuff they sold here was stuck in a sort of time-warp – much like the sisters themselves – stacks of old LPs, hardback books by dead and dreary authors like Walter stodgy Scott, cameras that looked as if they'd come out of the ark, yellowing maps in broken frames, tarnished metal candlesticks, beaded satin evening bags.

Nothing she'd be seen dead with, in short, so she mooched up to the counter with the top, proffering a £5-note and pocketing the penny change. 'Look after the pennies,' her mother always said, 'and the pounds will look after themselves.' Patently untrue – like most of what her mother believed.

As she made her way to the door, she all but collided with Wrinklie One, who had emerged from the private storeroom with a large object in her hands: a pink jewellery-box, with a ballerina on top. Karen stared in disbelief. It looked absolutely identical to the one she'd been given by her father as a child, to celebrate her reaching double figures. Mesmerized, she scrutinized it more closely. Yes, the same pink leatherette, the same three drawers, painted with pink roses, the same slender little ballerina dressed in a real net tutu and silk top. '*Oh!*' she breathed, rooted to the spot. All sorts of questions were swarming in her head: was it for sale? Did it play the 'Dance of the Sugar-Plum Fairy' when you wound it up? Did the dancer twirl around to the tune, as hers had done so tirelessly? But she couldn't seem to speak. Her throat was blocked with pain and pleasure mixed.

'Nice, isn't it?' the woman said, clearing a space on the shelf.

Karen nodded dumbly, following in her wake.

'And it's brand new, you know. It's not often we get things in such good condition. A lady brought it in yesterday – said it was given to her daughter as a present, but the daughter didn't like it.'

Didn't *like* it? That had to be a crime.

'Thought it was too babyish, she said.'

Babyish? Even if you lived to be a hundred, you could never outgrow a box like this. She had cherished hers, right on through her teens. Day by day, month by month, the ballerina had come to play an increasingly important role in her life, as confidante, as soul-mate, as the sister she had never had. Tatyana, she was called – a name chosen by her father, which seemed to suit her cherry lips and exotic jet-black hair. And she had needed Tatyana more and more as things got worse at home, believing that as long as the little dancer was standing guard on top of the pink box, life wouldn't blow apart.

Wrong. Completely wrong.

So in a fit of almost madness, she had chucked the jewel-box out – consigned Tatyana to the rubbish bin, along with all her other stuff. She'd only done it because she was so angry with her mother – with life, with death, with heartbreak – that she didn't care if she destroyed herself and everything she loved.

Yet here was her soul-mate back again, and looking every bit as perfect as she'd done when they'd first met. Her father had crept into her bedroom on the day of her tenth birthday with a big parcel in his hands, wrapped in fancy paper and tied with a silver bow. 'For my Sugar-Plum,' he'd whispered, kissing her on the mouth. She could smell his smell of aftershave and cigarettes; taste his breakfast on her lips: coffee, bitter marmalade.

'Does it still work?' she blurted out, finding her voice at last. 'I mean, is there a key and …?'

'Yes, three keys in all. I've taped them securely to the inside of the lid. That way, they won't get lost. But I can wind it up, if you'd like to see it in action.'

'OK,' she said, feigning a casual shrug. She'd learned long ago that if something meant a lot to you, then best to hide the fact.

As the familiar tune tinkled out, the ballerina began twirling round and round, arms uplifted, face serene. In her mind, Karen was dancing too, holding out her skirt and prancing round the room, as she had done so often as a child. 'Bravo!' her father cried. 'You're so graceful on your feet. Daddy's little dancer, Daddy's little Sugar-Plum.' He had tied the silver bow in her hair, his hand brushing across her ear, lingering on her neck. His hands were so strong they could unscrew the tightest lids, or mend her bike, or carry her upstairs, as if she were still his little baby. But they were also soothing hands, which could stroke softly down her skin and ...

'Well, I must get on,' the woman said, retaping the key to the inside of the lid, before stumping off to serve another customer.

Only when she'd gone, did Karen dare to think about the price. A new, unused item was unlikely to be cheap. At least a tenner, she reckoned and she only had six quid left, now that she'd bought the top. Perhaps she could ask for a refund, and wear her old grungy black tonight instead of the sexy leopard-print. Anthony would hate it, but she'd play any stupid game he liked, to compensate.

Finally steeling herself to look at the price-tag, she let out her breath in a gasp. £29.99. Daylight robbery! She strode up to the counter. 'That jewellery-box – it *can't* be thirty quid! That's ridiculous for a charity shop. I mean, it's more than it would cost in Debenhams' or—'

'It certainly is *not*,' Blue Twinset interrupted. 'As I've told you already, it's brand new, and real leather into the bargain.'

'No, it's leatherette – I know it is. I used to have one just the same.'

'I'm sorry' – the other sister was now chipping in, her voice rising in displeasure – 'It's actually marked "real leather" on the bottom.'

'Fuck!' Karen mumbled, going back to check. Yes, the sisters were right, curse them. As a child, she had loved the word 'leatherette', which she took to be a female version of leather: soft and pink and tender – all the things her mother never was. Having replaced the box on the shelf, she lifted the lid, as she had done so many times before, to admire the little mirror inside and the nest of tiny compartments on the top. These compartments were empty, but hers had been crammed with trinkets and her store of lucky charms: a shamrock, a black cat, two lucky silver horseshoes and a tiny silver wishbone, each nestling on its couch of cotton wool. She had *needed* luck, back then – not that it had lasted long. The charms had gone the way of the box: dumped amidst old, soggy, oozing teabags and mouldy, black banana skins.

Next, she opened all three drawers in turn. Empty again, but already she was restocking them with all her childhood treasures: bangles, bracelets, pendants, magpie feathers, magic shells, letters from her father after he'd disappeared from home. Tatyana had protected all the booty, forever poised on tiptoe, as if ready for all comers. The red ballet shoes were tied with ribbons, not real, but painted on. She had longed for her *own* ballet shoes; yearned to have long jet-black hair, piled up in curls on top, instead of a boring mousy bob. And a scarlet smile, fixed permanently in place, so that she'd be cheerful all the time. Tatyana never had moods, as *she* did, nor did she hide in the airing cupboard specifically to sulk, or cry for days over nothing. And she never screamed blue murder at her mother. She didn't have a mother – lucky sod.

She reached out to touch the three small keys taped inside the lid: one for winding up the ballerina, and two to lock the drawers – the first keys she had ever owned, which made her feel wonderfully grown-up. Keys kept secrets safe, and the letters from her father were a secret. 'Don't tell your mother I keep in touch,' he always wrote before he signed his name, adding a row of kisses underneath. He even sent the letters care of Auntie Anne, who, as his sister, could be trusted not to sneak.

Wrinklie Two had just shuffled over and was regarding her suspiciously, as if she were a child with sticky fingers about to do some damage. 'Well, do you *want* this, dear, or not?'

'Could I have it a bit cheaper?' she asked, blushing as she spoke. Two customers were listening in, which made her feel embarrassed. She loathed the way she blushed still, like a gormless adolescent. She was meant to be grown up, for heaven's sake, now that she'd left the hostel and was living on her own.

'We're not allowed to reduce our prices. It's against company policy. But we do have a January sale. The only problem is, I very much doubt that a box like this will still be around by then. It's bound to be snapped up almost straight away by someone looking for a Christmas present.'

'Could you put it by, while I try to get the cash?' She had lost

Tatyana once already; mourned her ever since. The thought of losing her a second time was like a physical pain.

'No, that's not allowed either, I'm afraid. But we're open till half-past five today, so you might be lucky, if you come back later on.'

How could she drum up thirty quid in just a matter of hours? No good asking Anthony. The only time she'd begged him for cash (when she was behindhand with the rent), he had refused to lift a finger; said he paid for all the booze and nosh, *and* for the hotel, and that had to be his limit – sorry. But some of her friends might help – Pam, perhaps, or Bridie. It they lent her just a fiver each and she got a refund on the top, she'd be halfway there already.

She rushed over to the counter, where Wrinklie Two had just rejoined her sister. 'Look, I'm sorry,' she said, thrusting the bag into their hands, 'but I don't want this any more. Could you be an angel and give me the money back?'

'We don't give refunds,' the sisters said in unison, as if they had rehearsed this line before.

'But I haven't even left the shop.'

'Makes no difference. You've paid your money and been given a receipt, which means the transaction's valid. Now, would you kindly move out of the way, dear. This gentleman is waiting to be served.'

'Thanks for nothing,' she muttered, casting one last lingering look at the box before marching to the door and slamming it behind her.

Triumphantly she placed the box on the battered chest of drawers. It seemed to transform the room, so that you no longer saw the stained, uneven floorboards, or the damp patches on the walls, only the posh pink leather and the stylish ballerina. And once she had wound Tatyana up, the air was filled with sweet, silvery sounds that drowned the drone of the traffic and the noise of the kids next door. Now she had her soul-mate back, life could only improve. She would find a better job, and a quieter place to live, maybe meet a girl who'd like to share; perhaps even win the lottery and splurge the lot on clothes.

Self-consciously, she raised her arms above her head and began twirling around the room to the 'Dance of the Sugar-Plum Fairy'. She kept bumping into the chest of drawers and banging her legs on the edge of the bed, but she didn't care – she was dancing for her father; could hear him calling out 'Bravo!', praising her, admiring her. Not until she was dizzy and the whole room spinning round with her, did she finally give up, collapsing on the duvet, out of breath.

It was time to stop, in any case. She was meeting Anthony much earlier than usual, and she still had to change and put on her war paint. Anthony hated make-up. He was always worried about it getting on his shirt and all hell breaking loose at home, but she couldn't seem to face the world without blusher and mascara.

She was just applying a second coat of Wonder-Lash, when the doorbell rang loud and long. She froze. No one ever called. She was too ashamed of this squalid room to bandy her address about. It must be the police – come to bang her up! She'd assumed she'd got away with it – disguising herself in glasses and a headscarf, skulking in a corner until the coast was clear (one sister in the storeroom and the other serving customers), then quietly sliding the box into her capacious plastic laundry bag and sidling out of the shop. She had heard no cries of 'Thief!', no angry footsteps pounding in pursuit, as she had hurtled round the corner and up the hill to her street, yet someone must have seen her, none the less.

The bell rang a second time – viciously, accusingly. She wouldn't answer, pretend she wasn't here. She sat utterly still, closing her eyes, as if shutting out the coppers. But suppose they broke the door down? That would be even worse. The landlord would come rushing up, alerted by the noise. He'd throw her out – he detested her already – and she would land up sleeping rough.

Better to brazen it out, tell the cops it had all been a mistake. She'd meant to pay – honestly – but another customer had come up and started chatting, and it had simply slipped her mind. And, yes, of course she planned to return the box – in fact, she was on her way this minute. It was only five to five, so she would have time before they shut.

Jumping to her feet, she darted to the door and flung it open, explanations ready on her lips. No one there. They must have gone down to the landlord to fetch the master key. She could see herself stretched out on the pavement amidst a load of other dossers, smell the reek of beer and piss, feel the cold night air sneaking down inside her sleeping bag to grope her private parts.

Doubling back into her room, she grabbed the box, plunged it into the bag again and hurtled down the stairs with it, praying she wouldn't collide with the police.

Once outside, she slowed her pace, scared of arousing suspicion. It was dark, in any case. The sun had set an hour ago, and the murky winter's afternoon seemed to belch out fog and shadows with every clammy breath. The sky hung low, weighed down with greyish-purple clouds that looked as if they were bruised. She had come out without her coat, and her hands were numb already; her feet cold and chafing in her stupid slingback shoes. She kept glancing round in terror, expecting any minute to be nabbed by the police. The bag was banging against her legs, heavier with every step, like a boulder made of lead. The whole thing was pointless anyway. The sisters would never believe her story about forgetting to pay for the jewel-box, yet how could she replace it without them noticing? The shop was shutting any minute, so there wouldn't be many customers to provide a bit of cover. And of course they would recognize her instantly, dressed as she was in the very top they had sold her.

Her steps faltered to a halt. The plan was naff, so why risk her neck? Yet if she slunk back to her room, the coppers might be lying in wait – and her landlord, too, most likely. Perhaps she could lose herself in the huge building site that had been disfiguring this stretch of road for the last three months or more. The old Victorian pub had been torn down, to make way for a huge apartment block that would eventually stand twenty storeys high. The whole site was barricaded off, but she remembered seeing a couple of gaps where someone small could just about squeeze through. Skulking along the length of the fence, she found the larger of the holes and managed to worm her way in, trying not to graze herself on the rough edges of the wood. She stood precariously on the makeshift wooden platform, gazing down in horror into the vast excavated pit below. It was a scene of total chaos, with no sense of any building taking shape; only sheets of rusting iron, piles of earth, lengths of rotting wood, and great pitted holes filled with muddy puddles. A gang of men, wearing hard hats and fluorescent yellow jackets, was working in the glare of floodlights, their shadows moving eerily like figures in a dream. They seemed dwarfed by the scale of the project – worker-ants surrounded by gigantic cranes and soaring scaffold-towers.

A month ago, she had watched a vicious iron ball on a chain crashing into the brave but puny pub, each vicious thwack removing more of the fabric, until it collapsed in a mass of rubble. Her father's death had been like that – swingeing blows coming thick and fast, destroying her whole existence, reducing *her* to rubble. The death itself was more than she could grasp. Fathers didn't die – not at forty-two; not when you'd hoped to see them again, every day for the past three empty years. *How* he died was a mystery. People refused to tell her anything, because of what he'd done. Her mother called it criminal, but her mother was so bitter she didn't understand. He *had* touched her, yes – stroked her breasts, let his finger slip between her legs – but that was just his special way of showing her how deeply he felt; the outward sign of inner love. And he had never gone too far; never done a single thing she didn't like or want. He was her lover in the best sense: he loved her more than any man ever could or would. His death had left her naked. And what upset her most was that she hadn't sent a wreath. If she had known about the funeral, she would have stripped every flower from every bed in every garden in the land, and dispatched them by the truckload.

Furiously she wrenched Tatyana from the bag and hurled her into the chasm. She couldn't see where she landed – didn't even care. 'Good riddance!' she yelled. 'I didn't want you anyway. What's the point of dancing when my father's just a box of bones?'

She sank down on to the platform, holding her head in her hands, but immediately straightened up again, straining her ears to listen. She could hear the well-loved tune – the 'Dance of the Sugar-Plum Fairy' – ringing out above the site, every note distinct. Impossible. The whine of the electric drills drowned all other sounds; the clank of the cement-mixer; the brute clash of iron on iron. Could she be hallucinating? No, everything was in focus: the sharp metal teeth of the earth-digger, the grey sludge of fresh-laid concrete, the gleam of the scaffolding where it caught the light of the lamps. And the tune was still trilling out, the familiar lilting rhythm as catchy and consoling as it had sounded in her room. Was this her father's doing, his private signal to her, assuring her he was with her still, protecting her from beyond the grave?

She glanced around, as if half-expecting to see his burly form; hear his gravelly voice, hoarse from all the smoking. He must be there in spirit, guiding and advising her, because her mind was clear, at last, as if a brilliant light had switched on in her head, after months and months of darkness and confusion. Anthony was finished. She wouldn't be meeting him tonight, or *any* night. She didn't need him, didn't even like him – certainly didn't like the things he did.

The music rippled on, as she stood, no longer looking down, but up towards the sky, the stars. 'My Sugar-Plum,' her father breathed from some realm, way up high, 'I'm with you always, my little love – my precious, only bride.'

Fall

'Good afternoon.'

'Good afternoon,' she responded automatically, looking up from the bench to see the well-groomed, elderly gentleman who always took his constitutional in this particular part of the park and at this particular hour. They had never exchanged names, of course – nothing so familiar – just recognized each other as lone souls, killing time.

'Nice weather, isn't it?'

'Yes, lovely.'

Was it lovely, she wondered as he strolled on through the drifts of fallen leaves? October had always been her favourite month, but having celebrated her eightieth birthday earlier this year, she was more than usually aware that, beneath its golden glory, autumn was still the season of decay. Her mother, grandmother and great-grandmother had all died at eighty-one, which surely must be more than mere coincidence. She feared something in the family genes that might affect her, too, within the next eighteen months – or less.

Leaning back against the bench, she watched a yellow leaf flutter from the plane tree, then spiral in slow circles, as if it refused to end its life cycle. Every leaf, she'd noticed, fell in a different way. Some slumped directly down in a hopeless sort of fashion, giving up on life. Some were indecisive – vacillating, dithering, unsure of their direction or their fate. Others seemed adventurous, scurrying along the ground, far from their parent tree, or lifting off into the air again, like intrepid little parachutists bellying in the wind. And the trees, too, varied hugely in how they responded to the season. The beeches, for example, had hardly changed in colour, whereas most of the horse chestnuts had turned a brittle brown, and one small, stunted birch had only a few stray leaves left, clinging sadly to its mottled limbs. It was much the same with people. Her two dearest friends, Annabel and Madge, had both been in their coffins now for close on fifteen years.

In fact, the near-naked tree reminded her of Annabel in the last months of her illness, sitting half-undressed at home, wearing shabby, scanty underclothes that revealed rolls of sallow flesh, and with patches of pale, blotchy scalp showing through her thin and straggly hair. And her hands would shake continually, as the last leaves on the sickly birch were trembling even now, perhaps anticipating the same dire fate that had befallen their companions. One fell as she sat watching, dropping abruptly to the ground with an air of stern finality.

Deliberately she transferred her gaze to the sturdy oak that stood beside the bench – a much healthier tree, with a luxuriance of foliage, still mostly shiny-green. The leaves were rustling in the breeze and shimmering in the sunlight, so that the whole tree seemed astir. She envied its solidity, its massive girth, the anchor of its roots plunging deep into the earth. She tried to imagine herself with roots, and immediately felt less frail. No more risk of tripping on loose paving stones, her legs giving way beneath her; no more early-morning vertigo, as her bedroom turned a nervous somersault. But there would, of course, be a downside – she would have to stay put in one particular spot, no longer able to walk to the park or wander round the shops. A fair exchange, she wondered? Difficult to say.

'Mind if I join you?'

A young girl had stopped beside the bench, arms crossed, brows drawn down. *Laura*, she thought, with a jolt of rare excitement, as she gazed at the dishevelled clothes and blaze of red-gold hair. 'Please do,' she said, patting the battered wooden slats by way of invitation. She would happily sit next to Laura for all eternity and, although this was a much younger version, there were still striking similarities: the same tiny (enchanting) gap between her two front teeth; the same dark, sleek, tidy eyebrows, in contrast to the wild mop of wiry hair.

The girl sat down heavily, jabbing her shoes in the dirt. 'Bother you if I smoke?'

'Not at all.' Nothing about Laura had ever bothered her, except the fact she was unobtainable. She closed her eyes, to savour their first meeting. Yes, already she was there again: in New England, in the fall – the five-hour flight contracting to five seconds – she and Laura standing side by side, admiring a whole mountainside of maples. The trees were flaming in a trumpet-blast of colours: vermilion, amber, crimson, topaz, russet. The entire holiday had been tinged with red and gold: torrid sunsets setting the whole sky alight, the blaze of real log fires, heaps of glowing pumpkins, piles of tawny apples, shaggy bronze chrysanthemums running riot in the gardens. And Laura, too, continuing the theme, with her exuberant hair and crazy clothes: orange sweatshirt teamed with scarlet jeans; madcap yellow coat – *Vermont* yellow, which meant deeper and more vibrant. Returning to London, Laura-less, everything seemed weak and faint, as if the whole country had been stricken with anaemia.

'Warm today, in'it?' The girl was trying to light her cigarette, cupping her hands around the lighter and flicking at it irritably.

'It certainly is.' In Vermont, she'd been permanently flushed, as if she'd had a blood transfusion; Laura's own impetuous blood careering round her arteries, scorching all the dross away. Laura had changed the world for her – *and* changed several words. Until that particular autumn, 'Fall' meant only sin and shame: Adam's fall from innocence and grace, his expulsion from Paradise, along with guilty Eve; humanity's former happy state banished at a stroke. But once Laura had exploded onto the scene, 'fall' took on new, convulsive meanings: falling in love, falling under someone's spell, falling into temptation, falling into despair, falling ill because her passion wasn't returned – or even so much as *noticed*, come to that. Laura had been a youthful not-quite-forty; she an already fading fifty-nine. A whole generation between them; a husband and twin boys between them; the vast Atlantic Ocean between them – a bleak, forbidding ocean. And, even in America, they'd been strangers, more or less, bonded only by the fact that they were staying at the same hotel and booked on the same excursions. In fact, their total fortnight's intercourse had comprised nothing more than the exchange of a few pleasantries, when they happened to rub shoulders in the lobby, or sit behind each other on the coach.

'I'm skivin' today.' The girl blew out a plume of smoke, twisting one leg round the other.

'I beg your pardon?'

'Off work. Just couldn't face the aggro.'

'What sort of work do you do?'

The girl shrugged. 'Rubbish work.'

Could *any* work be rubbish? After her retirement from the bank, she had longed for even the lowliest of jobs, so long as it brought company and colleagues, a sense of purpose, a reason to get up. But this girl was barely twenty and thus couldn't understand. So many things she knew now, she hadn't known at *that* age: that there wasn't any truth, either in science or religion; that the health of teeth depended on the health of gums; that love brought more pain than pleasure, and that high heels always exacted their revenge.

'I'm Sharon, by the way.'

'Oh. Nice to meet you, Sharon.' Everyone used Christian names these days, even doctors and dentists. Yet *they* were still 'Dr' and 'Mr', which didn't seem quite fair. For most of her life she'd been 'Miss'– considered now almost a badge of shame. People assumed that because you were 'Miss', you had never been in love; never prey to the sort of delirium that could shrink planet earth's whole teeming populace to one small, slim-boned female. That first evening in Vermont, she had sat in the hotel dining-room feasting on the pith and core of Laura, consuming her in great intoxicating gulps, along with the four-course meal. And everything on the menu just happened to be gold that night: corn on the cob, honey-roasted chicken, sweet potatoes, braised squash, pumpkin pie.

'And *your* name?'

'Cecily.'

'Come again.'

'Cecily,' she repeated. 'It means "blind one" – well, according to the *Book of Babies' Names*.'

The girl swivelled on the seat to peer into her eyes. 'You're not blind, are you?'

Yes, in a way, she thought. In Vermont, she'd been completely blind to reality; had actually dared to hope that she and Laura might somehow get together, despite the hulking husband, the raucous, clingy twins, the smug gold wedding ring. Certainly, in her fevered mind, she and Laura spent their nights together. That first frantic kiss – she was experiencing it now again – all the concentrated colour of the blazing maple trees pouring into her body, leavening its pale and passive flesh. She was tempestuous yellow, sizzling scarlet, cascading molten bronze. Sleep was out of the question. Indeed, she had hardly closed her eyes the entire fortnight of the trip. With Laura dazzling beside her, it would be a crime to waste a single second in dull unconsciousness.

Sharon flicked a worm of ash off her jeans. 'See that big tree there?'

'Yes.'

'What's it called? I don't know the names of trees.'

'It's an oak – an English oak – and probably twice as old as I am, at a guess.' Did oaks get tired, she wondered, of living on their memories, looking back, regretting? 'It may surprise you, dear, but the whole of Britain was once covered in oaks like that. And even as late as Henry VIII's time, a third of the land was still forested with oak-woods.'

'How d'you know?' the girl enquired suspiciously, as if used to being duped.

Yes, how *did* she know, Cecily reflected? By trusting books and historical accounts. Yet such trust might be misplaced. After all, so much of what she'd once believed had proved erroneous. 'One thing I *am* quite certain of is that there are four hundred and fifty different kinds of oak tree in the world – white oaks, black oaks, cork oaks, holm-oaks …'

'You've seen them all, you mean?'

She laughed. 'Oh, no.'

'But you've travelled a lot?'

'Yes, quite a bit.'

'I ain't been nowhere.'

'That's a shame. Maybe you will when you're older.'

The girl gave a derisive snort. 'And who'll cough up the cash, I'd like to know?'

Cecily all but said, '*I* will.' She didn't need her savings any more. Why not hand them over, so that this unschooled child – Laura's double physically, yet so different in both age and education – could see something of the world? She was aching to transform the girl, endow her with intellect, discernment; turn her into the woman she had idolized – and lost.

'So, what's your favourite country, then?' Ash was falling on the jeans again – tattered jeans, worn thin around the knees.

'Oh, America, no question. And New England in particular. In fact, I can narrow it down even further. There's a small town in Vermont called—'

'Oh, look – them squirrels!' Sharon gestured with her cigarette. 'They're so close I could almost touch their tails. You'd think they'd be scared, with us two sittin' here.'

'No, they're very tame. And, of course, they love the acorns. As do many of the birds, especially the jays. It's amazing, when you think about it, how much other life oak trees support. All sorts of different creatures – squirrels, spiders, oak-moths, gall-wasps, and every type of bird – live in, or on, them.'

Sharon shot her a guarded look. 'Are you a teacher or some-thin'?'

'No, just interested in wildlife.'

'So I s'pose you come here often, then?'

'Most days, yes.'

'Lucky sod!'

'It can be boring, you know, without a job.'

'Not as borin' as slavin' nine to five.'

'Can't you find something more …fulfilling?'

The girl yawned hugely in response, turning her face up towards the sun. 'Weird!' she said, grimacing. 'It feels really hot – like summer.'

'According to the News, it's the warmest late-October day since they first started keeping records.'

'Yeah, I heard that too. And Prince poncy Charles has to go and spoil it. Says it's due to global warmin', and we'll all pay for it in years to come.'

Years past, not years to come. Global warming had already taken place. In 1984. In Wilmington, Vermont. Laura's dangerous fire had ignited the whole cosmos, left it scorched and torrid.

Sharon was still gazing at the tree, where, even at this moment, a couple of jays were hopping from branch to branch, in their search for the choicest acorns. 'I'd like to be a bird myself. Then I'd fly away.'

'And where would you go?'

'Somewhere no one could soddin' find me, that's for sure.' The girl tossed her cigarette end on the ground. 'Shit! I'm completely out of fags now. That's my last – fuck it! I suppose *you* don't smoke, by any chance?'

Cecily smiled at the very idea. So many things she had never done: been drunk – or even rude or loud – shared a bed, given birth. She watched a woman strolling past with two babies in a pushchair; an entire world in themselves. Children were so powerful, could chain a mother down, prevent her even contemplating other sorts of attachments. Perhaps she should have *declared* her love; not restricted herself to banal remarks about the weather or the coach-trips. Strange how every detail still vibrated in her head, two long decades on. That dinner-dance the last evening in the hotel; the knife-sharp pain of watching Laura cheek-to-cheek with Hamish. She had murdered him a thousand times, but he would keep resurrecting; his hateful, hairy hand clamped against his wife's bare back. The dress was backless, strapless – and she sat transfixed, trying to wrest her eyes away from the exquisite, dangerous curves.

Finally she retired to bed, having neither dined nor danced. Another fevered, sleepless night, shattered by wild dance-music mocking in her head. The next morning, late for breakfast, she rushed down in a turmoil, desperate for her fill of Laura, to last her through the starving days ahead. Her love-feast had been interrupted by a callously cheerful waitress bringing waffles and a jug of maple syrup. 'Thanks,' she'd murmured vaguely, still so intent on Laura she'd kept pouring and pouring the syrup until it overflowed her plate and actually trickled across the tablecloth and down on to her lap. And at that very moment, Laura rose to leave, laughing and joking with Hamish and the twins, and totally oblivious of the fervent glances cast at her from the table-for-one tucked away in the corner. Stricken, she remained sitting where she was, trapped in sticky sweetness; spooning up the syrup from her plate, even scraping it off her lap, needing to swallow every smallest trace, mouthful after mouthful …

'Ta-ra! I'm off to Tesco's.'

'For maple syrup?'

'*What?*' With a bewildered shrug, the girl heaved herself off the bench and slouched away along the path.

Watched her depart, Cecily changed the clumsy, plodding gait into Laura's graceful stride. Laura had moved like a dancer, with elegance and poise. Even her posture was imposing: head held high, back imperiously straight. Though she also had a childlike streak, and could skip and jump, bounce balls about, and play leapfrog with her boys. And on one excursion – a day-trip to Mount Snow – she'd suddenly kicked up her heels and raced ahead along the path, leaving Hamish and the twins behind, as if impatient to break free of them. In her mind, she'd followed, running at full tilt until she'd caught up with the yellow coat, taken the eager hand; she and Laura eloping as they sped towards the mountain top, together and alone at last, escaping ties, convention.

Skittish little flurries of leaves began falling in a sudden gust of wind. She reached out to try to catch one the exact shade of Laura's hair, and with Laura's same exuberance. Eluding her grasp, it was carried on the breeze and began dancing in the air – frolicking, cavorting, refusing to come to rest.

On impulse, she rose to her feet. She, too, would dance, as she had longed to do since that final harrowing night at the hotel. Self-consciously, she looked around, to ensure she was alone. Yes, nobody was watching, save the squirrels and the birds. Venturing across the expanse of grass, she held out her arms – to Laura – and, suddenly, astonishingly, romantic, yearning music began throbbing through the park. For twenty years, she had waited for this moment: to feel her body pressed against those forbidden, willing breasts; Laura's maple-scented breath warm against her face; her ardent blaze of autumn hair out-shining even the sun.

Rhythmically, bewitchingly, they went waltzing through the drifts of whispering leaves. No risk of falling – not with Laura there. She was too young to fall, in any case – a girl again, in love again, experiencing the first and only passion of her life. All thought of death was banished; all choking fears about the great beyond. Time had stopped, this instant, as she and Laura dipped and twirled amidst the rustling trees. And, as they danced, the insipid browns and bashful yellows erupted into Vermont gold and crimson; the grass aglow, the clouds aflame, the entire tame and tepid park now scalding, incandescent.

And suddenly she understood that Laura's love could help her to survive, like a revivifying wonder-drug, conserving her for many winters more, to be the last blazing, brilliant, tenacious leaf still clinging to a life-sustaining oak.

Kentucky Fried

'Was it good for *you*, darling?' Graham reached out to squeeze her hand. He was still flushed and out of breath.

'Yes, wonderful,' she murmured. No man should ever need to ask, especially a husband of ten years. Ten years; a thousand lies. Did one more really matter?

'Hey! Is that the phone?' He leaned up on one elbow, poised to run.

Leave it, she longed to say. Make love to me. Again.

'I'd better get it. It might be Tom.' Scrambling into his dressing-gown, he disappeared downstairs.

She turned over on to her back, all the feelings dammed inside her, aching to explode. Her skin was sheened with sweat; her whole body restless and alert, like a racehorse at a starting gate. She slipped a finger between her legs, biting her lips, so she wouldn't make a sound. The walls were thin and the neighbours might complain. Graham often shushed her. 'Ssshh!' was such a putdown.

The finger didn't seem enough – too feeble and too small. If only she could *tell* him what she wanted, but that would be bad-mannered. She hated the thought of appearing ungrateful and demanding, when he was so good to her in other ways.

'No, I'm sure she won't mind. I think she's going out herself.'

What wouldn't she mind, she wondered, as she heard his voice rising from the hall. She stroked her other hand across her breasts. The nipples were erect still, clamouring to be touched.

'Hold on, and I'll ask her.'

Hastily she returned both hands to her sides, as the bedroom door clicked open. Once Graham had come, he immediately lost interest, and assumed she did the same. But their reactions were quite different. He was a gas-stove, she an electric hob. Switch them both off and whereas the saucepan on the gas-stove would instantly go off the boil, that on the electric hob continued to seethe and sizzle.

'It's Angus, darling. He's been let down by his golf partner and wants me to play this morning. Would you mind?'

"Course not. I shan't be here in any case.'

'That's what I thought.'

Her body was still begging to be touched, but Graham was pacing around the bedroom, making arrangements with Angus: they'd meet for coffee in the lounge, tee off at half past ten. She had always thought of golf as a low-libido sport, along with billiards, bowls and ping-pong, whereas football, rugby and wrestling were more macho altogether. Then, further up the scale, came the extreme pursuits like bungee jumping, skydiving, white-water-rafting, hang-gliding. She tried to imagine being married to a white-water-rafter. Would they plunge and soar in perfect unison, shoot the rapids together?

'Want to go first in the shower?'

'No. You go ahead.' Once he was out of sight, she ran the tip of her tongue round and round her palm, in slow, caressing circles, then up and down each finger and, lastly, between the fingers, taking her time gently to nuzzle and probe. Tongues were such amazing things, lodged in the cave of the mouth, yet connected to more intimate parts by an ingenious sort of current that, even now, was sending tiny (exquisite) jolts from her fingers to her pelvis. Often, when she and Graham made love, her tongue felt under-used, fretful and caged up; craving to find release with some equally responsive tongue. The white-water-rafter's, perhaps. Yes, quicker than the thought, it began flicking in and out between her legs, as she lay frothing and churning, a wild wave about to break.

'All yours,' said Graham, towelling his hair as he strolled back in.

'Thanks,' she said, glancing down at her chest. The nipples were still hard and stiff, like tiny pepper-mills. Strange he didn't notice.

She watched him apply a thick layer of greasy sun-block. Graham never took risks, especially since his oldest friend had been diagnosed with skin cancer. Today, the forecast had promised highs of ninety and, even at this early hour, the day was already hot. She shifted position on the bed, until she was lying directly in the pool of sunlight streaming from the window. The rays were like a lover's hands, fondling every curve and crevice of her body. She closed her eyes and, as a deep scarlet shutter engulfed her lids, she imagined scarlet gasps and cries escaping from her open mouth as the sun penetrated, scorched.

'Have you seen my tie – the striped one?'

'No.' All she could see was the top of the white-water-rafter's head, bobbing back and forth as he crouched between her legs, still rasping with that tongue of his. She pushed him off, tried to concentrate on Graham. 'It's far too hot for a tie.'

'Try telling that to the Royal Berkshire!'

Of course. She'd forgotten the dress code: jackets and ties in the clubhouse, even in tropical conditions.

'Shall I get breakfast?' he offered, buttoning his blazer. 'I'm in a bit of a rush.'

'I'll do it,' she said, not moving. He had his back to her now, so she grazed her teeth, to and fro, along the inside of her wrist. Teeth were every bit as versatile as tongues.

'You seem tired, my love. ' He came to sit beside her on the bed. 'Don't get up on my account. I'll just make some toast or something, and you can have a lie-in.'

Not much joy in a lie-in on her own. Reluctantly, she swung her legs off the bed and, after a perfunctory wash, pulled on shorts and a top, and went barefoot to the kitchen. Opening the fridge, she stood for several moments in front of the open door, letting its frosty breath cool her overheated body. 'Calm *down*,' she muttered, removing three eggs from the rack. 'It's over now. That's it.'

She placed the eggs on the worktop, returning to the fridge for the low-cholesterol spread. Everything they ate these days seemed to be divided into his and hers: his Benecol, her butter; his skimmed milk, her cream; his tofu, her full-fat cheese. One of the disadvantages, she'd found, in marrying a much older man was that he had developed health problems, while she remained frustratingly fit. Graham's cholesterol wasn't dangerously high, but he had to be ultra-careful with his diet.

She cracked the eggs into a basin, carefully separating the

whites from the yolks – only whites were allowed. She beat them with unnecessary force, angry with the anaemic, flimsy mixture. No colour in it, or richness, no hint of satisfaction.

While the pan was heating, she laid the table, banging down the plates and cups. They, too, were white and delicate. Nothing in this kitchen seemed attuned to her present mood; prissy pastel walls, blinds drawn down to bar the sun, dried flowers on the windowsill, lacking sap and succulence. Even the garden was parched; the lawn brownish-dry and cracking, from the long period of drought.

'It's ready, Graham,' she called, dishing up the egg-white omelette and sprinkling it with low-sodium salt.

He joined her at the table, immaculately attired in the blazer and a pair of linen trousers. 'Aren't you eating, my love?'

'I'm not hungry,' she shrugged.

Not for food, in any case.

As she stepped out of the house at last, the sun pounced on her and pawed her, glaring in her eyes, blazing against her back, drawing a rush of perspiration from every inch of skin exposed. The sheer force of the heat dazed her into submission; all her plans dissolving as she melted in its embrace. Shopping was out of the question. The only possibility was to lie on the grass and flop.

She dawdled down the hill towards the common, aware of her thighs rubbing moistly against each other with every step she took. It was an agreeable sensation wearing almost nothing – no underwear, no tights, just sandals and a gauzy dress.

Once she reached South Heathside, she found her way obstructed by a cordon of traffic cones and barriers, with diversion signs indicating an alternative route. She paused to watch the group of men re-tarmacing the road, surprised they should be out in such fierce heat. Yet far from covering themselves, they were all naked to the waist; their bare torsos glistening-damp, their hair dark and drenched with sweat. They were shouting to each other over the noise of the machines – a thudding, juddering descant, interspersed with high-pitched beeps, together with whining sounds and soft seductive hissing from a pair of diesel rollers.

She moved a little nearer, intrigued by a huge lorry, the entire back of which was rearing up – up and up, like a giant erection – tipping fresh supplies of tarmac into an open metal mouth that drew it down, drew it in, as if never satisfied. This black ejaculation was followed by a whole series more, as spurts of boiling tarmac gushed onto the road from the steel jaws of the machine. Immediately the men began to smooth it with their shovels, and she transferred her gaze to their brawny backs and sinewy arms; the muscles rippling and pulsing as they worked. Clouds of steam were rising from the tarmac, the acrid, febrile smell of which hung heavy in the air. Although it clogged her throat and choked her lungs, she still longed to be one of the gang, part of all that heat and noise and danger, and operating those brute machines herself. She tried to imagine sitting in the cab, with panting engines and throbbing motors vibrating underneath her, as she controlled massive rollers or hulking wheels, or operated levers that made rampant lorries rear aloft. The only incongruous object was a wheelbarrow: a helpless-looking, creaky thing that seemed to belong to another era. Like *Graham*, she thought, quickly suppressing the thought as shamefully disloyal.

For the last few minutes, the foreman had been observing her, and now came slouching over, wiping his face on a piece of dirty rag. 'Anything wrong?' he asked.

She shook her head, riveted by the mass of tattoos that covered every inch of his stomach, arms and chest.

'You can't come this way. The road's closed. Didn't you see the signs?'

'Yes,' she muttered, unable – and unwilling – to tear her eyes away.

'You need to take the Compton Rise diversion.'

'I know.' His body seemed to pulse and writhe as she peered, entranced, at the tangled maze of anchors, snakes and hearts.

Suddenly, on impulse, she squeezed through a gap between two of the steel barriers and gripped him by the arm, tracing the coils of one long rippling serpent from his hot, perspiring shoulder to his belly.

He looked nonplussed, embarrassed, standing with his head down, while her hand went lower still. Then, all at once, he steered her off the road towards the grass verge of the common, continued on, until he found a screen of bushes, then threw her down on the rough, uneven ground and began stripping off her dress. She could feel prickly bits of leaf and twig pressing into her naked back as she watched him unzip his jeans.

His body felt colossal after Graham's; his full weight bearing down on her, his huge hands hot and heavy on her breasts. The reek of sweat from his underarms had displaced the smell of tarmac, and she was inhaling beer and onions on his breath. As he moved against her, the anchors seemed to jab and thrust, penetrating deep inside her, while the serpents looped and undulated, sinuous against her skin.

'Bite my nipples,' she ordered. *She* was now the foreman, demanding instant obedience from her gang of willing men.

'Yes, harder.'

'Now flick them with your tongue.'

'That's good. It's great! Go *on!*'

'Now take the whole of my breast into your mouth.'

'Fantastic! And the other one.'

'No, don't come yet. I'm not ready. Hold off until I tell you.' He could damned well do what *she* wanted; accept *her* rules and timing, for a change.

Another man appeared – a great lout of a guy, with a shaven head, who was standing by the bushes, already unbuckling his belt, obviously keen for a share of the action.

'Wait your turn!' she snapped. She didn't want to rush; needed time to relish all the varying sensations: her wrists pinioned in a fierce, hurting grip as the foreman's bristly stubble chafed against her breasts; his nails clawing down her back, then a convulsive, violent shudder blazing from his groin to hers, as she shouted, 'Yes! Oh, *yes!*'

As he clambered off, she remained stretched out on the grass, glancing up at the heat-haze shimmering in the sky. It seemed to drift and quiver downwards, until it fluttered through her body, cell by sensuous cell.

'Jesus fucking Christ!' the second bloke exclaimed, staring at her nakedness. He had left his hobnailed boots on, and his trousers fell in folds around his ankles as, awkwardly, he straddled her.

'Don't talk!' she barked, drawing him towards her. 'And lie still until I say.' She needed to get the feel of him first: the strange smoothness of his bullet head underneath her hands; the chain around his neck, entangled in his chest-hair; the wet fullness of his lips.

Only after several minutes, did she allow him to bore in. Immediately she bucked and thrust against him, and he responded with a string of shouted expletives.

'Shut up, I said! We're doing this in silence.' It was a powerful feeling, shushing someone else, seeing them submit.

For the second time that morning, she came at the exact same moment as the man – unheard of in her marriage – but she, too, kept silent, deliberately, letting her body do the shouting. Then abruptly she kneed him off, to make room for the next: a lad of seventeen or so, and the only one of the workmen wearing his fluorescent jacket. *He* was just a stripling, and kept the jacket on – perhaps to conceal his puny chest. He seemed bashful altogether, leading her deeper into the undergrowth, to ensure they were well hidden. In contrast to the previous guy, his hair was exceptionally long and tied back in a ponytail that kept thumping up and down against her shoulder, like a second ardent lover joining in. She adapted herself to its rhythm, her body moving in time with it, then suddenly putting on a spurt as it began spanking – faster, faster – in a wild impetuous climax.

Afterwards, she let him lie against her, enjoying the feeling of the fluorescent jacket against her naked breasts – a delicious shiny clamminess. But he was soon embarrassed by the other men, who had now come over, excited by her cries, and were squeezing between the tangled shrubs, to watch.

Once the lad had slunk away, a small, swarthy bloke lunged forward and took her from behind. He kept up a non-stop commentary in some alien tongue she couldn't understand, although this time she didn't silence him. She *liked* the barbarous sound of it, which seemed to match his violent, jerky thrusting and the strange guttural roar snarling from his throat when, finally, he collapsed against her back.

After two more guys – an Asian and a Scot – she called a halt, at last. These men had work to do, so she snapped her fingers, sent them back on-site.

'But I'll be here again tomorrow,' she told the foreman, who was hanging around and clearly still aroused. She scrambled up, exhausted, from the ground, brushing bits of leaf from her thighs. 'We've only just begun.'

'So how was golf?'

'Fantastic! Angus and I were neck and neck until the eighteenth, then I birdied and took the game.'

'So I hope he bought you lunch.'

'No, actually he didn't. His son was playing in a cricket match, so he had to get back to watch. In fact, I've been in for quite some while and was beginning to get worried. You're much later than you said.'

'Sorry. I ... lost track of time.'

'But was the shopping trip successful? Did you get the dress you wanted?'

'No. Nothing seemed to suit me.'

'You're too hard on yourself, my sweet. You look beautiful tonight.'

'What, in this old thing?'

'Yes, in that old thing. It's what's underneath that counts.'

She moved towards him, kissed him on the cheek – a chaste, loving, contrite, guilt-clogged kiss. 'I love you, Graham. I love you more than anything. It's terribly important that you know.'

'But of course I know. And I love *you*. It goes without saying.'

'No!' she insisted. 'It *doesn't*. Love's so ... so difficult.'

'What *is* all this? You sound quite overwrought.'

She pulled away. 'It's nothing. I'll get supper. You must be starving if you missed lunch.'

'Well, a bit peckish, I must admit. What are we going to have?'

'Not sure yet.' She opened the freezer, stared in at the haddock fillets, white and tame and safe; the skinless, boneless (joyless) chicken breasts. Wearily, she opted for the fish – poached in meagre low-fat milk, as usual, and served with some starveling sauce.

As she stood at the sink peeling onions for the sauce, the gang of workmen suddenly burst in. They had finished work, downed tools, then stopped off at the Kentucky Fried for a giant-sized bucket of chicken, along with a load of chips. They seated themselves at the table, gnawing on the chicken pieces, brushing breadcrumbs off their lips with dirty, callused hands, tossing the bones behind them before dipping in again.

The smell was tantalizing: flagrant grease, shameless fat, audacious, brazen spices. She put her knife down, went across to join them. Within seconds she was tucking in herself, crunching wings and breasts; the crispy, oily texture of the coating a perfect contrast to the yielding, succulent softness of the chips. She crammed another dozen chips in all at once, savouring the luscious film of grease adhering to her tongue and teeth; the triumphant feeling of fullness and excess.

She was so intent on the sensations, she barely noticed Graham slip into the kitchen. But he came towards her, put his hand gently on her shoulder. 'So have you decided, darling?'

'Decided *what?*' she asked, rising to her feet, alarmed.

Patting his stomach in response, he gave a rueful laugh.

'Oh, your supper, you mean,' she said, glancing over her shoulder at the delicious depredation on the table: crumpled bits of paper, half-gnawed bones, the scattering of crunchy, savoury crumbs. 'I thought we might have something different, for a change – Kentucky Fried Chicken and chips.' The cholesterol count would be lethal – enough to kill her husband there and then.

'You're joking, of course.'

'Of course,' she murmured, wiping her ravished, grease-emblazoned hands on her torn and oil-stained dress.

May

'Damn, damn, damn, damn, *damn!*' Slowing to a halt, Jenny snatched up the map from the passenger seat and checked the name on the signpost. Yes, as she'd feared, she was headed in the wrong direction. *Again*. Her map-reading skills were minimal, but then she was used to Patrick navigating.

Furious at the thought of him, she wrenched at the steering wheel and tried to turn the car round in the narrow, rutted lane, but succeeded only in stalling the engine and eventually landing up with her back wheels in the ditch.

'Look, for God's sake, get a grip,' she muttered to herself, winding down the window and taking in a few deep breaths. The air was warm and scented, the hedgerows were frothing with cow parsley, and the fringes of the field beyond spangled with polished buttercups. Yet she was polluting both the weather and the scenery with her own toxic cloud of anger and frustration. If she only managed to calm down, she could still enjoy this lush May afternoon, despite the fact she was incorrigibly lost. Everywhere she looked, different shades of green were eagerly unfurling: thrustful shoots of new spring wheat; translucent, tender beech leaves; lusty nettles rampant in the hedge. There was no sound except the birds: sweet, silvery trills and deeper, husky notes, neither of which she was able to identify. It was Patrick who was the authority on birds.

Sighing, she restarted the engine and, having extricated the car from the ditch, retraced her route until she reached a fork in the road. Should she go straight on, or bear right? By now she was so thoroughly confused, she might as well decide by tossing a coin. If only there were somebody to ask, but for the last few miles there hadn't been a single sign of human habitation, just fields and woods unfolding on either side, until they lost themselves in the hazy blue horizon. It was as if she had reached a land where no one lived, not even sheep and cows. And, as she squinted at the map again, she had a sudden strange suspicion that this was territory *beyond* maps, and that Patrick might be wreaking his revenge by dissolving all its boundaries and landmarks, in order to trap her in its coils.

Shivering, despite the heat, she made herself drive on, opting for the right fork, but regretting her decision once the road began to peter out into a narrow, puddled cart-track. However, she followed it for half a mile in the hope the track might lead on to a farm, only to be thwarted by a heap of ancient farm machinery, rusting where it lay, and blocking any hope of further progress. Was Patrick working another ominous spell, picking up whole villages and transferring them to distant counties, so that she would never, ever reach her destination; never find Briar Cottage, or its owner, Phyllis Potts? If so, she was doomed to spend the entire weekend driving round in endless circles, in an empty country devoid of humankind.

Briar Cottage.

Dusk was falling, so she could barely make out the letters on the gate, but she traced them with her finger to make absolutely certain. Yes – Briar Cottage – no mistake. And she had to admit it did look rather idyllic, with its thatched roof, whitewashed walls, and riot of flowers in the overgrown front garden. Yet it was with a sense of trepidation that she walked up to the door. Inside, it could be different: dark and poky; even dirty or dilapidated. Several of her friends had rented cottages on spec, only to be severely disappointed. One unlucky couple had even encountered bed-bugs, and returned home covered with bites.

She prayed the key would be there – under the brick, behind the small stone cat, as Mrs Potts had promised. If not, it would mean driving another seven miles, and dragging the poor woman from her supper or her bed.

No need for that, thank God. And, as she slid the key into the lock and opened the front door, she let out a sigh of sheer relief. Even in the gloom, she could see how clean and comfortable the place was. And, once she'd switched the lights on, she stood surveying the cosy sitting-room, with its flagstone floor and brightly patterned rugs; its broad-shouldered, squashy sofa, piled with patchwork cushions, and the charming lattice windows looking out to a sweep of shadowed hills. Only one thing missing – Patrick.

Determined not to dwell on him, she explored the cottage further, admiring the solid pinewood cupboards in the kitchen, and the matching table, complete with welcoming fruit-bowl. The fridge and oven both looked new, in contrast to the dark oak beams, hung with strings of onions and bunches of dried herbs, as if she'd driven not to Shropshire but to Provence.

Elated, she bounded up the stairs. The bedroom had a high brass bed, covered with a splendid quilt, hand-stitched from squares of silks and velvets in a kaleidoscope of greens and golds. Bugger Patrick! Let him stew. She could enjoy herself without him in this enticing little haven.

Returning to the sitting-room, she unzipped her bag and unpacked the provisions she'd brought for this first evening, all seriously affected by the long drive in the heat. The loaf of bread was already dry and stale, the chicken pie smelt tainted, and the cheese was sweating yellow droplets through its wrappings. Well, she'd dump the lot and feast on the fruit in the kitchen: a veritable cornucopia of peaches, plums, apples, pears and grapes. And, as for the wine, she would simply drink it warm. She was too tired to go and chill it; too tired to lift a finger. All she intended doing for the moment was to stretch out on that sofa and toast the fact that she had actually arrived.

She had barely swallowed a mouthful of Chardonnay, when she heard a car drawing up outside. She tensed, fingers gripping the glass. Patrick! In pursuit of her. Perhaps he'd come to apologize. Or to announce that things were over between them and he was returning the eternity ring she had given him just days ago. 'Eternity' seemed heavily ironical in light of this morning's quarrel.

She sat frozen where she was, listening to the rat-tat-tat on the door. Then, suddenly, she leapt up to her feet. She *had* to see him, if he'd driven all this distance. Even if he were burning with resentment, they could discuss things, make it up, spend the night together in that benevolent brass bed.

Flinging open the front door, she came face to face not with Patrick but with a small, plump woman, dressed in gumboots and a denim skirt; her ship's prow of a bosom emphasized still further by a tight, ribbed sweater in a bilious shade of yellow.

'Phyllis Potts,' she announced. 'You must be Jenny. Pleased to meet you.'

'Oh … hello.'

'Sorry I couldn't be here when you arrived. I always like to greet my guests in person, but you *did* say afternoon.'

'Yes. My fault entirely.' She was still reeling from the disappointment; trying to switch her thoughts from tangled sheets to twisting roads. 'I tried to ring you several times, but—'

'I know. You got the answerphone. I've just picked up all your messages. Poor you, getting lost – and lost with a vengeance, by the sounds of it! Pity I wasn't at home, then I could have given you directions. But one of our bullocks got loose and created havoc in the vicar's precious flowerbeds. Why it *had* to be the vicar, when his wife's the keenest gardener in the village, God only knows!'

Jenny laughed, warming to this woman. 'Come in,' she said, 'and have a glass of wine.'

'No, I won't disturb you. I'm sure you and your gentleman friend would prefer to be alone.'

'He's, er, not here.' She cleared her throat, opting for a lie. 'He … went down with some virus thing. One of those bugs that come on out of the blue. But we didn't want to cancel, so …'

'Oh, what a shame. I'm sorry. But I'll leave you in peace, in any case. You must be deadbeat after all that driving. I'll just fetch a few things from the car, then I'll be on my way. I made you a cake, which I meant to bring round earlier.'

'A cake? How kind!'

'Well, I was baking anyway. I just hope you've no objection to chocolate sponge.'

'Sounds wonderful! I love anything with chocolate in.' This must be Wonder-Woman – home-made cakes, overflowing fruit-bowls … 'Can I help?' she asked as Phyllis dived towards her car.

'No, you stay where you are.'

When she reappeared, Phyllis was holding not just a cake-tin but a large bunch of hawthorn blossom, wrapped in a sheet of newspaper. As its pungent, curdled scent began choking through the room, Jenny shrank against the wall, feeling instantly faint. Phyllis was saying something, but it was her mother's voice she heard: a series of hysterical shrieks exploding in her ears.

'You stupid little fool! Don't you realize it's unlucky to bring may blossom inside?'

'But I *picked* it for you, Mum. It's a present. For your birthday.'

'Present? Are you mad? That stuff's a curse, and brings sickness and death to any house it comes to. Get it out! Get it out, before we're all struck down!'

'But it took me hours to—'

She was silenced by a slap across her face, a face already scratched and smarting from the thorns. She had braved those thorns to please her mother, who never had the money to buy flowers for herself. Yet now she was being punished: stinging blows raising great red patches on her legs.

She fled, the bunch of hawthorn still clutched against her chest. Its prickly stems seemed to be clawing at her dress, tearing holes in the flimsy cotton fabric, which would bring another thrashing from her mother. Ramming the evil things into the dustbin, she slammed the lid on top and stood, sobbing, in the back yard, terrified by what she'd done.

Two days later, her grandmother fell ill. By Sunday, she was dead. '*Your* fault!' her mother howled.

'Jenny, are you OK? You've gone quite pale.'

She clung to the wall for support. The whole room had started spinning as she watched her grandma's coffin lowered into the grave, heard spadefuls of earth thud-thudding on the lid, and God's harsh voice accusing from the sky, 'Your mother's right. *You* killed her!'

Somewhere, in another world, her arm was gripped securely and she was being led across the room and sat down on a chair. Disoriented, she opened her eyes; saw not black-garbed mourners, but an expanse of yellow sweater.

Phyllis's voice seemed to come from far away. 'Whatever's wrong?' she asked. 'You've gone all cold and sweaty Are you sure you haven't caught that bug – the one your boyfriend has?'

Jenny gave a shaky laugh. 'No, I … I'm fine. I haven't eaten since breakfast, so it's probably just hunger-pangs.'

'Well, let me get you something – a sandwich or ...'

'No, honestly—' Jenny broke off in confusion. Why say 'honestly', then lie? She almost *wanted* to admit the truth, having kept this shameful secret for over twenty years. 'It was actually the may blossom,' she blurted out, blushing as she spoke.

'The *what?*'

'That hawthorn you brought in. I can't bear it in the house.' And she began recounting the whole story, hardly knowing why she was confiding in a stranger, when not even Patrick or her closest friends knew that she had caused a death.

'So, you see, I've always lived in terror of the stuff.' There was a relief in having confessed, a relief overlaid with shame. Wasn't it absurd to have allowed a guileful superstition to entrap her since the age of eight?

Phyllis clearly thought so. 'But that's *nonsense*, Jenny,' she said in her emphatic voice. 'Your mother was completely wrong. And so are all the other folk who think may blossom's unlucky.'

'But if it's such a widely held belief, it must have *some* foundation.'

'Well, it all sprang from the notion that Christ's crown of thorns was made from hawthorn twigs. So, because it caused Him suffering, people assumed it must be bad. But there's an equally strong tradition that says it's actually a sacred tree that brings blessings and good fortune, on account of the fact it touched Our Saviour's head.'

'Really?'

'Yes, really. And long before Christianity it was seen as beneficial. Way back in Greek and Roman times, people used to carry it at weddings, as a token of good luck for the newly married couple. And they tied it to babies' cradles, to protect children against sickness and death.'

'Just the opposite, you mean, to what my mother said?'

'Absolutely. And, on a more practical level, it's been used in herbal medicine for centuries. In fact, one of my friends is a practising herbalist and she was telling me the other day how versatile the plant is. It cures heart conditions, kidney problems and a whole host of other things, she said – even insomnia and depression.'

'Well, I suppose we'd better drink to that,' Jenny said uncertainly, reaching for the Chardonnay. 'Please do stay and have a glass of wine.'

'OK, why not? The old man's watching the football, so he won't miss me for a bit. But I suggest we cut the cake, so that you're not drinking on an empty stomach.'

While she went to fetch a knife, Jenny approached the bunch of may blossom, lying on the dresser. The tiny flowers might look innocent enough, but for her they were still treacherous; the stems fiercely armed with spiky thorns, which seemed all the more malicious for being concealed beneath such handsome, glossy leaves.

Phyllis returned with a knife, two plates and a second glass. 'I see you're reassessing the hawthorn,' she smiled, cutting two large chunks of cake, and passing one to Jenny. 'And so you should! Us country folk see it as an emblem of hope, because it marks the end of winter and the coming of spring. And it's called the lovers' flower, because of its long association with marriage and fertility. And, actually, when you come to think about it, the smell *is* quite earthy, isn't it?' She gave a sudden throaty laugh. 'Perhaps that's why your mother couldn't stand it, like Cromwell and the Puritans. Too sexy for them by half!'

Jenny chewed her cake reflectively. 'Well, she was certainly puritanical. In fact, sex was never mentioned in our house. Though she must have had her fair share of it, since she produced six children in as many years!'

Phyllis gave another booming laugh. 'I'm one of five myself – all girls. And things got pretty hairy, I can tell you, with seven of us crammed into our tiny house. But I used to escape every summer to my Auntie Bridget's place. She lived in the wilds of Ireland and always invited me to spend the month of August with her.'

'My boyfriend comes from Ireland.'

'Oh, really. Which part?'

'Not the wilds. He's a Dublin man. But he's interested in all the old traditions.'

'Well, he'd have loved my Auntie B. There was nothing she didn't know about mythology and folklore. That's how I first learnt about the may trees. She had a couple growing near her house and she believed the fairies lived in them. In fact, it's a common belief in Kerry that the Wee Folk favour hawthorns and protect any land they grow on. In return for their protection, she used to plait these crowns of may blossom and leave them out for the fairies overnight. If the crown was gone by morning, it meant the fairies had approved of it and would shower blessings on the house.'

'Phyllis, surely you can't believe that?' Jenny put her glass down with unnecessary force.

'Who knows? There are lots of things we can't explain, but that doesn't mean they're not true.'

'It depends on what you mean by truth.'

'I can't define it, Jenny, and nor, I suspect, can anybody else. But the older I get, the more I think we should be open to possibilities beyond logic, reason and even common sense.'

In the ensuing silence, Jenny's mind was less concerned with logic than with her absent lover. Her former anger was now curdling into guilt. If she were honest with herself, the appalling row had been more her fault than his. She had yelled at him with no cause whatsoever, beyond the fact she was stressed and over-wrought. But that stress was due to work, and to the problems with her mother, so it was quite unfair to take it out on *him*. On the other hand, he had definitely overreacted in refusing to come away. That was punishment too far. 'More wine?' she asked, making a deliberate effort to concentrate on Phylllis rather than on Patrick.

'No, I'd better be getting back. But are you sure you're OK? You still look a bit washed out.'

'I'm fine now, thanks. And it was really good to meet you.'

Phyllis lumbered to her feet, grabbed her car-keys and the cake-tin, then picked up the bunch of hawthorn. 'I'll take this out of your way. I intended putting it in a vase on the bedroom windowsill, but I don't want to give you nightmares!'

'No, leave it,' Jenny said, surprising herself even more than Phyllis. 'If it brings blessings to a house, well … I could do with some at present.'

'Are you sure it won't upset you?'

'Yes,' Jenny said, with more conviction than she felt. 'And thank you for the delicious cake. Thanks for everything.'

Once Phyllis had gone, she sat sipping her wine, aware of the cloying scent of may blossom, now heavy in the air. That smell had always seemed a stench, rather than a fragrance: the rank and rancid stench of death. Phyllis saw it as sexual, but for *her* it was oppressive, and no way would she allow it in a bedroom. All she was taking upstairs was a mug of hot milk and a Mogadon, to help banish thoughts of Patrick.

At 2 a.m. she was still awake, since neither milk nor sleeping pill had worked. Instead she felt both restless and exhausted; her body craving sleep, whilst her grasshopper mind continued jumping from one worry to another. She longed to phone Patrick, just to hear his voice, but was it really fair to wake him in the early hours? Besides, anything she said in her present vulnerable state might only make things worse.

Dragging herself from bed, she stood by the window, staring out at the darkness. The silence was so intense, she actually missed the traffic that droned more or less continuously past their London flat. At least it made her feel connected to a busy, purposeful world, whereas here she seemed superfluous, a mere speck in the vast landscape.

Her stomach rumbled suddenly, reminding her that all she had eaten in the past twenty-four hours was a bowl of Shreddies and a slice of chocolate sponge. Maybe she'd go and raid the fruit-bowl and have another cup of milk.

Halfway down the stairs, she was assaulted by the smell of may, now more pungent still. She hesitated, a surge of fear rising almost instinctively, as the odour seemed to seep into her pores. Struggling to ignore it, she went on down to the kitchen, helped herself to plums and grapes, warmed more milk, then took her midnight snack into the sitting-room.

She sat munching plums and sipping milk, one wary eye on the hawthorn. It was wilting now and some of the frail white blossom had already fallen on the floor in milky drifts. If it really cured depression and insomnia, she ought to take it up to bed with her. And she was certainly in need of help from a so-called lovers' flower, to heal the rift with Patrick. He was the only man she had ever loved, which made their present separation all the worse.

On impulse, she got up, unwrapped the bunch from its newspaper, hands shaking as she did so, and took it into the kitchen. Hunting through the cupboards, she eventually found a vase, filled it with water and thrust the hawthorn in. After all, if a plant had been considered sacred since Greek and Roman times, and in a score of different countries, could all those varied cultures be universally wrong? Perhaps, in the cold light of day, Phyllis's tales of blessings and good fortune would seem completely fanciful, but here, in this deserted place, in the spooky middle of the night, anything seemed possible. Even Yeats had believed in fairies, for God's sake, and *he* was considered a leading intellectual. In fact, was it any more rational to believe in God (as some three-quarters of the world did) than to believe in the powers of the Wee Folk?

Self-consciously she glanced around, as if in search of invisible presences – powerful spirits that could rescue her relationship. If Patrick took her spiteful words to heart, she might have destroyed all chance of a future life with him.

The thought was so unbearable, she snatched up two twigs of hawthorn and began frantically trying to plait them into a crown – an act of desperation, and totally illogical. Yet making offerings to the fairies had worked for Phyllis's aunt and, as Phyllis herself had pointed out, there might be truths and possibilities *beyond* the grip of reason.

Fashioning a crown, however, was much harder than she'd realized. The recalcitrant twigs didn't seem to want to bend, but kept obstinately springing back at her, thwarting her attempts to twist them into a circle. Having dislodged clouds of blossom and scratched herself on the thorns, she finally went in search of pliers and some string. Both took a while to locate and, even with their help, the resulting crown looked decidedly skew-whiff and sadly short on blossom.

Yet it was with a sense of real achievement that she carried it upstairs and left it on the bedroom window-ledge. Whatever else, she had overcome her fears to an incredible degree: not only handling the loathsome plant, but actually tolerating its presence just outside the windowpane. Even without the agency of fairies, there was magic in the fact that she had broken the hawthorn's spell, at last.

She was woken by rays of sunshine nuzzling at the curtains, as if clamouring to come inside. Opening her eyes, she reached for her watch: 12.25. Impossible! To have slept for over nine hours in a strange bed, in an unfamiliar house, and without Patrick's comforting presence beside her, was something of a miracle.

Bemused, she went downstairs to the kitchen, where she was confronted by the mangled remains of the hawthorn, sitting on the table beside the pliers and the string. Only then did she remember the crown, feeling immediately embarrassed by her credulity last night. How could she have been so gullible as to go along with some Irish superstition?

Having made a cup of tea and demolished another slice of cake, she returned upstairs to wash and dress. As she drew back the bedroom curtains, she noticed to her astonishment that the hawthorn crown had gone. She stared at the empty window ledge, rubbing her eyes in disbelief. The crown *must* be there; it must be! The ledge was too high up for any prowling cat or fox to have dislodged it, and too wide for it to have fallen off. Nor could it have blown off, since there hadn't been a breath of wind last night, and the weather was still sultry and quiescent. None the less, she peered down at the ground below, to make absolutely certain, but there was no sign of any prickly circlet, or even broken twigs. Could some bird have carried it off – a buzzard or a crow, perhaps? But that made no sense either. No creature would be tempted by a tangled mass of thorns.

She sank down on the bed, totally perplexed. Other questions were jostling in her mind. Why did she feel so different: upbeat and energized, whereas normally if she took a sleeping pill, she would wake fuzzy and lethargic? And all the worries oppressing her last night – the anguish over Patrick and the future of their relationship – seemed to have completely disappeared. She was no longer even anxious about the impasse with her mother, or the mounting pressures at work. It was as if every problem in her life was now open to solution.

Suddenly, on impulse, she began hurling things into her case and pulling on her clothes. There wasn't time to wash. She had to drive back *now* – this instant – to activate the blessings showered on this morning. Those blessings were indisputable – as strong, as real, as the beating of her heart, though transmitted through some agency she couldn't understand. If she tried to claim they had been granted by the fairies in return for a hawthorn crown, she would be derided as a crackpot. She *had* no explanation; couldn't even begin to say how the crown had vanished, or why she felt so extraordinarily empowered. All she knew was that if she went home straight away, her bond with Patrick would not only be cemented, but endure throughout the span of both their lives.

Seizing her case, she ran downstairs, scrawled a note for Phyllis, grabbed her bag and jacket and slammed the door, replacing the key beneath the brick before getting into the car.

As she drove off down the winding line, she suddenly spotted a bank of hawthorn in full bloom; the mass of creamy flowers resembling a lacy wedding veil flung across the hedge. She hadn't even noticed it when she'd arrived here in the dwindling evening light. But now it was shining in the sun; its heady scent attracting bees and butterflies.

Stopping the car, she scrambled out and started picking armfuls of the stuff – a child again; a London child, with no trees near her home, delighted by the prospect of free flowers. Now, as then, the thorns tore her dress and scratched her hands, but this time she didn't care. She was returning not to punishment and thrashings but to happiness and peace. Hawthorn was the flower of love, and she had a strong, deep-seated instinct that the minute she got home, Patrick would rush to greet her – and greet her with a ring.

The wedding would be next May, with the hawthorns in full bridal attire, bestowing sacred blessings on the marriage.

And, as she drove away – to Patrick – she saw herself reflected in the mirror: a shower of blossom-confetti in her hair.

Barbecue

Pink with indignation, Muriel heaved herself out of bed, stumbled to the window and peered down at the next-door garden. Yes, as she'd thought, another barbecue – that wretched couple disturbing the whole neighbourhood as they hammered in the stakes for the marquee. The dratted thing was a fold-up affair, stored in the garden shed, but it seemed to come out every weekend now, to impress their swanky friends. Neither of the pair were dressed at all appropriately, she noticed with distaste: Piers in skimpy shorts that revealed far more than was decent, and Yvette in a quite scandalous bikini. And clearly neither had heard of skin cancer. Every time the sun so much as glimmered, they'd be out there in a trice, exposing acres of their naked flesh not only to its dangerous rays, but to any hapless neighbour watching from upstairs.

She looped back the curtain, to get a better view. It was not that she was nosy. Indeed, when the refined, fastidious Barlows had owned the house next door, she would never have dreamt of snooping. But then the Barlows entertained their guests in the privacy of the dining-room, whereas these two laid on public displays and so were more or less *asking* to be spied on. Half the contents of the house had been dragged out to the garden: crockery and cutlery, little tables, parasols, cushions, tartan rugs. And the deckchairs and recliners had already been set up, forming a large circle round the barbecue. Did they *have* to start the preparations quite so early? Of course, in the normal way she would have been up and dressed long since, but she had been banking on a lie-in, after a sleepless night wrestling with a pulled muscle in her leg.

All hope of a nap expired, however, as the hammering continued and, to make matters worse, Yvette switched on the radio and turned the volume up. Muriel rapped her fingers on the sill – a useless little protest, lost in all the racket. She was subjected to their raucous noise every minute of the day. If it wasn't the radio, it was the television set – or *sets*, she ought to say, since they appeared to own a good half dozen, judging by the hullabaloo she heard coming through the party wall: car-chases and gunfire, jingles from advertisements, chimes from Big Ben, theme tunes from the soaps. Of course, if you lived next door to a couple called Yvette and Piers, there was bound to be some sort of friction. Such frivolous, un-English names were simply spoiling for a fight – so different from the Barlows, who'd been Elizabeth and John: Biblical, traditional and utterly dependable.

Yvette laid down her mallet and sat back on her heels, displaying an ample expanse of thigh. 'Shall we stop for breakfast, darling?' she yelled to Piers above the din.

'Yes, *do*,' Muriel muttered under her breath. 'Then perhaps I'll get a few minutes' peace.'

Not a chance. She might have guessed they would eat outside, with the radio as threesome. Since the day they'd first moved in, two endless months ago, they'd taken most of their meals in the garden, presumably in a bid to accelerate their tans, which were now a shade of deep mahogany. 'Meals' wasn't quite the word, though. Most of the time it was pizzas, delivered in huge, square, cardboard cartons by foreign chaps on motorbikes, who came roaring up the street, causing yet more aggravation. Clearly Yvette couldn't cook. Indeed, she probably couldn't boil an egg, since breakfast was usually croissants.

Muriel leaned out further, to check this morning's menu. Yes, a whole pile of the greasy, foreign things, plonked on the patio table, along with a bowl of orange fruits she didn't recognize – certainly nothing as commonplace as clementines or tangerines. The couple were obviously loaded. Each one of their fancy barbecues must set them back several hundred pounds, what with the mountains of meat they bought, the exotic fruits and elaborate ice-cream-cakes, the cocktails and champagne. Yet half of it was wasted – scores of uneaten chicken legs tossed into the wheelie-bin, along with sausages and steaks; whole pineapples and melons, barely touched, discarded amongst empty tins and teabags.

And it was just the same with the newspapers. Even as she watched, Yvette unfolded the *Sunday Times*, while Piers was already skimming through the *Mail*. Every single day, they ordered a whole stack of papers, read a section here, a section there, then disposed of the entire week's-worth on the Monday. Monday was rubbish-collection day and she made a point of being out there in the street when the dustcart rumbled up, so she could see for herself the extent of their extravagance.

Suddenly, there was the sound of high-pitched barking as Fifi burst out of the house and jumped up on Yvette's lap. Muriel never failed to wonder at the dog, which seemed not to be made of flesh and bone, but only of a mass of fluffy hair. The creature was hardly more than toy-size, yet its coat was quite extravagantly profuse, and even its small pendulous ears resembled miniature hearthrugs. If one were going to have a dog (and frankly she'd never been keen on a species that combined the maximum of noise and mess with the minimum of charm), then why not go for a manly breed, such as a boxer or retriever, rather than a foppish little thing that resembled a walking powder-puff?

'*Hygiene!*' she exclaimed, as Yvette went to fetch a brush and began grooming the pampered brute – yes, right there on the breakfast table. She had seen them groom the dog before and been stunned by the devotion lavished on the process. Of course, she couldn't make out what was said, not from this far off and with music blaring out, but the cosseting and coddling were unmistakable. As Yvette primped and titivated, she accompanied each brushstroke with affectionate pats, loving little squeezes and butterfly kisses planted on the small wet nose. And Piers joined in as well, leaning forward to nuzzle the dog, or fondly scratch its ears. Both breakfast and the barbecue appeared to be forgotten; nothing else existed for them but their beloved only child. At last, the task was finished and, with a final sweep of the brush, Fifi's fringe was scooped back from her face and tied in a topknot with a large pink satin bow. Muriel shook her head in wonderment. She wouldn't be surprised if the spoilt little minx had its own designated room in the house, to store its stock of bows: rainbow-coloured polka-dotted, tartan, lurex, even hound's-tooth check – a different style and colour every day.

Suddenly she was a child again, sitting in the chilly bedroom while her mother brushed *her* hair – though with resentment and annoyance, rather than affection. She could actually feel the pain in her head, as her hair was tugged and de-tangled, then plaited far too tightly, so that it was pulling at her scalp. And there were certainly no satin bows, just plain old rubber bands. Children were expense enough, without wasting yet more money on frivolities.

Yvette rewarded Fifi with a large buttered piece of croissant, while Piers offered her a sugar lump – the doting master and mistress indulging their precious petkins. Fifi yapped her thanks. Diminutive she might be, but her bark wouldn't have sounded out of place on an Alsatian or Great Dane, and could be heard by the Park-Davisons, as far away as number five. They had recently complained – quite fruitlessly, of course, since Yvette would no more shush her darling dog than turn down that dreadful music. Both were in full cry: Fifi pleading for more titbits, whilst a so-called singer squalled disastrously off-key on the heart-shaped, red-plush radio.

Muriel let the curtain fall, limped from window to door, and took refuge in the spare room, which faced towards the front. Although the bed was lumpy and the once vivid poppy wallpaper had now faded to a lethargic pink, those were trivialities compared with the chance of blessed peace.

She sat up in confusion, glancing with horror at the bedside clock. Nearly half past twelve! How on earth could she have slept so long? And wasn't that the doorbell? Who on earth could be ringing it so loudly – indeed ringing it at all? She never had any visitors, and it wouldn't be a tradesman on a Sunday. She struggled out of bed, pausing in dismay as she glimpsed herself in the mirror. She could hardly deal with callers when she wasn't even dressed and her hair looked such a fright. Inching to the window, she concealed herself behind the curtains, trying to see who was there.

'Yvette!' she murmured, barely able to believe her eyes. Never, since the couple moved in, had either of them approached her; never exchanged a single word with her, let alone turned up on her doorstep. So what could the woman *want*, for heaven's sake?

All at once, a flush suffused her cheeks. Wasn't it obvious –

calling round at lunchtime on a Sunday, and dressed up to the nines like that in a blue silk party frock? She must have come to invite her to the barbecue! As a way of making amends, perhaps, for all the noise and disruption over the last two months. Muriel's glow of pleasure deepened to a blush of shame. Clearly she had judged the pair too harshly. She had to admit she wasn't her usual self. She felt constantly out of sorts, these days, and thus liable to snap or be judgmental. Thank God she'd kept her annoyance to herself; a public confrontation would have wrecked any chance of being included on the guest list. And it *would* be rather wonderful to attend a barbecue – something she had never done in her entire seventy-seven years.

She closed her eyes, saw herself gliding in and out of that showy green marquee; eating in the open air, instead of in her small, dark, poky kitchen – the thrilling sense of danger from glowing charcoal, billowing smoke. Yes, the porky tang of sausages was sizzling on her tongue, and she was biting into best rump steak, meaty juices running down her chin. 'Do have a couple of chicken breasts,' a deep male voice persuaded, as she was passed a steaming platter, freshly cooked for her alone. Next, she was offered corn on the cob, deliciously sweet and buttery (though a serious challenge to her teeth). Then, after a brief pause to aid digestion, came a feast of luscious desserts. Not her usual Instant Whip (made from a packet and tasting of soapy nothing), but elaborate frozen gateaux, studded with whole strawberries and smothered in double cream. And no boring apples or cut-price black bananas, mushy in the middle, but young, firm, blushing mangoes and musky golden papayas.

With trembling hands, she pushed the window open and called out in a breathless tone, 'I'll be down in a couple of minutes, Yvette! Just give me time to get dressed.'

If they were to see her in her nightgown – an ancient thing in pea-green nylon, with a darn on one of the sleeves – they wouldn't want her in their perfect garden, with its padded swing-seats, its sundial, and its beds of exotic flowers, tended by a proper high-class gardener who came every Tuesday afternoon in a van marked, 'Lotus Landscape Design (Chelsea Medal-Winner)'.

'OK,' Yvette bellowed back. 'But don't be long.'

Feverishly she rushed to her own room, tore the nightie off, struggled into her underclothes, pulled on her loosest frock, so she wouldn't have to bother with fiddly belts or buttons, and slipped her feet into her best white summer sandals. While she dressed she kept glancing down at the next-door garden, her elation increasing by the second. The setting looked quite magical, with silver streamers looped between the bushes, and huge bunches of balloons (in the shape of stars and flowers, no less) hanging from the apple trees. Several guests had already arrived – young, stylish types, in amazing clothes, giving tinkly little laughs as they greeted each other with extravagant embraces. Perhaps *she* would be embraced – which hadn't happened for close on four whole decades.

An elegant young man, dressed in smart cream linen trousers, was doing the rounds with a bottle of champagne. Champagne! The very word sent a shiver of excitement tingling down her spine. She never touched alcohol – the doctor had forbidden it – but today every rule would be broken with glorious impunity. Indeed, a whole magnum of champagne seemed to be dancing through her body, in a veritable Highland Fling of bubbly spume and fizz.

'*Hurry*!' she reproved herself, as she ran a comb through her hair. 'You're keeping Yvette waiting.' Yet she just couldn't tear her eyes away from that tantalizing scene next door: the great stack of meat still waiting to be grilled, the piles of tropical fruits – everything from hothouse grapes to outlandish pomegranates. All she'd planned for lunch today was a hard-boiled egg and salad, or beans on toast, if the eggs were past their sell-by date. Couldn't eggs be sold singly instead of in half-dozens? No one seemed to cater for people living on their own. Today she *wouldn't* be alone, though, but mingling with distinguished guests – maybe television presenters, or interior designers: people who owned racehorses or villas in the sun. The notion was so thrilling, she all but lost her footing as she went tripping down the stairs, ignoring all her aches and pains in her haste to reach the door. Flinging it open, she greeted her neighbour with a radiant smile.

'Look, I don't even know your name,' Yvette said apologetically, 'but—'

'That doesn't matter. I'm free. I'd *love* to come. It's awfully kind.'

Yvette looked noticeably disconcerted. Perhaps she was a

stickler for the proprieties and wanted introductions first. 'I'm Muriel – Muriel Hemmings. And you're Yvette – I know that. I've heard your lovely husband call you many a time.'

Yvette's frown cut deeper. 'Muriel, forgive me, but I haven't time to chat. I'm out of my mind with worry. We seem to have lost our little dog ...'

'Fifi?'

'Yes, Fifi.' Her voice took on a note of desperate hope. 'Are you telling me you've seen her? You've *got* her here? Oh, please say yes!'

'No, I *haven't* seen her,' Muriel said tonelessly. 'Well, not since earlier this morning.'

'She might be in your garden, though. There's a small hole in the fence. I need to have a thorough search, to put my mind at rest. She could be in the shed or—'

'The shed's locked.'

'Yes, but she's so agile and determined, she can worm her way into anything.'

'She couldn't be here in the first place. That hole in the fence is so tiny, no creature could get through.'

'Muriel, I'm at my wits end! On top of everything else, we're expecting fifty guests. Some of them are here already. My husband's doing his best to cope, but I should be with them myself.'

And *I* should be with them myself, Muriel said silently. With an angry gesture, she motioned Yvette inside, led her through the house and out into the garden.

'Do you mind if I look everywhere?'

'Please yourself,' Muriel muttered, making no attempt to help. Her garden was so overgrown, it was doubtless full of hiding-places for disobedient dogs. She didn't have the strength to keep it tidy, or the money to waste on Lotus Landscape Design. While Yvette tramped her way across the weeds, she remained standing by the fence, fighting a surge of dizziness. The champagne she hadn't drunk was churning in her veins; the steak she hadn't tasted curdling in her stomach. She could *smell* the meat now, smell the smoke – an acrid, greasy, choking smell, the smell of disappointment.

Wretchedly she sank to her knees, until her eye was level with the small hole in the fence. Peering through, she watched the throng of guests. They were all tucking in, as *she* should be – munching chicken, swilling champagne, holding out their glasses for a refill and their plates for fresh-cooked steak. A buzz of conversation rose above the fence, as friend greeted friend effusively, exchanging jokes and laughter.

'I can see her!' she said suddenly, her face pressed against the scratchy wood. 'I can see your little dog.'

'*Where*?' Yvette was tearing over, her voice tremulous with relief.

'By the barbecue.' No, that wasn't quite correct. Fifi was *on* the barbecue. Her mass of fluffy white hair was slowly singeing and shrivelling, drifting into the air in a cloud of powdery flakes. The thicker fur on her rump and tail took longer to scorch off, but finally the last remaining shred had charred to cindery ash. The succulent pink flesh beneath was soon broiling to perfection on the glowing, red-hot charcoal. Piers tended it with care, sprinkling it with herbs, basting it with oil, and frequently turning it with cooking-tongs, to ensure it was evenly browned. Then he took his knife, sliced it into slivers and passed the pieces round. At first the guests were hesitant, chewing only warily, but caution changed to pleasure in this new, exotic treat, whose unusual taste and tenderness intrigued their gourmet palates.

'She's *not* there,' Yvette whimpered, all but pushing Muriel over, as she applied her eye to the peephole. 'How could you play a trick like that?'

'She is, she *is*!' Muriel insisted, her gaze focused on the morsels – hands reaching out, teeth masticating – fillet-steak-of-Fifi churning to a squelchy pulp in people's throats and bellies.

Yvette had one last look. 'Are you blind or something?' she snapped. 'Of *course* she isn't there. And, anyway, if she *had* turned up, Piers would have come rushing round to tell me. You've raised my hopes for nothing, which is downright cruel – not to mention crass!'

Was she cruel? She hoped not. And crass? Most probably. All she really wanted was the bows – satin bows and silk bows, tartan bows and rainbow-coloured bows, hound's-tooth-check and polka-dotted bows. And that gentle brush singing through her hair, and the titbits as reward, and the fondlings and caresses, the loving little squeezes, the butterfly kisses planted on her nose. But, most of all, of course, the loving, doting mother.

'You're right,' she said. 'She's *not* there. It was just a … foolish hope.' And, turning on her heel, she walked slowly, stiffly, sadly back indoors.

Wedlock

'Jo, you *must* get dressed! It's fearfully late.'

'Coming,' she called from the bathroom, still trying to dislodge an obstinate piece of carrot from her tooth.

'Everyone will be in the church by now.'

'*My* friends won't,' Jo remarked, sauntering out in her bra and pants. 'If they get anywhere on time, it's a bloody miracle.'

'Well, my friends *will*,' her stepmother retorted, with a disapproving frown. 'Quick – let's get you into your dress.'

'Hold on a tick. I need to put my deodorant on. I'm sweating from sheer nerves.'

'*Perspiring*, dear, not sweating. Only men and horses sweat.'

Jo made a neighing sound, her jokiness disguising genuine fear. Pre-wedding nerves were normal. Weren't they? 'Damn! Where the hell did I put the stuff? It must have walked off on its own.'

'Borrow mine. I'll fetch it.'

Jo was glad of even a few seconds on her own. She didn't want an ageing, fussy bridesmaid – didn't want a bridesmaid at all. It seemed desperately important to have this time alone, before she joined her life to someone else's, for ever and ever and—

'Here you are, dear. It's a nice one – Estée Lauder Youth Dew.'

'Thanks.'

'Now what about your tights?'

'I'm not wearing them. I'm hot enough.'

'Jo, you *must* wear tights for a wedding.'

'Why? Is it a law of the land?'

'Don't be silly. And please do get a move on. It's ten to twelve already.'

'Brides are always late,' she said, wriggling her bare feet, with difficulty, into the stiff white leather shoes. 'It's our prerogative.'

'Not *that* late.' Shirley took down the wedding gown from its padded satin hanger and held it out towards her. 'Careful! Don't tread on the train.'

As she stepped into the wide-skirted dress, Jo suddenly felt as if she were entering a cage; the prison door slamming shut as Shirley zipped her up. The brocaded fabric was extraordinarily heavy, weighing her down, enclosing her in a luxurious white padded cell. When she'd tried it on at the fittings, it hadn't seemed so cumbersome, yet now it was squeezing all her organs, almost preventing her from breathing.

'You look absolutely beautiful!' Shirley said, standing back to admire the effect.

Jo fidgeted in embarrassment. 'Absolutely beautiful' was way over the top and, anyway, according to the fairytales, stepmothers hated beauty in a stepdaughter.

All at once, there was a bellow from downstairs. 'Shirley! Jo! What the hell are you two playing at? We should have left hours ago. The driver's doing his nut!'

'Nearly ready, Dad,' she shouted back. They had left him with the gin bottle, but he sounded anything but mellow.

'Oh, dear,' Shirley tutted. 'He can't take stress.'

Don't criticize my father, she was just about to shout, but Shirley was advancing on her again, this time with the veil.

'No, wait! My ear-rings first.'

'We haven't time for ear-rings. It's a good half-hour's drive to the church and, at this rate, the vicar will be pacing up and down, wondering where on earth you are.'

'Look, Edward bought me those ear-rings, especially for today.'

'Well, hurry up, for heaven's sake!'

Jo dashed over to the dressing-table and endeavoured to sit down, but the dress was so stiff and full, it didn't seem to want to bend. Still standing up, she opened the tiny box, withdrew the diamond shamrocks, then fiddled about for a moment, trying to put one on. 'Shit! The holes in my ears have closed up – I suppose because I haven't worn ear-rings for such ages. And these ones are for pierced ears, so I just can't get them in.'

Shirley made a noise between a sigh and a groan. 'I've got

dozens of the clip-on sort, including a gorgeous little seed-pearl pair that'll look perfect with the dress. Wait a sec and I'll fetch them.'

'No, I must wear Edward's. The shamrocks are for luck and, anyway, the diamonds match the ring.'

Another shout erupted from downstairs. 'For God's *sake*, Jo! Are you getting married or aren't you?'

'Look, I'd better go and calm him down.' Shirley teetered out in her high-heeled sling-back shoes. She was wearing a vile shade of green and far too many frills. Though who was *she* to talk? Her own dress seemed ridiculously elaborate. In fact, when she examined herself full-length in the mirror, the reflection staring back at her bore no resemblance to the ordinary self she knew. Her dark hair had been twisted up on top, instead of hanging tousled round her shoulders. And her make-up looked too thick, almost like a mask. Normally, she didn't wear lipstick or foundation – only a lick of mascara – but Shirley had insisted on giving her the full works. ('It'll look better in the photographs.') And the dress itself made her seem much older: a doomed figure in some Spanish Tragedy. What would Edward think? He rarely saw her in anything but jeans. But then it was his status-conscious family who had insisted on a big wedding in the first place.

She walked slowly to the window, glancing out at the small back garden, with its apple tree, its square of lawn. She had climbed that tree, dug the soil for worms, planted a nasturtium patch, measured out her childhood in daisy-chains and hopscotch. Today it looked forlorn: the leaves yellowing and drifting down, the grass parched from the late summer heat. She turned back to the room, trying to drink in every feature, so she could imprint them on her mind: the bookshelf with its Beatrix Potters, the patchwork quilt Aunt Eve had sewn, the corkboard on the wall, with its mass of photographs, depicting her and various school-friends from kindergarten to sixth form. This was the only room she had ever had – the only home she had ever had – yet she would be leaving it in just a matter of minutes. Though it *wasn't* really home now, not with Shirley there, putting her stamp on the furnishings and colour scheme, even chucking out the old sheets and towels. Tomorrow, no doubt, the photos, quilt and Beatrix Potters would also end up in the bin, dumped as so much trash.

Shirley panted up again, her green eye shadow already smudged. 'Your father's in a dreadful state. And the driver's in a tizzy, as well. He's got another booking after this and says he—'

'Look, if I go and fetch a needle, could you jab it through each ear? You'll see the little marks where they were pierced originally, so it'll only take a second to open up the holes again.'

'Jo, are you out of your mind? You'll get an infection and land up with a raging fever on your honeymoon.'

'Of course I won't. I'm tough.' She *had* to wear the diamonds – not just for good luck, but because diamonds were for ever, so the adverts said. 'For ever' still seemed frightening – a path winding up a steep and dangerous mountainside, until it lost itself in mist. 'OK, OK, I'll sterilize the needle first, but it'll only waste *more* time.'

'Jo' – Shirley's voice was wire wool – 'we haven't time to be sterilizing needles. Once I've fixed your veil, we're off.'

'But—'

'No "buts". We're leaving in one minute flat.'

Yards and yards of tulle suddenly descended on her head, blinkering her, blocking out the view. Images of gags and blindfolds flitted through her mind. 'Ow!' she cried, as Shirley fixed the wreath on top with what felt like sharp steel needles. 'You're hurting.'

'Well, it's got to be secure. You don't want it falling off.'

She wasn't sure she wanted it at all. Weren't wreaths for funerals?

'Right, got your bouquet?'

'It's in the hall.'

'Good! Let's go.'

Shirley preceded her down the stairs, Jo walking with exaggerated care. This wasn't her – this was some impostor – the daughter-in-law Edward's parents would have chosen, had they been given a free hand: a sophisticated woman in her twenties, not a crass kid of nineteen, and someone with a decent education, and what they called 'background' (which meant upper class, top drawer.) They disapproved not just of her, but of the fact that Edward had proposed a mere seven days after meeting her. He'd known after seven *minutes,* so he claimed. Which was one of the reasons she loved him – *and* loved the proposal. He'd actually gone down on his knees and recited a Shakespeare sonnet, then whipped a little box from his back pocket, opened it with a flourish to reveal the diamond ring, slipped the ring on her finger, and said she was never, ever to take it off, not even in the tomb. She'd been in the middle of cooking supper and the burgers she was frying had frizzled to a black, charred mess. Who cared? She would burn a million burgers for the sake of romance like that.

Her father was waiting in the hall, looking hot and flustered; his ill-fitting morning suit straining over his stomach. He approached her almost shyly, lifting her veil to give her a bashful kiss. 'You look sensational,' he whispered.

'Thanks, Dad,' she whispered back. It seemed imperative to whisper, so they wouldn't be overheard. Fortunately Shirley was out of earshot, checking her hair in the mirror, and putting on her large green feathered hat. But after today, it would be her father and this woman on their own – she an occasional visitor. And it was clear where his priorities lay. OK, he'd given her a kiss, but already he had turned his back and was fussing over Shirley again – did she have her car-keys? Did she know the way? She would remember, wouldn't she, to turn off at junction 9? 'You'd better go ahead of us,' he added, 'so you're in the church by the time we arrive, and can reassure the others. They'll all be having kittens, imagining we've broken down, or I've had a heart attack.'

Don't rub it in, Jo thought. I know it's all my fault. She had disappointed both her parents by always being late – late for school, late for appointments, even late being born, according to her mother; still clinging on to the safety of the womb a whole ten days after she was due. Would the *new* baby be late? The loath-some creature was expected this very week, keeping her mother a virtual prisoner up in Perth. A pregnancy at the age of forty-six carried the risk of complications, and they feared she might not get back home in time if she travelled such a distance.

Jo loosened one of the hairpins digging into her scalp. At first, she'd wept and stormed, but now she felt something close to relief. At least the day would be more peaceful without the ex-wife and the current wife spoiling for a fight, and without snide attacks on her mother as villainness-in-chief – walking out on her family because she'd fallen for a hairdresser half her age, who'd landed her with his love-child. It was the hairdresser that rankled as far as Edward's parents were concerned. If she had run off with an Oxbridge don, or a surgeon, or a judge, all would have been forgiven, no doubt.

Shirley was still racing around like a rabbit on adrenaline, locking up, turning any lights off, fetching her bag and gloves, and finally seizing the wedding bouquet and tweaking one of the roses into line, as if it, too, needed discipline. 'Careful now – don't crush them,' she said, handing the flowers to Jo.

I'm not a child, Jo didn't say, wondering how red roses could feel so burdensome. She longed to have her hands free, longed to be wearing casual clothes, longed to scrub her face clean, kick off the crippling shoes. Tonight, with Edward, she would be naked, unconfined, just warm skin against warm skin. 'Roll on tonight!' she murmured.

'I'm off, then, you two. See you soon. Good luck, Jo!'

'Thanks,' Jo muttered, frowning in annoyance as her father kissed Shirley goodbye. And a longer kiss than *hers* had been.

All three of them walked out to the front path, Jo still moving stiffly, like a creature which had grown a shell and had to drag the unwieldy thing around wherever she might go. Having waved Shirley off in their scarlet Ford Fiesta, her father took her arm and led her out to the waiting car – a vintage Bentley in weddingwhite. The chauffeur held the door for her and took charge of her bouquet, while she manoeuvred herself into the back, encumbered by the bulky folds of her dress. Her father scrambled in the other side, his reassuringly solid thigh nudging against her own. 'OK, pet?'

'Yes, fine.' Any minute she would be leaving his official care, leaving this street, leaving her home town. He'd be 'giving her away', as if she were an object or possession, and probably glad to do so, now that he had Shirley in his life. Once, there'd been just the two of them, after her mother left. Had he forgotten that era completely, forgotten just how close they'd been, united in their grief? If only he hadn't remarried, he could have come and lived with her and Edward in their smart new garden flat – the ideal situation: her husband and her father under the same roof. OK, she was probably a total wimp, but she still didn't feel quite old enough to leave a Dad behind.

As they turned into the High Street, he begged the chauffeur to make up for lost time. 'If you could you step on it, Ron, we'd really be obliged.'

'I'll do my best, sir,' the fellow said, putting his foot down hard. 'Though this old lady's a wee bit temperamental and doesn't do much more than sixty-five.'

Jo stared at the back of his head: neatly clipped grey hair beneath a navy cap. He must see so many weddings – bride after bride after bride transported in his car. But he'd be aware merely of the externals: the forced smiles, the gorgeous dresses, the impeccable façade. Marriage was like an iceberg, with only the tiny top part open to public scrutiny. Underneath were dangerous depths and currents that could sweep man and wife away. Her parents' marriage had foundered. Suppose she'd inherited a gene from them – the unhappy-marriage gene? No, that was daft. Edward worshipped her and was everything she wanted: easy-going, funny, bright – even rich, for God's sake. She was the luckiest girl in the world.

She sank back against the luxurious leather seat. Most of this extravagance was being paid for by his family. As was their ritzy honeymoon. This time tomorrow, she and Edward would be wandering hand in hand along sand as fine as gold-dust, or sipping exotic cocktails beneath the shade of leafy palms. It was hard to believe, as she gazed out at the dreary stretch of motorway: lorries clogging the inside lane, scrubby grass withered on the verge, an overcast and sluggish sky threatening further rain. Although they were now bowling along at quite a pace, she had an extraordinary feeling that she would be stuck on this same stretch of road for the remainder of her life; high-speed cars roaring past, as the decades ticked away; the thrum of the engine and the whine of the wind reverberating in her ears until she was too old and deaf to hear. '*What*, Dad?' she mouthed, her father's last remark drowned in the snort and rumble of a huge pantechnicon.

'I said I'll miss you, darling,' he repeated, clasping her hand in his hot, red, knuckly one.

She nodded, terrified she'd cry. Everything was about to change, just as it had changed for *him*, a year ago, after his remarriage. You had to learn to compromise in marriage. Where you lived, what you wore, when you ate, how you ran your finances or chose your holidays – all would now depend on what a partner thought. She would even change her name. She tried it out: Mrs Pemberton-

Jones. No, that *couldn't* be her. It was too swanky, too grown-up again. None of her friends were married, nor even wished to be. 'How could you promise to shag just one bloke for the rest of your life?' Lucy had demanded.

'Why not?' she'd retorted fiercely. 'Edward's great in bed.'

'Yeah, but you'll get sick of the same routine.'

'I *shan't*.'

'I mean, blokes are all so different. And variety's the spice of life.'

Lucy was a slut – everyone knew that. If she wanted to sleep with half the office, that was her affair.

'I hope you'll be really happy, pet. Edward's a good chap.'

Again she nodded, not trusting herself to speak. How could her father know what Edward was like, when, in some respects, he was a stranger even to *her*? Perhaps other people were always unknown quantities, or did marriage bring you closer? Her best friend, Lorraine, believed that sex was the closest you could ever get to anyone, and that you didn't need marriage vows, just a double bed. And, yes, when she and Edward made love, she did feel really special; his key in her lock, opening and exploring her. She'd had only one other bloke before, and he was a complete non-starter, whereas just thinking about Edward lit her up inside, as if the nineteen candles on last month's birthday cake were flickering and sparkling in her stomach. It was the other stuff that rankled: his parents always nosing around – turning up at Edward's pad and fussing about stupid things like why he hadn't defrosted the fridge, and did he know the cups were chipped? And his maddening younger brother who called her Freckle-Face, and the snooty sister, Kate, who had borrowed her best skirt, then spilt red wine all over it. But then taking on your husband's tribe was simply part of the deal.

'You'll phone from Tobago, won't you, darling?' Her father squeezed her hand again.

''Course.' She pictured a palm tree in their honeymoon suite, sprouting telephones instead of dates or coconuts.

'Otherwise I'll worry.'

'It's OK, I understand.' She knew he wanted to say more, but couldn't find the words. He had never been one for emotion. That was her mother's forte.

'Thank God we're making good time,' he said, peering at his watch.

'How late *are* we?'

'Well, we should have been there ten minutes ago, but don't worry – it's not far now.'

'Shit! They'll all be going bananas.'

'Don't worry. Just try and relax.'

'I can't. Everybody's staring at us and it makes me feel a prat.' Ever since they'd started out, other drivers had been smiling or waving, some even tooting their horns; all attracted by her get-up and by the beautiful old car, its wide white ribbons fluttering in the breeze. Did they envy her, or pity her, she wondered? Getting married was like entering an unknown land with neither passport nor map. If only she and Edward could stay as lovers and simply lark about.

'Well, let's play "I Spy",' her father joked. 'And pretend you're a little girl again, who doesn't care who's looking.'

'OK. I'll go first. I spy with my little eye something beginning with ...with ... K.'

'Kettle.'

'Don't be silly.'

'Kestrel.'

'Oh, come on, Dad, you wouldn't see a kestrel on a motorway.'

'Yes you would. They hover over the verges, searching for food. *And* I've seen a buzzard.'

'Buzzard doesn't begin with K.'

'Well, er, let me think ... Knee.'

'No.'

'Key, then.'

'Give up. My brain's on strike.'

'KitKat.'

'*Where?*'

'On that lorry, in huge red letters. You must be blind if you can't see it.'

'As they say in the song, "I only have eyes for you ..."'

'Thanks, Dad. You're a true romantic. Right, *your* turn.'

'I spy with my little eye something beginning with—'

'Wait! I need a pee.'

'Oh, *no!*' he cried. 'Can't you hang on?'

'No, I'm desperate. That awful feeling's suddenly come on – that you've just got to go or—'

'Look, we're almost there. It's only another mile or two.'

'Yeah, but they might not have a loo in the church.'

'They're bound to.'

'Well, even if they do, I can't just disappear when everyone's been waiting for me so long. I'd die of shame.'

Her father shook his head in exasperation. 'Why the hell didn't you go before we set out?'

'Oh, *Dad*! You sound like Shirley.'

'Well, didn't *she* remind you?'

'No.' Her mother would have done. That's what mothers were for: to make sure your bladder was empty before all important functions, and that your shoes were polished and you had a nice clean handkerchief. Though, of course, proper mothers would be present on your wedding day, instead of in the labour ward.

'Excuse me, madam,' the chauffeur interjected. 'Forgive me butting in, but we're coming up to a service station. I could pull in there, if you like.'

'Yes, *please*.'

'Jo, for heaven's sake, you can't get out in all that fancy gear.'

'Dad, I haven't any choice. It would be worse if I had an accident.'

'Christ!' he groaned. 'Not that.'

Suddenly she laughed. Wetting her pants on her wedding day – what next? She jiggled on the seat, relieved to see the SERVICES sign. And, as they drove into the car-park, she kept her hand poised on the door-handle, ready to leap out the minute they'd come to a halt. Throwing back her veil, she made a dash for it, not waiting for the chauffeur to come round and do the honours.

'Careful!' her father called. 'Don't let that dress trail in the dirt, or Shirley will go berserk.'

'It's OK,' she shouted back, looping up the flowing gown, and attracting more stares in the process.

It was a good fifty yards from the car-park to the café, and a spiteful wind was tugging at her hair, threatening to dislodge the pins. Now she wished she *had* worn tights. The recent heat wave had given way last week to a moody, grey September, and her bare legs were distinctly cold.

'Hey, look, Mum!' a small boy yelled. 'They're having a wedding here.'

She grinned, despite herself. Edward's parents would be mortified if their grand reception at High Pines Country Club were downgraded to the Little Chef.

All the toilets were engaged, but there was no queue, thank God, just one woman waiting, who said she could go first. 'Your need is greater than mine,' she laughed. 'You can't keep the bridegroom waiting.'

'I'm afraid I already have! But he's a patient sort, I'm glad to say.'

'You're lucky! My old man goes through the roof if I'm even a second late.'

'Really?'

'Oh, yes. Mind you, he wasn't always like that, but men are unpredictable.'

'Not all of them.'

'Yes, *all* of them, believe me. You marry one you think you know and land up with a stranger.'

Just at that moment, a cubicle came free. With a quick word of thanks, Jo darted forward and squeezed herself into the narrow space, cursing the dress as she tried to pull her knickers down. Still, at least she'd only had to wait a minute, and should be back in the car in just a couple more.

Having straightened her clothes, she charged out of the ladies' room and veered left along the passageway, trying to find the exit. But this particular corridor didn't look familiar, and she eventually found herself face to face with a small blue door, which certainly *wasn't* the way out. Disoriented, she pushed blindly at the handle and all but fell into a cleaner's cupboard, full of mops and pails. 'Bloody hell!' she muttered, staring at the clutter: dustpans, disinfectant, a box of rubber gloves, and a pair of fluorescent orange overalls, hanging on a peg.

Suddenly, impulsively, she stepped into the cupboard and closed the door behind her, enclosing herself in the dim, claustrophobic space. There was barely room for her voluminous wedding finery, but already she had begun to tear it off. She tugged first at the wreath, discarding it in a shower of hairpins, then stripped off the veil, bundling it up any old how and tossing it into an old red plastic bucket. Next, she struggled out of her dress, almost ripping it in her haste. She couldn't bundle *that* up – it was too stiff, too self-important, and seemed to have a life of its own, still standing to attention. Angrily she shoved it right to the back of the cupboard, then took down the orange overalls, climbed into them and zipped them up. They were far too big – a man's pair – but delightfully loose and baggy, although they did look rather peculiar teamed with white wedding shoes. Tomorrow she would be back in her old trainers – no more high heels, high style. And her make-up she'd get rid of now. She rummaged for a J-cloth and kept rubbing at her face with it, until most of the lipstick and foundation had come off. Finally she combed her hair with her fingers until it was hanging loose and straight again and free of the last of the hairpins. Her old self was back, thank God.

Pushing the cupboard door open, she bolted down the corridor, no longer looking for the exit but for the bridge across the motorway that would take her to the other side. She hadn't got a penny on her, so she would have to hitchhike back the way she'd come. Lorraine would give her a bed until she decided what to do. And her father would forgive her – grudgingly, eventually. As for Edward – no, she dared not even think of Edward, nor of the romantic diamond ring still shrieking on her wedding finger. The guilt was just too huge: a great mushroom-cloud of self-reproach, remorse, regret …

Ah – she'd found the stairs that led up to the bridge, and was already teetering up them, hampered by her shoes. And now she was on the bridge itself and refusing to look back – or down – just running, running, running, away from shackles, fetters, wedlock.

If all men were unpredictable, then best not to take the risk.

Dandelions

'I don't like the look of that sky, Brianna. Mark my words, it'll be bucketing down before you reach the station. Why don't you stay the night?'

'Mum, I *can't* – I've told you. That meeting in the—'

'Well, stay another couple of hours and catch a later train.'

'But it's just as likely to be raining then, as well.'

'There's no need to snap. I'm just concerned about you getting wet. You *do* have an umbrella, I presume?'

'Yes,' Brianna lied, knowing her mother's efforts to find one would only cause still more delay. 'I'll be fine. It's not far.' Another lie – the walk took half an hour.

'And don't forget, next week you're coming earlier.'

She was hardly *likely* to forget when they'd been over it a dozen times already. 'Don't worry. It's all settled.'

'Well if you have to go, you have to, I suppose.' Her mother opened the front door, only to close it again, barring the escape-route. 'Look, are you absolutely sure you can't make it on the Wednesday? It would mean a lot if you could take me to that appointment.'

'But I thought that woman you met at church was—'

'Oh, Angela's no use! She'd bound to turn up late. And that car of hers is an absolute disgrace. Dog hairs all over the seats, and the ashtray overflowing.'

'At least she's *got* a car. I can't really help without one.'

'You could arrange a taxi, couldn't you? There's this nice little man in the village who—'

'Mum, I'm sorry, but I just can't get away on a weekday – not with my job as pressured as it is. And I simply must leave now. Otherwise I'll miss the train.'

'Off you go, then. It was silly of me to ask. I should have saved my breath. You've never got a minute, have you, to do anything but work?'

Brianna suppressed a scream of rage. Hadn't she been there all damned day, for heaven's sake? Her mother could at least say thank you, instead of issuing reproaches.

As she set off down the lane, she kept turning back to wave. That was part of the whole ritual, as if her mother liked to leave her with the image of a poor, pathetic figure abandoned on the doorstep by a, yes, endlessly busy daughter.

The minute she rounded the corner, she broke into a run, although there was no real relief in beating a retreat, when she was left struggling with a curdled mass of anger, guilt and pity, all seething and bubbling like the yeasty scum on fermenting beer. And 'shoulds' and 'oughts' kept snaking round her head, hissing out more venom-clouds of guilt: she *should* have stayed the night; *should* have been more sympathetic; *should* have coaxed her mother to eat the food she'd brought (expensive food from Fortnum's, which had necessitated a special journey on her precious one day off). Instead, she had tipped the whole damned lot into the waste-bin, once her mother started complaining about pâté being a health-risk and shop-bought quiche a con. Other people's mothers actually *cooked* for their daughters, or took them out to lunch, especially when they'd been travelling for over two-and-a-half hours on a crowded tube and a moody, stop-start train.

The rain began in earnest after only a few minutes, yet there were still two miles to go. Did her mother have to live in such a godforsaken place? With no means of local transport other than the bus (notoriously unreliable), of *course* she'd feel cut off – isolated, lonely and all the other words that played the same refrain: 'Poor me. All alone.' She wouldn't move, though, not even into Guildford. She *liked* to make things difficult, to test her only child's devotion. 'If you really cared, you'd come down twice a week, pressured job or no.'

Was she mean? Undutiful? Downright selfish, even? Yes, all of them, most likely. Her mother was in desperate need of company –

that was incontestable. 'But why should *I* provide it? It's her own fault if she hasn't any friends. She's driven every single soul away but me.'

Stopping a moment to button up her jacket, she cursed her folly in not bringing a proper mac. But when she'd set out this morning, the sky had been reasonably clear. Besides, one didn't expect protracted April showers in the second week of June.

On finally reaching the station, she made an immediate dash for shelter and stood huddled under the platform roof, wringing the water from her long mane of dripping hair and peeling off her sodden rag of a jacket. She had barely caught her breath when a voice crackled from the loudspeaker-system. 'This is a customer announcement. South West Trains regret to inform you that the 18.53 service to London Waterloo has been cancelled, due to non-availability of staff. We apologize for any inconvenience caused.'

'*Fuck!*' she muttered under her breath – not that anyone was listening. Apart from her, the platform was deserted; no one else 'inconvenienced', not to mention hungry, tired and drenched. According to the station clock, it was 18.46. The Sunday trains were only one an hour, which meant hanging about for sixty-seven minutes, on a station with no facilities whatever: no waiting-room, no toilets, no refreshment bar. Well, at least there was a seat, and some musical diversion in the form of the deluge drumming on the roof and the plop-plop-plop of water-drops leaking from a hole.

She sat gingerly on the bench, which had broken slats and a black scribble of graffiti behind it, on the wall: 'Ted loves Sally.' 'Piss off, wild boy.' 'Kirsty likes it up the arse.' Unfolding the *Sunday Times*, she tried to immerse herself in an article on the Kyoto protocol, but it was impossible to concentrate. Her mind was more concerned not only with her mother but with what awaited her at home. She wouldn't be back till half-past ten, and there was a mass of stuff to get ready for the morning, mainly connected with the crucial Monday meeting. According to the Head of Department, all their jobs were on the line; indeed, the very future of the college was at stake. She had tried to explain the situation to her mother, but someone who'd never had a job, never worked to deadlines, simply couldn't understand. In any case, her mother preferred to talk about herself: the pain in her left leg, the rudeness of her neighbours' boys, the uneven pavement outside Clarke's, just waiting to trip her up.

Brianna refolded the paper and stuffed it back in her bag. It was *vile* to be so lacking in compassion, and only went to show what a rotten daughter she was. She took a deep breath in, exhaled it in a long, shuddering sigh, trying to clear her mind of the whole exhausting cycle of resentment and remorse, annoyance and regret. At least she was mercifully alone now, with no mother making demands; no frantic boss warning of a showdown. In fact, a stifling Sunday silence seemed to have descended on the land; the station still deserted; not a soul in sight.

Even the rain was easing off, at last; glints of sunlight breaking through the clouds. As if seeking an escape from herself, she walked right to the end of the platform, where the concrete finished and a tangle of brambly scrub took over, interspersed with weeds and flowers: cow-parsley and chickweed, stinging nettles, willowherb. She stooped to pick a dandelion, admiring the way the showy yellow flower-head had closed against the rain. If only *she* had that same knack, in order to protect her hair from downpours. She also envied the fact that dandelions reproduced themselves non-sexually, never requiring pollination from any outside agency. That, too, would come in handy in her present man-less state, when she was longing for a baby, but had no obvious means of conceiving one

She started picking a whole bunch of the flowers, in tribute to her father, who'd been passionate about nature study and a champion of the dandelion. 'It's not a weed,' he'd told her, 'but a valuable plant that gives us food and wine.' Indeed, now she came to think of it, he and the plant had certain things in common: bright, cheerful, easy-going, resilient and strong. And neither her father nor the flower ever gave themselves airs or demanded special treatment, but simply adapted to their circumstances and flourished where and how they could. If he'd had a grave, she would have piled it high with dandelions, but his ashes were still in their original container, which took pride of place on the mantelpiece. Her mother refused to relinquish them – *or* the role of widow – even after twenty years.

'You don't understand, Brianna. I loved your father so much, I couldn't even contemplate starting again with someone else.'

Love was such an equivocal word, bandied about without a thought, and often meaning very different things: dependency and need, possessiveness, obsession ….

She put her flowers down for a moment, in order to pick a dandelion clock. They, too, were growing freely, mixed in with the flowers. She began puffing at the downy seed-head, reciting 'He loves me, he loves me not' with each and every puff. The final puff was 'loves me not', which was demonstrably untrue of her father. He had adored her from the moment of her birth: a squirming, red-faced infant, bawling at the universe. He had even chosen her name, over-ruling her mother's preference for Melanie or Jean. OK, Brianna was a mouthful (and had resulted in sporadic teasing from silly girls at school), but as the feminine form of his *own* name, Brian, it had forged a bond between them from that first day of her life. Her mother had been jealous, of course; craved such love and closeness for herself. In fact, the dandelion clock was a rather fitting image for her mother: delicate and vulnerable, with the same thistledown grey hair. Yet what an irony that her lusty, vigorous father had been the one who actually died, while her weak and wispy mother soldiered on.

Shrugging, she strolled back along the platform, still holding her 'bouquet'. Her hands were stained with the milky sap oozing from the snapped-off stalks, and had a bitter medicinal smell – the smell of pain, of death.

Suddenly, she was back there in the hospice, being led into the parlour by an ice-block of a nurse: white uniform, white voice. The room itself had died and looked all pale and stiff, with drawn blinds, plastic flowers, and stale and sickly air that made you want to throw up. The nurse spoke in a whisper, as if they were in church. 'Your daddy's passed away,' she said – a rotten lie, since he was hideously dead. Barely able to breathe, she crept towards the couch-thing where they had arranged her darling father – what remained of him: stiff grey face, moulded out of candle-wax, mouth clamped shut, glassy eyes, fixed in a ghastly stare.

She didn't cry. Not once. You cried about stupid things like losing your purse or failing an exam, not when you were paralysed inside. Her friends now lived in a different world, fussing over homework, buying clothes and make-up, giggling over boys. And her mother was enclosed in a rigid, black-edged blisterpack, cut off from everyone. Anyway, she didn't want her mother. The only parent who had ever mattered had vanished overnight. Which meant everything else was pointless. Why bother going to sports days, if he wasn't there to cheer her on, or auditioning for school plays when he wouldn't be in the audience? Even toffees disappeared. They had always shared a bag between them on their way back from the paper shop, but if she ate one on her own now, it blocked her throat and choked her. And her nature books sat gathering dust on the shelf. The only reason for learning things like the Latin names for dandelions, or how to tell a kestrel from a sparrowhawk, was to make him proud of her.

Angrily, she gazed out at the fields beyond the station. The countryside was preening in its prime of June perfection, as it had the day he died; the grass long and lush and sappy, the trees a jubilant green, with no foretaste of decay. *Everyone* had lied – not just the nurse and priest, but the trees, the sun, the hayfields – pretending it was summer, pretending life went on.

She slumped against the station wall, turning her back on the railway line. She was no longer waiting for a train. There *was* none. The trains had stopped; the entire living world shuddered to a halt.

'Welcome aboard this 19.57 South West train service from Horsley, calling at Effingham Junction, Cobham and Stoke D'Abernon, Oxshott, Claygate, Hinchley Wood ...'

'Damn!' she mumbled, looking up from the notes she was making for tomorrow morning's meeting. One of those wretched recorded announcements, disturbing the peace. It was hard enough trying to work in cold and clammy clothes. Her skirt was clinging to her legs, and drops of water from her hair kept falling on to her notebook, smudging her neat writing into tears. As for her summer sandals, they were so waterlogged they had started to disintegrate.

Having listed all the stations to Waterloo, the booming voice now embarked on a different tack. 'Please familiarize yourself with the security notices posted in each carriage. If you see anything suspicious ...'

Look, for heaven's sake, she interjected silently, there's nothing to see, and no one *on* this train but me, as far as I can tell. Can't you just pipe down and let me get on with my work?

'Please notify a member of staff immediately.'

A member of staff? Who were they kidding? The previous train had been cancelled on account of a *lack* of staff, and this one wasn't exactly crawling with helpful, cheery employees.

'Customers should note that next weekend, June 23 and 24, major engineering works will affect many services on this line. No trains will be running between Surbiton and Guildford in either direction. A replacement bus service will be in operation, departing at hourly intervals from ...'

She groaned aloud. Whatever the impediments, she *had* to be there next Sunday for her mother's sixtieth; flowers and gifts in hand. And she had promised to be earlier than usual. Fat chance! If she set off at midnight the day before, she might just arrive in time for lunch.

The announcement finally crackled to a stop, but she sat staring into space, battling with the 'oughts' and 'shoulds' once more. Perhaps she ought to stay the whole weekend, knowing how much her mother hated being on her own. Except that would mean missing Madeleine's party – one of the best bashes of the year. She should put her mother first, though, especially on such an important birthday; forget her own petty social round.

'Welcome aboard this 20.05 South West train service from Effingham Junction, calling at ...'

Lord! *Again*? For whose benefit, she'd like to know, since no one had got on, either here or at Horsley.

'Our next station-stop is Cobham and Stoke D'Abernon. Security notices are posted in each carriage ...'

She couldn't see a security notice anywhere, only a series of random doodlings scratched into the window-glass, as if some bored delinquent had been busy with his knife-point.

'If you see anything suspicious ...'

She glanced around: smeary, rain-streaked windows, scuffed floor, blue plush seats. Hardly suspicious, any of it.

The minute the obdurate voice shut off, she made an effort to return to work, trying desperately to banish her mother, along with Madeleine. But the respite was short-lived.

'In the interests of security, passengers are advised to keep all personal items with them.'

That was so much verbiage. Would people really part themselves from precious bags and briefcases?

'We are now approaching Cobham and Stoke D'Abernon Please mind the gap between the train and the platform edge.'

More unnecessary advice. Next they'd be told to wash their hands after using the train toilet. (Except there *wasn't* a toilet, as she knew from bitter experience.) It was all part of the nanny-culture that seemed to be spreading like a virus: weather girls exhorting you to slather on the sun-cream; outbreaks of hysteria were you fool enough to light a cigarette. If the trend developed further, recorded announcements would worm their way even into private homes: the fridge ordering you to stock up with fruit and vegetables; the electric kettle squealing, 'Beware! Boiling water scalds.'

Instead of continuing with her notes, she began jotting down the needless repetitions Perhaps she'd write to the area manager, claiming a breach of human rights. There were probably genuine grounds, for goodness' sake: noise pollution, intrusion on her private space, increased risk of a heart attack, due to sheer frustration. Or maybe she'd try to be creative and work the lines into a poem, a soothing ditty that might lull her off to sleep.

'Our next station-stop is Oxshott.
We are now approaching Oxshott.
Our next station-stop is Claygate.
We are now approaching Claygate.'

Hardly a great work of art. And, in any case, the rhythm was broken at Surbiton, where the announcement was far longer, running through the whole rigmarole again and even adding a few extras for good measure. 'Change here for Thames Ditton and Hampton Court. Our estimated arrival time at London, Waterloo is 20.45.' And the security notice was repeated, of course, although perhaps with slightly more reason, as half a dozen people had struggled into the carriage – mostly bedraggled, dripping figures. The improvement in the weather had proved inconsiderately transitory, and the rain was now pelting down once more, causing further distraction as it lashed against the windows.

'We wish you a pleasant journey this evening, and we hope you enjoy travelling with South West trains.'

That was really stretching credibility. Could *anyone* enjoy lumbering along in a dirty, draughty carriage, while subjected to these constant interruptions? She tossed her notebook back into her bag, capped her pen, and sat tapping her fingers irritably against the edge of the seat. Work was out of the question and, as for poetry, forget it.

'If you require any assistance, I'm located in the rear of this train.'

'Good God!' she exclaimed out loud. All this time, what she had assumed to be an automated recording was actually a living, breathing person – obviously one with delusions of grandeur who liked the sound of his own voice. Or perhaps a demoted pilot, since he was using aircraft-speak. All those 'Welcome aboards' and allusions to his 'staff'. She half-expected to see a stewardess come tottering along with the drinks trolley, or to hear the bloke announce that they were cruising at an altitude of thirty thousand feet.

Instead, he piped up with the same old spiel, once they stopped at Wimbledon. By now, she knew it off by heart and mouthed it in tandem with him: '… calling at Clapham Junction, Vauxhall and our final destination, Waterloo.'

But there was an additional little coda, to keep her on her toes. ' No – correction, ladies and gentlemen: we have an additional stop at Earlsfield today.'

'Which means, I suppose,' she snorted, 'that you'll have a field day *there*, as well.'

In actual fact, he restrained himself till Clapham, where the smug, chatty, totally maddening voice began reprising the whole saga.

'Welcome aboard this …'

As the security notice was repeated yet again, she tried to rally her strength for the second part of the journey, by tube this time: Jubilee Line to Baker Street, then change to the Metropolitan. There were bound to be delays, not to mention Sunday evening drunks. It would be nice to snatch forty winks before coping with such hindrances, but no chance of peace with that garrulous guard on board. The wretched fellow was now reeling off the whole palaver about the engineering works, including the times of the replacement buses, where customers could board them and …

Suddenly, on impulse, she leapt to her feet, grabbed her things, dandelions and all, and marched down to the rear of the train, determined to find that self-important loudmouth and muzzle, if not strangle him. Didn't he realize people were busy and had better things to do than listen to his one-man show? If he was so hungry for attention, couldn't he retrain as an actor, or enter for a talent contest? Any minute, he'd be giving them his personal history: 'I grew up in East Acton, over a hardware shop, with a brother, Jack, a sister, Peg, and Sooty, the black Labrador.'

As they stopped at Vauxhall with a sudden shudder, she banged her knee against a seat and yelped in sheer frustration. She'd deliberately sat at the *front* of the train, so she would be close to the barrier when they arrived at Waterloo, and could nip out double-quick. But, of course, for the purposes of finding the guard, she had to walk the whole way back, which wasn't easy when she was carrying so much clutter and the train kept lurching about.

'If you see anything suspicious,' the windbag was intoning again, for the benefit of the few passengers who had just got in at Vauxhall, 'please report it to a member of staff, or to me. This is your guard speaking and you'll find me in ...'

'I know where to find you,' she hissed, striding into the last carriage and finally confronting the source of her fury as he turned away from the microphone. Her irate retort withered on her lips as she stared at him in shock. Her *father*! Returned from the dead. No – impossible. Her father was ashes in a plastic pot. Yet this man was so extraordinarily like him, in build, in height, in colouring, she remained gazing at his face, transfixed, as she took in all the details. The same curly crop of mid-brown hair, and open, smiling manner; the same small, white, even teeth; the same slightly bulbous eyes, in the same shade of slatey blue; the same strong, straight nose and jutting chin. She hadn't seen her father since she was a gangly adolescent, yet he seemed totally unchanged – actually preserved at the age he'd died. But not the pallid wraith in the hospice, whose face felt marble-cold when she'd tried to kiss it back to life. *This* father had warmth and colour in his cheeks, brightness in his eyes, an alert, concerned expression.

'Can I help you, madam?'

The voice was different, of course – nothing like her father's sonorous burr – yet—

'Madam, are you all *right?*'

She nodded, shook her head, so totally confused, she was unable to formulate a single word. She yearned to hug the man, run off with him, weep on his breast, sit on his lap, forbid him ever, ever to leave her, or allow anyone to burn him to a cinder and put him on a mantelpiece.

'Is there anything I can do to assist?'

Yes, she pleaded silently. Hold me. Touch me. Keep telling me you love me and that you're here to stay. For ever.

'Madam, if you're unwell, I suggest you—'

'I'm not unwell,' she blurted out. 'I feel better than I've done in years.' Tears were streaming down her face – the first tears in two long decades; dry, unproductive decades. 'I know they're dead,' she sobbed, thrusting the bunch of wet and wilting dandelions into his outstretched hand, 'but ...but things can resurrect.'

Birth-Day

'Happy birth-day, angel,' Sandra whispered, bending over the cot.

The baby gazed up at her unblinkingly, with lustrous, china-blue eyes.

'It's such a special day, darling, we're going to celebrate. But first it's time for your feed.' The milk was already prepared and waiting in the bottle-warmer, though actually she loathed the bottles and longed to be able to breastfeed. According to the books, babies deprived of mother's milk could miss out on vital nutrients.

Settling the baby on her lap, she smiled down at her with mingled love and pride. No child could be less trouble. Penelope never refused to suckle, never developed colic, didn't even scream when she was hungry. Ruth next door had a very different infant on her hands – a fussy, finicky bellower, who kept the entire family awake at night. But then boys were much more trouble – sometimes downright bolshie. She was lucky to have had girls; all pretty and petite and perfectly behaved. Even now, while she was busy feeding Penelope, there wasn't a sound from Emily or Florence, who were playing quietly downstairs, and wouldn't dream of interrupting her or arguing with each other.

'Shall we take you to see your sisters?' she murmured, once Penelope had finished feeding. 'We could change you down there, by the fire, then Florence can help to dress you. You know how she loves to play "Mummy".'

The baby seemed to understand; the intense blue stare focused on her face with an answering depth of devotion. Sandra carried her downstairs, being extremely careful not to trip. She dared not take the slightest risk with this precious little life.

Emily and Florence were sitting one each end of the sofa, as placidly as she'd predicted. Seating herself between them, she changed the baby's nappy, allowing both girls to help. 'Shall we put on your best dress, Penelope, my sweet? Then the three of us can have a little birth-day party. Yes, Emily, you can choose the— *Damn!*' she said, interrupting herself. 'Wasn't that the doorbell?'

Neither girl replied, but at a second insistent peal, Sandra shot to her feet, bundled up all three dolls, thrust open the sideboard door and quickly stuffed them inside. Then, trying to calm her breathing, she went to answer the door.

'Oh, Mavis – it's you.' Sandra shrunk at the sight of the woman: a busybody mother-of-four, who lived at number nine.

'I hope I'm not intruding, but I haven't seen you for such ages, I was beginning to get worried. I did phone several times, but no one ever answered, which made me even more concerned. Are you *OK*, my dear?'

'Yes, fine.'

'You don't *look* well, I have to say.'

Sandra shrugged. 'Just a bit tired, maybe. You know, after the … birth.'

'Yes, of course. I was horrified to hear about it. Can I come in?'

No, Sandra ached to say. Mavis was not only a nosy parker but a pillar of the local church, and had probably come to invite her to join some ghastly prayer-group. 'I'm … rather busy, actually.'

'Busy? But Father Peter told me you were still convalescing.'

'No, I'm … better now.'

'Sandy, dear, you really shouldn't push yourself. It was only a couple of months ago, and that's nothing really, after such a tragedy.'

Sandra said nothing, determined to shift her mind from the whole affair, as she had in fact been doing most successfully. She stared out at the front garden, fixing her total concentration on the brilliant crimson berries on the cotoneaster bush. Red as blood. No, blood was a forbidden subject, along with—

'Look, I'm freezing to death on this step. Why don't I come in, just for a few minutes, then we can have a little chat.'

Mavis was actually stepping into the hall, uninvited, unabashed. 'You look all-in,' she clucked, shaking her head as she peered closely into Sandra's face. 'Now, listen,' she continued, as she headed for the sitting-room, 'if there's anything I can do to help, you only have to ask.'

Sandra darted after her, suddenly realizing that the baby's shawl and nappy were still lying on the sofa. Hastily stuffing them under a cushion, she motioned the wretched woman to a chair and sat down opposite, praying that the visit would be brief. She had no intention of offering tea or coffee, in case Mavis followed her out to the kitchen and saw the tins of baby-milk and the box of Farley's rusks, not to mention the carrycot and pram.

Mavis settled back against the cushions, as if she planned to stay all morning. 'Sandy, dear,' she said, her voice clotted with concern, 'I do have some idea of what you've been through. It must be quite horrendous to lose a baby so late on in the pregnancy.'

Sandra gripped the arms of the chair. She had tried so hard to bury all the memories, yet Mavis seemed determined to dig them up again, like a careless dog scrabbling with its clumsy paws to unearth a tiny corpse. And, yes, all at once, she was there again – in the labour ward, panting and gasping through twenty-six hours of contractions, only to expel a deformed, dead child.

'I wonder if you've considered going to see a counsellor? It can help to talk, you know.'

Talk? What for? There'd been enough chit-chat in the maternity ward, where they'd put her, cruelly, when she'd developed an infection, claiming it was the only free bed in the place. Couldn't they understand what torture it was to be surrounded by radiant mothers feeding their living, breathing, triumphantly normal infants?

'I mean, especially as you've lost three in succession. That makes it so much worse.'

Sandra said nothing. What was there to say? In the silence, she noticed Mavis glancing surreptitiously round the room. All right, so it wasn't as clean as usual, but she had other claims on her time – making the girls new clothes, dressing and undressing them, wheeling them round the garden in the pram. Christmas had been particularly busy, what with filling three stockings and helping the two older ones make paper-chains and decorate the tree.

'Do they have any idea why it happened?' Mavis asked, worrying at the subject again: that tireless dog still foraging for its bone.

Sandra gave a sudden squawking laugh, the sound startling her as much as it did Mavis. 'Well, the obstetrician told me I was simply a bad layer.'

'A bad *what*?'

'Lay-er. As in hen. Some hens go all broody and hatch whole clutches of eggs, while others…' She let the sentence trail away. With all due respect to her obstetrician, the analogy wasn't apt. The best layers in the hen community were those that *didn't* go broody. And, in any case, the term 'bad layer' surely applied more to problems in conceiving a baby, rather than bringing one to full-term. None the less, the phrase had upset her considerably, made her feel inadequate, not a proper woman; 'childless, fruitless, fallow' branded on her forehead for all the world to see.

'But wasn't there anything they could do to prevent it happening again – I mean, once you'd lost the first one?'

Since the interrogation showed no sign of abating, Sandra decided to open up, if only in the hope of getting rid of her visitor. 'Actually they didn't take the first one very seriously. I lost it at eleven weeks, you see, which the doctor said isn't that uncommon – it's a tricky stage, apparently. So if it's your first miscarriage and there's nothing basically wrong, they tend just to say "better luck next time".' An eleven-week-old foetus was still small enough to fit inside a goose-egg, yet the pain had been so fierce and lasted for so long that by the time the ambulance arrived, she was in a state of total panic, and then made things worse by actually biting one of the ambulance men on the wrist. She felt horribly ashamed now of harming such a kindly soul, when he was only trying to help her onto the stretcher, but extremes of pain had turned her into an animal, baring its teeth at the vet. And the journey to the hospital had seemed to take forever, the ambulance siren shrilling, and Thomas and the driver swapping football stories (having discovered they were both Chelsea fans), while she lay jolting and weeping as baby Florence bled steadily away.

Mavis was cuddling one of the plump, pink cushions – presumably so accustomed to having a baby on her lap, she had reached instinctively for a substitute. 'And what about the second time?' she prompted, obviously eager for further gossip, to pass on to Father Peter, not to mention half the road.

Who cared? If it gave them pleasure to tittle-tattle, good luck to them. 'Well, *that* time, I started bleeding even earlier on, so they took me into hospital to rest. They thought I'd be there for just a couple of days, but it was more than a couple of months, in fact, before the haemorrhaging stopped. Then, when I finally went home, it restarted the very next day and...' No need to spell out all the gory details. She had actually miscarried on a trolley-bed in the hospital corridor, with only a flimsy screen between her and people passing. Again they were short of beds and short of staff, so Emily had plopped into a chamber pot unremarked, unsupervised.

Abandoning her cushion-baby, Mavis leaned forward to take her hand. 'Sandy, I just can't tell you how sorry I am.'

The hand felt hot and damp. And no one called her Sandy except Thomas.

'And what with Thomas leaving on top of everything else,' Mavis added, as if reading her mind. 'It was Father Peter who first told me he'd moved out, then later I bumped into Ruth, in Sainsbury's and she confirmed it.'

Sandra stiffened. If her husband couldn't cope with three lost babies, that was *his* affair. She had removed all his photos from the house, including their wedding photo, which for the last seven years had stood in pride of place on the mantelpiece. Now it was Emily and Florence who smiled down from the ornate silver frame.

'You must have been absolutely devastated.'

Sandra released her hand. What had hurt most, in fact, was that Thomas had gone off with a *good* lay-er – a divorcée with three children, who was now expecting his. And, on top of everything else, the new woman was a bimbo, with less brain than a teapot and a mass of cutesy curls.

'Greg was quite appalled. He said it made him feel ashamed of his own sex. But, look, talking of Greg, why don't you come round for lunch this Sunday? I know he'd love to see you.'

'I'm sorry, I'm, er, tied up this Sunday.'

'Well, make it the Sunday after. In fact, we've invited Father Peter then, so it would be great to have you both. And Father might be able to help – you know, put you on the prayer-rota, or even suggest a counsellor.'

'Thank you, Mavis. That's really kind, but I'm afraid I'm busy then, as well. And, in fact,' she said, rising to her feet, 'I have a fair bit on right now. So if you'll please excuse me ...'

Mavis remained sitting where she was. 'Sandy, I don't like the thought of you working so hard. You need rest and recuperation, not a hectic schedule.'

'I'm perfectly all right,' she said opening the sitting-room door and standing pointedly beside it.

With obvious reluctance Mavis followed her into the hall, still pouring out advice. '*And,*' she added, gazing directly into Sandra's eyes, 'it goes without saying that Greg and I always include you in our own prayers.'

'Thank you,' Sandra muttered, closing the door with undisguised relief.

The minute she was alone, she rushed back to the sitting-room to rescue the children from the sideboard. Despite their ordeal, there wasn't a murmur from any of them – in fact, they greeted her with their usual sunny smiles. 'Poor darlings,' she soothed, gathering all three of them into her arms and pacing gently to and fro, in case they *were* disturbed beneath their placid façades. 'I'm really sorry to have had to shut you in, but people just don't understand. We're all right now, though – on our own again. And if we're going to have that party, I'd better make a start on the cake.'

Which brought her back to the matter of the candles – a source of some anxiety all morning. Today, 30 January, was the day Penelope was actually due to be born, had the pregnancy run its full-term. In brutal fact, the infant kidneys had failed at almost twenty-eight weeks, and the little heart stopped beating, but, without that dreadful trauma, the new-born baby would be taking her first lungfuls of air at about this very time. Her first birthday, though, was a whole year away today, which meant that even a single candle on the cake would not, in fact, be right. On the other hand, the older girls loved to blow out candles, so should she opt for seven, perhaps: one for each successful month of the pregnancy? After all, why dwell on loss and heartbreak, when she could celebrate instead – as she had managed to do (with, admittedly, some lapses) since the beginning of December? 'What do you think, my poppets?' she asked Emily and Florence, whose blithe expressions confirmed the fact that seven would be perfect.

She took her little brood into the kitchen, putting Penelope in her carrycot and settling the two others on their miniature highchairs. 'Now you sit nice and quiet while Mummy checks the ingredients.' Opening the top cupboard, she took down various jars and packets, ticking each one off the list. 'Self-raising flour, caster sugar and icing sugar, vanilla essence, raspberry jam. That leaves just the eggs. Shall we go and fetch those together, darlings?' she asked the girls, knowing how they enjoyed these little errands.

The pram was ready and waiting on the patio. She laid Penelope in first, tucking the covers tenderly around her, then allowed Emily and Florence to sit at the other end, making sure they were warm enough before venturing down the garden path. This winter had been bitter, with heavy frosts and several falls of snow. However, today was bright and clear, as if even the weather was rejoicing in Penelope's birth-day; the sky a deep, contented blue, and every blade of frosted grass glistening in the sun.

The hens could hear her coming and started clucking loudly as she approached the chicken-run. She was still new enough to poultry-keeping to be nervous about her tiny flock. However, the breeder, Mr Townsend, had given her a wealth of useful tips, as well as helping her choose the birds in the first place. The only real perquisite, she had emphasized, was that they had to be good lay-ers. 'In that case,' he'd advised, 'I'd recommend either Black Rocks or Rhode Island Reds.' She had opted for the latter, since their laying record was slightly better and – so far – they'd lived up to it.

Once she reached the hen-house, she left the baby in the pram, then lifted the two girls out, reminding them again how to put their hands gently into the nest-boxes and withdraw the large brown eggs. They were so co-operative and docile they never scared the hens and, on this occasion, managed with a little help to find half a dozen eggs – exactly the number needed for the sponge.

The hens looked fit and well, thank God. She was doing every-thing in her power to ensure that they continued to lay well, even under her amateurish care. Their feed was carefully balanced; they were shielded from all predators, and she kept a constant lookout for the slightest sign of sickness. She had even bought a cockerel, so that, by the spring, she could hatch a load of eggs and fill the place with baby chicks. And, judging by the way the rooster preened and strutted, there was no doubt that he would do his stuff. Like *Thomas*, she thought, quickly suppressing the image of her husband with a red comb and wattle, and flamboyant shimmering tail-feathers, mounting his new fluffy hen, again, again, again.

'That's it, sweethearts,' she said to the two girls, checking on the sleeping baby before putting them back in the pram. As she wheeled it up the path, she was mightily relieved that there was no sign of Ruth in the next-door garden. Ruth and her husband objected strongly to the hens – the noise, the mess, the risk of attracting rats to the area, which might spread disease or endanger their two boys. What they couldn't understand was how vital it was for her peace of mind to have babies in the house and good lay-ers in the garden, and the promise in the hen-house of continual reproduction. If she was surrounded by fecundity outdoors as well as in, it reversed her own sterility, made her feel more womanly, rather than a barren non-producer who had failed to make the grade. Every egg her chickens laid increased her sense of worth, as did every cot-sheet washed and ironed, every nappy changed.

The cake was a triumph – golden-brown and springy, and as light as air inside. She had sandwiched it with best raspberry conserve, and iced it in white glacé icing, with a big pink 'P' on top. Now, with Penelope in her carrycot and Emily and Florence sitting watching in their chairs, she drew the kitchen curtains and lit the birth-day candles, the seven tiny flames creating a glowing little circle in the gloom.

'Now look, my loves,' she told the older girls, 'this may be hard for you to grasp, in view of the fact that Penelope's been with us for the last two months. But today is really the day of her birth – my official "due" day, as it's called – and that's what we're celebrating.' She glanced at the two faces, knowing that they understood and were indeed hanging on her words. 'So when you blow the candles out, I'd like us to say – the three of us together – "Penelope, welcome to the world!" No, not just yet – hold on a sec. First I need to put her on my lap, so she's part of the whole thing. That's it. All set. Right – *blow*!'

'Welcome to the … the…' she began, the last word of the sentence aborted in a howl of pain. Then, all at once, she smashed both her fists into the sponge, snapping the still smouldering candles, and savagely pummelling the cake until she had reduced it to a mess of sticky crumbs. 'You're *dead*, Penelope,' she sobbed. 'All three of you are dead. This is a death-day, not a birth-day.'

And above her storm of grief, she heard the rooster in the garden suddenly give tongue, mocking her sterility with a long, contemptuous *Cockadoodle-doodle-doodle-oooooooooooo*.

Suicide

'I'm sorry, Miss, but you'll have to get off. There's been a suicide.'

'A *what?*'

'A man jumped in front of the train. It was on the other line, but no trains are travelling in either direction for at least a couple of hours.'

'So where are we now?' Tessa asked, confused, having been ousted from the toilet by an urgent knocking on the door.

'Hitchin. We're not actually scheduled to stop here, but in the circumstances ...'

'So how do we get to London?' Immediately she regretted the question. It was surely deeply selfish to be worried on her own account, rather than concerned about the poor, unfortunate man.

'They'll provide alternative transport, but it may take some time to arrange. Now will you please get off, Miss. You're the last person left on the train, you know.'

She'd been deaf to the whole drama, closeted in a cramped and smelly cubicle while she attended to her face, applying blusher, lip-gloss, eyeliner, in the hope of impressing Jacob. She might as well have saved her time. Patience wasn't his strong suit, and she couldn't see him hanging about till nine or ten at night. 'I'm sorry,' she mumbled, gathering up her things.

'That's OK. Now, mind your step.'

Alighting from the carriage, she blinked against the glare. The sun was like a blowtorch, scorching down from a cloudless sky; all the more ferocious after the air-conditioned train. Surely not a day for suicide. Wouldn't people tend to take their lives in dreary

November or barren January, rather than mid-June? Yet the recent heat-wave had become increasingly oppressive, breaking all known records, threatening heat-stroke, sunstroke, forest fires; making even placid souls feel restless, out of sorts.

Hoisting her bag on her shoulder, she joined the throng of people milling about on the platform. The other train, stranded on the northbound line, was now empty of all passengers, but surrounded by police and paramedics. Was the body still on the track, she wondered, her stomach churning at the thought, or had it been blitzed to smithereens? There was barely time to speculate, as an impatient guard began chivvying the crowd along, in tandem with an announcement on the tannoy.

'Will everyone clear the platform, please. A bus-replacement system will be laid on outside the station. Kindly listen for further announcements.'

She shuffled along behind a mother with a pushchair and a brood of fractious kids. The baby's hysterical screams seemed to express the desperation of the suicide. Had he been out of work? A refugee? An immigrant? Someone jilted or betrayed? Pictures of his grieving mother, or guilty, shattered girlfriend kept jumbling in her mind with images of Jacob sitting in the restaurant on his own, fingers drumming restlessly, as he checked and re-checked his watch. Most other people were clearly equally concerned about their own predicaments, complaining on their mobiles, as they trooped out of the station.

'Look, I'm really fucked … There's nothing moving and …'

'Sorry, but I haven't a hope in hell of making it. You'll have to count me out.'

'It's utter bloody chaos here. I'm going to miss that meeting, so you'd better …'

She should have brought her *own* phone, which had Jacob's number programmed into it. She knew the code by heart, but not the actual number, which meant she couldn't even ring him from a call box. He'd be furious – with reason. She *was* disorganized, as he had told her more than once. This afternoon, for instance, she'd rushed from the office without a backward glance, leaving her mobile on the desk, and even forgetting her best shoes, which had been sitting on the floor all day in a Sainsbury's plastic bag. 'Look, he won't be in the restaurant yet,' she tried to reassure herself. 'It's only ten to six. You've every chance of making it, if the bus arrives in time.'

However, once she reached the forecourt, there was an air of general mayhem – no one giving instructions, no one taking charge. Half-a-dozen police cars were, in fact, parked along the slip-road, together with an ambulance, but the police themselves were sitting tight, offering no assistance. The station looked a one-horse sort of place, with very few amenities: no waiting-room, no café, not so much as a bench outside – although even a whole string of benches would have been woefully inadequate for such a spate of people. Some were arguing and shouting; others more resigned, fanning themselves with newspapers, or simply staring into space.

She stood fidgeting and fretting in the middle of the scrum, aware that her eye-make-up was already beginning to run, and rivulets of perspiration were trickling down her back, ruining her best silk shirt. It must be close on ninety degrees, and the only shade available (provided by two skinny trees) had long since been appropriated. She glanced at the people standing round about – an elderly couple, looking close to tears; a family group with three small boys, bickering amongst themselves; a cluster of teenage girls in skimpy shorts and tops, and several harassed businessmen, one using his black umbrella as a parasol. All these different types and ages connected by a tragedy, yet isolated, separate, cut off from one another.

'Bottle of water, ma'am?'

'Gosh, thanks!' She took it gratefully. A railway official was distributing several crates of bottles, perhaps fearing some of the passengers would faint. 'Hey, wait!' she called, as he moved on to the next group, 'Could you tell me, please, when the replacement bus is due?'

'Couldn't say. You'll need to ask someone else.'

Who? she wondered, as her gaze returned to the sea of anxious faces, all stranded and adrift. 'Surely,' she said irritably, 'you must have *some* idea?'

'Well, I'd give it a good hour – I mean, by the time they've contacted the bus company and—'

An *hour*, she thought, aghast. If only she could get hold of Jacob, put him in the picture. It was her own stupid fault for not memorizing his number. 'Well, how about the trains, then?' she persisted, tagging after the fellow as he continued on his mercy-round. 'Will any be running from another line – somewhere I could get to?'

'Your best bet is Stevenage. It's only four miles up the road, and there'll be services from there unaffected by the crisis – trains from King's Lynn or Peterborough that take a different route. But, of course, if you haven't time to wait for the bus, you'll have to go by cab.'

Could she *afford* a cab? The fare was bound to mount up pretty fast on crowded rush-hour roads. Yet how could she let Jacob down on his all-important fortieth? A landmark birthday, he'd called it, when they'd last met two weeks ago. Besides, she had his present with her – a small sculpted eagle's head, which she had chosen on account of its attributes. The eagle was the king of birds, magnificent and powerful, belonging in a higher world than puny sparrows, timid wrens.

'Excuse me,' said a voice behind her. 'Forgive me butting in, but if you're planning to go to Stevenage by cab, I wondered if I could join you and pay my whack of the fare? And if we roped in a couple of others, it would cut the cost for all of us.'

She turned to see a small, plump man, with a balding head and a reassuring smile. 'Great idea!' she said. 'I'm a bit pushed for cash, so that would suit me fine.'

'Count me in,' said another man, standing just beside them, perspiring in his formal pinstriped suit. 'I'm in a devil of a hurry, so even a few minutes saved would help.'

The three of them squeezed their way through the crush and took their place in the long, winding taxi queue. At least the cabs were arriving thick and fast, presumably coming from all corners to help out in the crisis. Scores of ordinary cars were also pulling into the forecourt, to rescue those lucky enough to have mobiles and kind relatives. Though no one offered a stranger a lift, Tessa noticed with dismay, despite the fact that many people were visibly wilting in the heat. The police seemed equally oblivious, still doing nothing, as far as she could see, but lounge in their patrol cars and observe the hapless mob.

The plump man raised his voice. 'Anyone going to Stevenage, who'd like to share a taxi?'

At least a dozen voices piped up, 'Yes.'

'I'm afraid we've only room for one more.' He gestured to a

small, slight lad, dressed in jeans and a garish orange vest. 'And that's you, sir, since you were next in the queue.'

'Thanks,' said the lad, flushing in embarrassment, perhaps at being singled out, or maybe at the 'sir'.

Tessa introduced herself. If they were going to travel together, they might as well be friendly. Frankly, she was relieved to have a plan of action and a leader in the plump man. There were now four of them against the world

'I'm Vincent,' he responded, offering her a pudgy hand. 'Pleased to meet you, Tessa.'

'Gary,' the young lad mumbled, shifting from foot to foot.

The pinstriped man was less forthcoming, and contented himself with the briefest of nods, before returning to his mobile.

'I suppose you've no idea how frequent the trains are from Stevenage?' Tessa enquired of Vincent.

'Well, usually it's about every fifteen minutes – and more than that in the rush-hour – though, of course, after this emergency some may not be running. But they don't all come through Hitchin, so we should be OK once we get there. It's really just a matter of how soon we get a cab. I'm expected at my nephew's twenty-first. But—' He gave a philosophical shrug. 'I don't imagine the world will end if an old codger like myself doesn't make it before the toasts. How about you?'

'Oh, just a dinner date. But it's my boyfriend's birthday, so ….' The term 'boyfriend' seemed too frivolous for someone as intense and distinguished as was Jacob – and, indeed, so old. The eighteen years between them wasn't just an age-gap, but a gulf in intellect, experience, culture, expertise. However much she studied, or read the tomes he recommended, she would never ascend to his Olympian heights. She sometimes secretly wondered if he had *ever* been a boy, even in his childhood. And to envisage him as a baby required still more of an imaginative leap. He was surely too fastidious to have puked and pooped and burped; too restless to lie passive in his cot. Even as a new-born, he would have been wrestling with the problems of the origins of the universe, or discussing the relative merits of various poets or philosophers.

'And *you*, Gary?'

'I'm workin',' he said, 'in Stevenage. So I need to get there double quick. I'm an hour late as it is, and my boss will go ballistic.'

'What sort of work do you do?' Tessa asked, in an attempt to draw him out. He still seemed extremely tense, standing with his fists clenched and nervously shuffling his feet.

'Short-order cook at a burger bar.'

Only then did she realize how ravenous she was, having worked through the whole of her lunch-hour, in order to get away at five. The tantalizing smell of burgers seemed to waft beneath her nose as she bit into the soft, white, spongy bun, tasting juicy meat, sharp, eye-watering onion, slithery melting cheese. But wasn't it rather crass to be indulging in food-fantasies, when a man had just taken his own life?

'How do you stand the heat in a kitchen, when the weather's this extreme?' Vincent mopped his face with his handkerchief. 'I've never known temperatures as high.'

'We all sweat like fuckin' pigs. But you get used to it in time.'

The pinstriped man had finally finished on his mobile, which he returned to his black briefcase, snapping the case shut with unnecessary force. 'I think it's absolutely disgraceful,' he stormed, 'keeping all these people sweltering in the sun. There could well be another fatality if someone had a heart attack. They promised to lay on alternative transport, yet there's not a sign of a bus.'

'These things take time, my friend,' Vincent said in a soothing manner. 'At least this queue's moving at quite a lick. Only three in front of us now. By the way, I didn't catch your name.'

'Neil,' the man said curtly, as if he resented sharing it. 'And the police are doing damn-all! Why the hell can't they get moving and help direct the crowd?'

'They're probably waiting for the British Transport Police,' Vincent explained in the same measured, peaceable tone. 'As far as I recall, if an incident occurs on railway property, the ordinary police aren't allowed to interfere.'

'So why are they turning up in droves, then? Just for the ride, I suppose. Or to relieve the monotony of a boring Thursday afternoon.'

'Now come on, old chap, you know that isn't true.'

Neil was about to retort, when four cabs pulled up at once. Rushing to secure one, he put himself in charge, commandeering the passenger seat, without consulting the others, brusquely telling the driver to 'step on it', then ordering him to switch off 'that damn racket'. Tessa fumed in silence. She had *liked* the sound of the music – a jaunty, folksy tune that might at least have relaxed them. There was no stopping Neil, however. Once settled in the cab, he launched into another barrage, turning round in his seat to address them with more vehemence.

'Suicide's an act of utter selfishness. Some fool decides to jump, and hundreds of ordinary people are totally fucked up – the train driver's traumatized, everyone's travel plans are up the creek, and the poor, unlucky relatives are faced with a quite ghastly death.'

Tessa took a sharp intake of breath. Didn't this guy have a grain of compassion? 'Maybe he *had* no relatives,' she pointed out. 'And that was his actual problem – he was all alone in the world.'

Neil's voice deepened in annoyance. 'Suicide's a power thing, not a cry for help – a way of turning one's aggression onto other innocent folk.'

'But he might have been deeply depressed. Or in terrible debt. Or even terminally ill. You know nothing at all about him, so what right have you to judge?' It was *Neil* who was hung up on power – the insolent way he'd taken command and ensconced himself in the front, while she and the two other men were uncomfortably squashed at the back. *She* was pig in the middle, of course, her legs pressing on the one side against Vincent's fleshy thighs, and on the other into Gary's bony knees. And it was so stifling hot in the small claustrophobic cab that her whole body seemed to be melting away in a flush and slosh of sweat. She would look a total wreck by the time she reached the restaurant – if she ever did. They seemed to be continually stopping and starting, stuck in constant jams and blocked at every roundabout. With such heavy, fouled-up traffic, God knows how long the drive would take, or how much it would cost.

'Look,' she said, returning to the attack, 'depression's an illness, just as much as cancer.' *She* should know. Jacob suffered from frequent depressive moods, and she always did her best to understand and sympathize. The very fact it was *she* who made the journey to see him every fortnight was proof of her concern. It saved him the stress of travelling, allowed him more free time.

'I agree with *you*, mate,' Gary said to Neil, unexpectedly joining in the argument, whereas up to now he'd been sitting all hunched up, alternately chewing his nails and fiddling with his hair.

'There's this guy I know at work and his brother topped himself. The whole family cracked up. The mother went to pieces, so eventually the Dad pissed off, because he couldn't stand the strain. And the sister had a breakdown and dropped out of her course. And the guy himself – Rick, he's called – is still in quite a state – has nightmares all the time, and keeps comin' out in hives. And all that bloody aggro because one selfish git is feelin' a bit down.'

'It's not a matter of being *down*,' Tessa said, infuriated. 'It's a chemical imbalance in the brain.' Jacob had been given antidepressants, which unfortunately had only made him worse. According to his psychiatrist, the make-up of the brain was so incredibly complex, it wasn't always easy to find a drug that worked. 'And anyway, in *some* cultures, suicide's considered quite OK. I mean, think of hara-kiri in Japan, or Indian widows who throw themselves on funeral pyres. Or what about those Eskimos who deliberately choose to stand outside the tent and freeze to death, because they're so old or sick or feeble they don't want to be a burden to the rest?'

'I don't like to contradict you,' Vincent said, with a placatory smile, 'but as a practising Catholic, I feel I must point out that suicide is gravely wrong, in *any* circumstances. Only God has a right over life, so if someone assumes that right for himself, most religions would condemn him out of hand – not just Christianity, but Judaism and Islam and even—'

'Let's keep religion out of it.' Neil rapped his fingers testily on the seat. 'I've never been in sympathy with all that medieval bunkum about burying suicides in unconsecrated ground. And the Law was just as bad, making it a criminal offence. You may not realize, any of you, that the last person convicted for a suicide attempt was actually already in prison for some other crime he'd committed. And because he tried to hang himself in his cell, he was sentenced to a further two years. And that was as late as 1960, would you believe?'

Tessa opened her mouth to respond to Vincent's point, but Neil pre-empted her, as usual.

'And what good did the conviction do but waste more taxpayers' money? No – as far as I'm concerned, people have a perfect right to do away with themselves, so long as they're not harming anyone else. Hurling yourself onto a railway track is exceptionally unsociable. Couldn't the bloody idiot have taken an overdose, or sat quietly in his car and poisoned himself with carbon monoxide fumes?'

'He probably didn't *have* a car,' Tessa said indignantly. 'Or enough pills to kill himself. Besides, a lot of people who take overdoses are rushed to hospital. Maybe he felt so desperate, he couldn't bear the thought of being stomach-pumped and saved. Or perhaps he didn't think at all, but simply jumped on impulse, because things had got so terrible.'

'But, that's just my point – he *should* have thought, then—'

'Look, if we can't agree, why don't we change the subject?' Vincent suggested diplomatically, burrowing in his briefcase for a bag of sweets. 'Anyone for butterscotch?'

Both she and Gary took one. Neil declined, too busy holding forth again.

'Whatever their mental state, people have a duty to consider the consequences of their actions. For instance, the driver of that train may never be able to return to work. He might feel he "murdered" the victim, and suffer guilt the rest of his life. And some passengers may develop phobias about travelling on a train again, which could also affect them long-term. And someone might have had a stroke, standing around in the heat, or been taken dangerously ill. And think of all the knock-on effects – people missing important events and letting others down. I'm due myself at a meeting tonight, where I'm making the keynote speech. If I'm not there in time – and there's not a hope in hell, if we creep along at this rate – that will seriously inconvenience everybody else.'

Tessa crunched her sweet into fragments. 'People *can't* always think straight – not when they're struggling with depression.' Jacob, for all his gifts and talents, could be almost brutal sometimes, in ignoring her own personal needs. But that didn't mean she blamed him. He was a poet and an artist, and had to be judged by different standards.

Neil gave a mocking laugh. 'Depression's become a sort of buzzword in our namby-pamby society – almost flavour of the month. *Everyone's* depressed these days – children, teachers, doctors – even cats and dogs, according to some ludicrous piece I read in the *Express*. But it's often just indulgence, or an excuse for bad behaviour. My grandparents' generation had a war to contend with, but they didn't mope about the place, saying they couldn't cope. They faced up to major challenges like bombing raids and blackout and severe shortages of food.'

Resignedly, Tessa leaned back against the seat. This guy was just too crass to understand. Jacob had once pointed out that it was sensitive, artistic people who were often the most vulnerable; those who felt things deeply, or lived on a higher plane: Virginia Woolf filling her pockets with heavy stones before walking into the river; Sylvia Plath leaving her children bread and milk, then turning on the gas.

'Shit!' wailed Gary, gazing out at the stream of traffic, now completely blocked. 'Another bloody hold-up. I might as well cut my losses and catch the bus back home from here. Any cash I earn tonight will be less than the bloody cab fare.'

'Don't worry, lad,' Vincent reassured him. 'I'll help you out.'

Well, at least *one* of the men had a heart, Tessa reflected, trying to shift her leg away from his hot and heavy one. She, too, was deeply concerned about the fare. Her financial state was precarious enough, what with the constant journeys from Cambridge, not to mention Jacob's sculpture. It had set her back a cool £200, but then she didn't want to skimp. You couldn't give a man like Jacob a Marks and Spencer tie.

She scowled at the brat in the battered car in front, who kept turning round and putting out his tongue at them. Her own tongue felt dry and parched. She hadn't had a drink in hours, and the tiny cube of butterscotch had done nothing to dull her hunger pangs – although she was actually feeling sick now from the constant jerky motion of the cab. She loathed the sense of being hemmed in on all sides, and the haze of heat and anger steaming from the road, as cantankerous drivers honked their horns and flashed their lights, while the sun beat down implacably.

'I'm sorry about the delay,' the driver said, with an apologetic shrug. 'But I'm afraid there's nothing I can do.'

Tessa glanced at the back of his head: neatly cut black hair, crisply collared white shirt. This was the first time he had spoken, but she wondered what was going through his mind – that the crisis was a boon for him, perhaps, since it would bring him extra work and higher fares. She shivered, despite the heat

'Are you OK, love?' Vincent asked.

She nodded. 'But I think I'll shut my eyes, if you don't mind.'

'Yes, go ahead – have a little nap.'

Napping was out of the question, but if she *pretended* to doze, it might at least ensure a little peace. She felt so dispirited, so tired, she simply didn't have the energy to argue any more.

She slumped wretchedly against the station wall, close to the departures board. Not that any train was scheduled to depart. New problems had developed on the network, due to the excessive heat, and every train to London was now seriously delayed. She'd been hanging around for over half an hour, but not a single service had yet left. Neil had finally stalked off to commandeer another cab, and even patient Vincent had decided to cut his losses and celebrate his nephew's birthday in a local Stevenage pub, rather than in Battersea. Gary, of course, had gone rushing off to work the minute he'd leapt from the taxi, tossing a handful of notes on the seat and muttering darkly that he'd probably got the sack already. So here she was, stranded on another station, this time all alone. Fumbling for her purse, she started counted her remaining cash. She had exactly 63 pence left, after paying for the cab – not even enough to buy a cup of coffee. Jacob would be sipping wine in Lorenzo's, his fury and impatience increasing exponentially. If only he were the type to listen to the local News, he might hear about the hold-ups, but he was probably deep in some weighty tome about metaphysical poetry or mankind's spiritual quest.

She wandered along the platform in search of a chocolate machine. It was probably the height of folly to splurge her last few coins on a Crunchie or a Twix, instead of keeping them for emergencies, but she was so ravenous she didn't care. Having inserted a ten and a fifty, she pressed the appropriate button and waited for her chocolate bar. In vain. Even her coins appeared to be lost, swallowed up in the system, with no hope of return. And there was little point complaining about such a trivial matter. The few available railway staff were already being besieged by crowds of frantic passengers, irate at missing meetings, dates, connections.

She suddenly caught sight of herself in the window of the waiting-room, recoiling in distaste. Her ponytail had come undone and her hair was tumbling round her shoulders in total disarray. There were black smudges of mascara underneath her eyes, and her silk blouse was badly creased as well as damp. God knows what Jacob would think. He liked women to be stylish, as he invariably was himself. His own hair was so thick and straight it stayed naturally in place, and his clothes never seemed to crease, let alone discolour in the wash, as *hers* so often did.

The man beside her was demolishing a sandwich: teeth sinking into the moist brown bread, tongue scooping up the cheese-and-pickle filling. She watched with increasing envy, tempted to snatch the sandwich from him – indeed, even knock him down, to claim the booty for herself. Perhaps it was wrong ever to judge a crime. If one were hungry enough, desperate enough, one could murder for a bite.

She moved away to avoid temptation, her mind returning to the suicide. Had they collected all the fragments of the body? Did someone have to identify their beloved spouse or son, with just those bloody fragments as a guide? And suppose—

'The delayed 19.07 to London, King's Cross is now arriving at platform number two. First Capital Connect apologize for any inconvenience caused by the late running of this train ...'

Apologize! She was so relived she could *kiss* the man making the announcement – kiss every single employee of First Capital Connect. As the train rattled into the station, she wove her way towards the front of the platform, trapped in the crush of people jostling to get on. There wasn't a hope of a seat, but she was elated by the prospect of actually getting to the restaurant before Jacob finally left. She did the calculations in her head. The journey to King's Cross should take just under half an hour, then fifteen minutes on the tube, followed by a ten-minute walk – six minutes if she jogged. 'Jacob, *wait* for me,' she prayed, uncomfortably aware that expecting him to hang about for a further fifty minutes was perhaps pushing things too far. Yet at least he had the distraction of his book, the solace of his wine, and surely he must have realized by now that some emergency had happened.

At last, she thrust a foot into the carriage, and was pushed further in by the press of people behind. Her leg was jabbed by the corner of someone's briefcase; someone else elbowed her in the ribs. But, despite the fact she was jostled on all sides, she held her breath, held her ground. However, they couldn't yet move off, as the doors were blocked by still more obstreperous passengers struggling to squeeze themselves on to the already jam-packed train.

Suddenly, impulsively, she pushed in the other direction, encountering both curses and resistance. But, head down, she fought her way to the doors again, hardly caring if she was bad-mouthed. She *wasn't* going to London, but back to her own room and bed.

Stepping down from the carriage, she sank shakily on to a bench, her mind in utter turmoil. For some incomprehensible reason, all the points that Neil had made were resounding in her head once more, although now with a quite different slant. She had challenged him on every issue, condemned him as a callous brute, yet, all at once, she could see the truth in every word he'd said. Depression *was* a weapon for controlling other people, an excuse for bad behaviour, a form of aggression, a selfish and indulgent act. Didn't she witness it with Jacob, on each occasion they met – the fact she must never make demands on him, never give him cause for worry, never even argue with him, let alone remind him that she, too, had a life? His finely tuned nervous system simply couldn't cope with stress, and since he needed all his resources for his intellectual life, he refused to run the slightest risk of endangering his mental health or suffering a crack-up. It was like a sort of blackmail – do what I want, or I'll plunge into the abyss.

Of course, *she* was not allowed low moods – they were *his* prerogative, as a 'sensitive', 'artistic' type, living on a 'higher plane'. Nor could she be a minute late, whatever her predicament. The *cheek* of the man, to tell her she was disorganized, when all he did was sit at home scribbling the odd poem. He didn't *need* a proper job; didn't have to worry about paying bills or rent, because he lived on his father's money, in his father's Chelsea flat. Yet he never thought to help her with the fares, or thank her for her time and trouble in travelling such a distance on top of a full day's work. And he dared to criticize her clothes, when she could barely afford any decent ones because, ever since the day they'd met, she lavished her money on *him*. And since she was forced to use the launderette, naturally her things discoloured. She didn't have the luxury of a washing-machine and tumble-drier – things *he* assumed as his natural right, along with his collection of precious first editions and his signed Howard Hodgkin prints.

Why had it taken her so long to see him as he really was? Because he was so much older, so much better educated? Or had she been blinded by his romantic looks, his high calling as a poet, his air of brooding melancholy? Fuck melancholy! It was *fun*, she wanted, for a change – simple, childlike pleasure – and a man who loved her as she was: messy, sweaty, scatty, lowbrow; a man who made the occasional joke, and wouldn't mind her reading *Harry Potter* instead of Schopenhauer.

Thrusting her hand inside her bag, she drew out the sculpted eagle's head. She had swathed it in layers of tissue, wrapped it in expensive birthday paper, tied it with silver ribbon – all in homage to her eagle-poet. But she had been blind in that respect, as well. Eagles might be strong and powerful, but they were also cruel and ruthless, and, in flying high, ran the risk of ignoring lesser species, throttling smaller talents, denying any simple creature its right to life and freedom.

Striding to the platform edge as the train finally pulled out, she hurled the heavy package on to the track. Let it buckle, let it smash – she didn't give a toss.

OK, she was wasting money on a crazy, reckless scale. She could have sold the sculpture, or given it to someone else. But it was *Jacob's* eagle, so it had to be destroyed. She was better off without it, better off without him. From this day on, she was going to be her self – her crazy, reckless, angry, wilful self – so that never in her life again would she become an eagle's prey.

Saviour

'Happy Christmas, dear.'

'There's nothing very happy about it.' Cautiously, Violet opened the door a little wider to allow the woman access.

'Well, what about this lovely Christmas dinner? *That* should cheer you up, I'll put it in the kitchen, shall I?'

'Yes, please. On the side here.'

'I'm sorry I'm so late. We've been rushed off our feet this morning.'

'That's all right.' It certainly *wasn't* all right. The meal had been promised for twelve noon, and she had deliberately cut out breakfast, to economize. It was now almost five to two, and she was feeling weak with hunger.

'Would you like me to take the lids off?' The woman's sharp eyes were roving round the room, lighting on the grease-encrusted hob, the pile of dirty underwear soaking in the sink.

'*I* can manage, thank you.' Violet didn't want this stranger in her house. The place was in a state – untidy, none too clean – so there was a danger she would be reported to the council. Next thing she'd know, she'd be declared unfit and carted off to a care-home.

'Well, enjoy it, dear, won't you.'

Yes, that she did intend. Any change from her usual lunchtime fare – bread and jam, or tinned spaghetti hoops – was welcome in the extreme. They kept offering her Meals-on-Wheels, but you couldn't be too careful. Once you let people into your home on a regular basis, they'd take it as a licence to snoop; realize that the heating didn't work, or track down the mouse in the sitting-room, and class it as a health risk rather than a companion. 'Is there anything to pay?' she asked, self-consciously aware of her shabby clothes and down-at-heel felt slippers. Lady Bountiful was dressed as if for cocktails, in a smart blue dress and jacket, and high heels

'No, it's completely free, my dear – subsidized by St Saviour's. We're delivering Christmas dinners to all the elderly housebound in the area, as part of the church's Community Outreach Project.'

Violet mumbled her thanks, disliking the thought of being subsidized, or, indeed, part of any 'project'.

'Don't thank me,' the woman smiled. 'Thank our lovely vicar.'

Lovely or no, the vicar never called and, were he to do so, she wouldn't thank him anyway. His church bells made a dreadful racket, yet her letters of complaint had been totally ignored.

Even now, the woman seemed in no hurry to leave, and was examining the dingy hall, her gaze lingering on the patch of mould just below the ceiling. 'Well, God bless you, dear,' she carolled, finally making for the door at last.

Violet didn't reply. God kept His distance nowadays. Once, He had been a living, breathing Presence, and she still missed that sense of closeness to a Father.

Shutting the door with a sense of relief, she shuffled her way to the sitting-room, opened the sideboard, and extracted a large dinner plate – one she hadn't used in decades: bone-china, with pink roses round the rim. Next she found a linen serviette, crumpled but good quality, a tarnished silver napkin-ring, and her best embroidered tablecloth, a little faded and tattered now, as *she* was. Painstakingly she laid up the small table, using the best cutlery, and adding a crystal wineglass only slightly chipped. There wouldn't be any wine, of course — water would have to do. It was the *food* that was important: all the traditional items she hadn't tasted in years. No point cooking Christmas dinner just for one, and it was extremely wasteful anyway when everything these days was sold in such huge sizes – puddings for a regiment, turkeys to feed a tribe. You couldn't even buy a single tangerine. It was either a dozen in a red string bag, or go without.

Returning to the kitchen with the plate, she began prising the plastic lid off the larger of the cartons, feeling a ripple of rare excitement. It was over a year since she'd had a proper meal, and, judging by the wealthy folk who frequented St Saviour's, this one would be special, something to remember throughout the coming year.

Only after breaking a nail did she finally succeed in opening the container, and stood staring in dismay at two small slices of anaemic turkey breast, swimming in watery gravy, three slimy Brussels sprouts, disintegrating into a grey-green mush, a couple of pallid boiled potatoes and a dab of greyish stuffing. In her mind, she had pictured a whole succulent turkey sizzling on its carving-dish, with legs and wings intact. And rich sausage-meat stuffing, moist with prunes and port. And certainly *roast* potatoes – plain boiled went with fish. And butter-glazed sprouts, served with tiny chestnuts. And chipolatas beautifully browned and wrapped in bacon rashers. All covered with giblet gravy, simmered for an hour or so with onions and the turkey liver, bay leaves and a bouquet garni. And what had happened to the *smells* – pungent, heady, spicy smells, always associated with Christmas? She stooped down to sniff the dinner, but there was only a faint aroma of overcooked and slightly bitter sprouts.

Perhaps the pudding would be better – although it took her some time to find out, since the lid on the second carton was still more stubborn than the first. Sucking her bruised thumb, she scrutinized the contents: a pale brown square of what looked like shop-bought cake, sitting in a pool of biliously lurid yellow custard. Surely Christmas puddings should be *round*? And *dark* – dark with fruit and rum. It was custard that was pale – custard made with fresh farm eggs and real vanilla pods. And where were the mince pies? Proper Christmas dinner always included pudding *and* pies, not just one or the other.

Stifling her disappointment, she transferred the meal to the china plate, where it seemed completely dwarfed – a child-sized portion, not rations for an adult. She should have used a tea-plate or a saucer, but if she messed around any longer, the already tepid food would be completely cold. And she couldn't waste money turning on the oven to heat up one small meal. Besides, she was starving hungry and might actually faint, as she had done, in fact, last week, if she didn't eat immediately.

However, starving or no, she intended to spin the meal out, make it last as long as possible by chewing every mouthful a minimum of twenty times, The gaping day stretched endlessly ahead, with nothing else to fill it.

Before sitting down, she fetched another jersey from the bedroom. She was already wearing several layers of woollies, but the day was damp as well as cold, and the sitting-room faced north. She also turned the clock-hands back to one o'clock. Christmas dinner at Aunt Augusta's house was served on the dot of one. *She* would be up at five, of course, opening her Christmas stocking, and trying to persuade her mother that they should leave for Grove End House the minute they had washed and dressed. She could never wait to get there. The turreted grey-stone mansion, with its extensive grounds and sweep of hills behind, was like something in a fairy-tale, and a world away from their own shabby basement flat.

As she pulled up her chair to the small and rickety card-table, it extended lengthways and widthways into the Grove End dining-table: a magnificent mahogany table that could seat a couple of dozen guests. And her three solitary cards – one from the local Pizza Place, where she had never set foot in her life – had gone forth and multiplied, so that now at least a hundred jostled for space on the mantelpiece. And she herself was no longer the poor relation, but a proper little lady, dressed in her cousin's party frock, and with staff to wait on her. Would Miss Violet prefer white meat or dark?

'Both,' she replied, wriggling in anticipation as Priscilla loaded her plate. You weren't allowed to start until everyone was served, and you had to hold your fork right, and sit up straight, and not blow your nose on your serviette. The television was playing to itself – some old film in black and white, with people sitting round a festive table. She turned them into Augusta's friends and family: moneyed types, with swanky clothes, who always forgot her mother's name and often ignored *her* altogether. Who cared? She was happy just to *be* here; looked forward to this Christmas dinner for months and months beforehand, crossing off the days on her home-made calendar.

'Wine for Miss Violet?' Carter asked. He was standing just behind her chair, holding the bottle of wine, with a white damask cloth folded over his arm.

Excitedly she nodded. She was allowed a tiny drop, enough to turn her water a magical rippling pink. Not that she could drink it yet. You couldn't so much as touch your glass until Uncle William had finished saying Grace, and he hadn't even started yet. After what seemed like half an hour, he bowed his head, at last, and recited the peculiar words, which she could never understand because they were in some foreign language.

'Amen,' everybody said. She knew what *that* meant: they could all start tucking in.

She began with the turkey, trying the dark meat first – deliciously bronzed outside – and following it with a mouthful of breast, which was so delicate and moist it slipped down in a trice. Next she cut off a piece of her roast potato, its coating brown and crackly, in contrast to the soft whiteness inside. Her aunt never did the cooking herself, but had very strong opinions on how it should be done. Potatoes, she insisted, must be par-boiled first, then roasted in dripping, to ensure a perfect result. And Brussels sprouts should be glazed with butter and served with tiny chestnuts, to disguise any trace of bitterness, and cooked for exactly fifteen minutes, so that they were neither too hard nor too soft. And, when it came to gravy, short cuts were simple laziness, and the Bisto her own mother used nothing short of a crime.

Violet cut a sprout in half and forked it in, along with a piece of chestnut. The tastes seemed quite exotic, especially as they never had vegetables at home. She moved her pile of stuffing to the very edge of her plate, so that she could eat it on its own; pick out all the different colours and flavours: pale sausage-meat and dark chunks of prune and walnut, morsels of pink bacon and shiny whitish onion slices, glinting shreds of bright orange grated carrot.

She had to keep reminding herself not to eat too quickly. You were meant to put your fork down between every single mouthful, which struck her as plain daft. If food was sitting on your plate, then best to gobble it fast, in case someone snatched it away. But here it wasn't worth the risk – she might be banished in disgrace and forbidden to return. And she must never, ever, use her fingers, Aunt Augusta said, to pick up the chipolatas (which she'd done on her first visit, much to everybody's horror). *Now*, she cut them into strips, holding each piece in her mouth as long as possible, so she could enjoy their greasy, porky taste, and the different, darker flavour of the crusty, slightly burnt bits.

She paused a moment to admire the decorations: a huge bunch of mistletoe, brought in by the gardeners from the grounds, a ten-foot-tall Christmas tree, hung with miniature glass birds, and wreaths of holly and ivy, festooned above the windows. They weren't just outward show. Aunt Augusta lived her whole life round the church, so even Christmas greenery was a religious thing for her. Mistletoe, she'd told them, could survive the harshest weather and, even if it seemed to die, would revive like Christ our Saviour. And the holly and the ivy were symbols of Eternal Life because they stayed green throughout the year and never shed their leaves. Eternal Life sounded rather frightening. Did it mean you'd have a million, million birthdays? But wouldn't you get bored, then, living all that time, or run out of food or money and have to go to the pawn-shop? And if mistletoe could come back from the dead, then why not her own father, who had died when she was two?

To cheer herself, she took a sip of wine, feeling wonderfully grown-up, but casting anxious glances at her mother, who always drank too much. If an argument broke out, or some frightening shouting-match, again they might be shown the door. The people on the television were beautifully behaved, not talking with their mouths full, and passing the salt and pepper without having to be asked. Even the two screen children sat as quiet as mice, the girl with long fair ringlets, the boy in a brown velvet suit. The under-fives at Grove End House were confined strictly to the nursery, Christmas Day, or no. Uncle William hated children, so her mother said, which seemed rather strange when he had three girls of his own.

Suddenly he caught her eye and, as she met his gaze, he shot her a look of such hostility and spite, she immediately kicked her chair back and hurtled into the kitchen. She stood leaning against the worktop, still seeing his blue eyes bulging from their sockets, as if any moment they'd pop out of his head and shoot straight into the turkey dish. It was clear he didn't want her here – maybe even wished her dead.

She shivered, as the cold gape of her father's grave seemed to suck them down as well. No, she mustn't think of death and graves – not on Christmas Day – but think only about the meal: the luscious second course, followed by the crystallized fruits that came in a big wooden box, perfect for a pencil case. And the other box, of Turkish Delight, which opened in a sneeze of sugar, and contained gluey chunks of pink and white that tasted sort of scented, and stuck gloriously to your teeth. And, after that, the walnuts and brazils, with their thick, rough shells like bark on trees, and then coffee for the grown-ups in tiny, pretty cups, and big fancy golden crackers, with proper toys in, not just paper hats ...

The BANG-BANG of the crackers sent her frisking into the other room, where she grabbed her plate, with its soggy sprouts and undercooked potatoes, and, returning to the kitchen, tipped the contents in the waste-bin. No need to save provisions for tomorrow. Grove End House was groaning with food: pheasant paté, chicken pies, pork and veal terrines, whole sides of honey-roasted ham ...

Back in place at the table, she watched Priscilla carry in the pudding, flaming blue and gold. Everybody clapped as the flames danced and flickered, danced and flickered, before finally petering out. The making of the pudding was another holy rite at Grove End House. It couldn't be made any old time, but only on 'Stir-Up Sunday' – the last Sunday prior to Advent. And it had to be made with exactly thirteen ingredients – neither more nor less – to represent Christ and His twelve disciples. And every member of the family and staff was required to stir the mixture, stirring from east to west, in honour of the Three Kings. If only *she* was there, so she, too, could have a stir. But they never went to Grove End House except on Christmas Day, and her own mother was too busy to make puddings, and couldn't possibly afford the three real-silver charms that were put into the mixture, and bought new again each year: a ring, a thimble and a coin. Whoever found the ring would be married within the coming year; whoever got the thimble would remain a spinster throughout their life, and the one who found the silver coin would have their wish come true.

And the wishes *did* come true – she had seen it happen year on year. In 1927, her cousin Grace had got the sixpence and wished for a new pony. Two weeks later, a piebald with a long white tail had turned up in the stables. And in 1928, Uncle Hamish had suddenly spluttered on his pudding, coughed the sixpence from his mouth, and wished there and then for a wife. His marriage to Aunt

Ellen took place the following June. And the Christmas after that, it was Mrs Forbes who had got the coin and immediately made a wish to live abroad. She was never seen again, but spent every subsequent Christmas in her new exciting home – a ranch in Santa Fe.

'Would you like pudding first, Miss Violet, or mince pie?'

A difficult decision. She screwed up her face in concentration, trying to work it out. 'Both together' might sound rude, or greedy. 'Mince pie, please,' she finally blurted out. Pudding was her favourite, so best to leave it till last.

She was given not just one pie but two, and a whoosh of thick whipped cream, which began melting in luscious rivulets. The hot shortcrust pastry crumbled in her mouth, its buttery taste mixing with the tang of brandied mincemeat. If only her stomach was as big as the house itself, then she could fill it up to the attics, and down to the cellars, to last her through the hungry days ahead. Once, aged six, she had nicked an extra mince pie from the kitchen, and stuffed it down her knickers, to take home. By evening, it was a mess of damp and smelly crumbs, but she'd devoured it just the same.

She peeled off one of her jerseys. The room was warm from the real-log fire crackling in the hearth, so there was no more need for several layers to keep away the cold. Eric had just replenished the logs, giving them a vigorous poke to set them fiercely blazing. If you stared at the flames for long enough, you could see pictures in the fire: scarlet birds with golden plumes, trembly orange flowers ...

'Ready for your pudding yet, Miss Violet?'

She nodded. Her mouth was still full, so she mustn't speak, but she watched in amazement as she was given an enormous piece – enough for three or four – and covered with a tide of velvety custard. The custard looked alive, quivering with eggs, trembling with rich cream, as it murmured, 'Eat me! Eat me!' Without need of further prompting, she spooned in the first mouthful of custard-coated pudding, then shut her eyes, so she could remember the tastes and textures right through to Christmas next: the satisfying crunch of nuts contrasting with the smooth dark mass of fruit; the tiny jolts of bitter sweetness from strips of candied peel; the kick of rum and brandy tingling on her tongue; the waxy, sticky sweetness of whole glistening glacé cherries, the smooth, soothing balm of the custard itself. But all at once, she spat the pudding out. Her teeth had encountered something foreign – hard and sharp, metallic.

She looked down at her plate. There, amidst the dark regurgitated mess, shone a tiny silver coin. Awed, she picked it up, rubbed it clean, examined it – not the magic sixpence of Aunt Augusta's day, but a 5p piece, and magic just the same. How could *any* coin have landed up in a St Saviour's Christmas dinner? They were obviously pre-prepared on a massive scale by some municipal caterers, so wouldn't they have checks in place, health-and-safety regulations, hordes of council inspectors poking their fat noses in? After all, they wouldn't want a lawsuit, were some old soul to break her dentures or swallow a foreign body. Yet somehow this one tiny coin had escaped their vigilance, and found its dogged way into her particular carton, which in itself was something of a miracle. They must deliver countless meals, but only hers – she'd bet her life – contained a silver coin.

She clutched it tighter in her palm, smiling in sheer triumph. Throughout her childhood she had longed to get the coin, yet never once, in all that time, had it actually occurred. In fact, neither she nor her mother had got *any* of the charms. She had never abandoned hope, though, praying every year for the sixpence in particular, to make her wish come true. And she was always well-prepared, laying in a store of wishes so she would be ready if it happened, like the jars of jams and jellies in the Grove End larder that took up five whole shelves – wished to have a brother or sister, or at least a dog or cat; wished her mother didn't drink; wished they lived in a palace and not in the Walworth Road; wished she had new clothes instead of cast-offs; wished to be plump and pretty, with blue eyes and a mop of curls, not a skinny scarecrow, with hair so limp it resisted even curling-tongs; wished sherbet lemons grew on trees, so you could pick them when you wanted.

Once she grew up, her wishes changed. At the age of twenty, she wished for a better job, and more cash for cigarettes, and an escape from her boss, who kept putting his hot hand on her leg and breathing cheese and pickle in her face. And she wished for romance, of course – not with *that* old fossil, but with a tall, dark, handsome sweetheart, who would kiss her sort of hungrily like they did in all the movies, and give her an engagement ring. Later still, her wishes changed again, so that now she wished for healthier lungs, and for *any* job at all. And, as for men, she had seen too much of marriage to want to be bullied like her neighbours, used as a servant or a punch-bag by some rude pig of a spouse. Instead, she wished her friends were still alive; wished she had a skateboard, to spare her aching feet, or a battery-heated nightdress to keep her warm at night.

Now, however, *none* of the wishes seemed to rouse her interest – certainly not the early ones, and not even the most recent. It was as if she had lived so long, she had outgrown all desires. Yet how could she simply ignore the coin, when she had been waiting every Christmas past to find it in her pudding? Wouldn't it be a shocking waste of this once-in-a-lifetime chance?

Indecisive, she sat listening to the silence. All around her, in the street, her neighbours must be eating Christmas dinner, pulling crackers, singing carols, yet not a sound of their festivities reached her in this room. No child was playing outside; no car purred past the house; no burst of music exploded from next-door, no bird piped up or church bell pealed, no plane droned through the leaden winter sky. Despite the row of houses crammed rib to rib the entire length of the road, it was if she were the only person left in the whole world, abandoned here in isolation, while life went on elsewhere.

Then, all at once, a wish formed on her lips: a wish to be at Grove End House again, not just for one short Christmas Day but for what Aunt Augusta called Eternal Life – yes, sitting at that blessèd table for ever and ever and ever. And Eternal Life wouldn't be alarming, as she had feared when she was young, because there'd be so much cheerful company – the whole throng of distinguished relatives she had so rarely seen in *this* life. Nor would it be boring, with the whole house to explore and its stables, orchards and fishponds, not to mention the fields and woods beyond. And the food would keep on coming through all eternity: breakfast after breakfast, dinner after dinner, then tea and supper and bedtime snacks, with sweets and drinks and iced buns in between.

Closing her fingers round the coin, she shut her eyes and sat up very straight. 'I wish,' she said out loud, her voice solemn with emotion, 'that this time next year I'll no longer be here, and I'll no longer be alone.'

Then, suddenly, through half-closed lids, she saw a dazzling ray of light illuminate the drab December day. Wonderingly, she bowed her head, knowing that her wish was granted and that *next* Christmas would be truly happy because, as well as the big family, her own father would be there – resurrected like the mistletoe – and she would feel his loving arms around her after eighty-seven years of waiting, and the two of them would sit entwined, the most honoured and triumphant guests in the bliss of Grove End Heaven.

Pet

'Can I help you, madam?

'Er, yes,' said Margaret, eyeing the salesgirl's prominent bump. Did this store employ pregnant women deliberately, as part of some new marketing technique? 'I'm looking for a present for a one-year-old.'

'Girl or boy?'

'Girl. It's her birthday next week, but I'm afraid I don't know much about babies, so if there's something you could suggest.'

'How about a pretty dress?' The girl steered her towards a rack in the middle of the shop. 'This would be the size you need, unless the child's exceptionally big.'

'No, average, I'd say.' It was difficult to judge. Clara looked quite puny in her cot, yet felt a ton-weight when picked up. But then she never felt at ease with a baby in her arms, not even her own great-niece.

'How about this frilled one, with the darling little matching pants?'

Margaret surveyed it dubiously. The precocious infant already had every conceivable garment, from a fairy outfit, including wand and wings, to a pair of miniature Levi's, encrusted with fake rhinestones. 'I'm not sure about clothes. She seems to have so many as it is.'

'Then a doll, perhaps. Or a cuddly toy. We have a fantastic range of animals. If you come this way, I'll show you.'

Confronted by the menagerie, Margaret stood in silence, her gaze straying from the array of bears (everything from polar and teddy to grizzly and koala), to more exotic creatures such as bison,

191

yak and porcupine. The dolls were equally numerous: china dolls and rag dolls, in various skin-tones from pink-and-white to black, with shades of cappuccino in between; dolls that wet their nappies, or spoke or cried or giggled; dolls that sucked on bottles, or came with fashion-statement wardrobes. And there was an impressive selection of doll accessories: cots and prams, bathtubs and high-chairs, even a Jacuzzi.

The choice was, frankly, baffling. If she opted for an Anglo-Saxon doll, would that be construed as politically incorrect? And any bottle-fed doll would meet with Rachael's outright condemnation. Her niece believed passionately that breast was invariably best, and intended feeding Clara for at least another year. Margaret sometimes feared that when the child began at primary school, she would still be trotting home for her thrice-daily fix of the nipple.

'Look, I'm sorry,' she said to the salesgirl. 'I don't want to waste your time. It's probably better if I have a little wander round and try to make my mind up.'

'Just as you please. But don't hesitate to ask, madam, if you do need any help.'

'Thanks. I will.' Margaret trudged self-consciously from rocking cradles to potties, wishing she wasn't so much older than everyone else in the shop. Apart from several pregnant customers (and at least three pregnant salesgirls), there were half-a-dozen young couples in sight, complete with progeny. One man standing near her was cuddling his baby with unashamed devotion, kissing every finger in turn, whilst whispering endearments in her ear. Rachael's Ted was just the same, doting on his daughter and passionately involved with her, changing nappies, singing bedtime lullabies and boasting about her achievements to anyone who'd listen: she had swallowed her first solids ('wonderful to watch'), learned to crawl ('a milestone'), cut her first tooth ('I felt profoundly moved'), taken her first step ('it seemed an actual miracle'). He kept her photo in his wallet and on his desk at work, and, according to Rachael, even got up at night, to be part of the ritual of breastfeeding. If he could have grown a pair of breasts himself, in order to offer Clara an alternative milk-experience, no doubt he would have done so. And he and Rachael had actually attended a baby massage course, so that their child could have four expert hands caressing every inch of her small body.

Margaret glanced at the young man again. He was still goo-gooing and kiss-kissing with no trace of embarrassment. Rather different from her own father, who had regarded babies – and indeed children generally – with a mixture of resentment and distaste. In fact, he had been away 'on business', for the greater part of her childhood, and although neither she nor her sister had any idea what that mysterious 'business' meant, it was clearly of infinitely greater importance than dandling a couple of infants on his knee, or spooning pap into a pair of drooling mouths.

All at once, she gripped the edge of the shelf, as a wave of burning heat went surging through her body; a volcano about to erupt. Oh, no, she thought, not *here*! Hot flushes seemed particularly inappropriate in this temple to the young and fertile. Her face had gone a deep brick-red and sweat was pouring down her back and chest, as she stood trying to gain control. What scared her were the palpitations that accompanied each flush. The doctor had reassured her that her heart was basically sound and that the flutterings and pulsings were just another menopausal symptom. She struggled to follow his advice: she must focus on some object, observing its colour, shape and size, and so divert attention from her symptoms and her self. The only thing in her line of sight was a row of plastic potties, some in garish colours, some in the shape of animals or cars. She fixed her gaze on a plain one in a soothing shade of grey – brilliant reds and purples only made the flushes worse.

However, far from growing calmer, she was suddenly plunging back in time, until she was an infant of two months again, being held out over the chamber pot by her fastidious, rule-ridden mother, who detested dirty nappies. The hard china rim was pressing into her bottom, and huge, harsh hands were gripping her so tightly her body felt as if it was breaking in half. 'No!' she screamed with her not-yet voice, knowing with her not-yet brain that it was a battle for supremacy – and one *she* was bound to lose. Her mother had the bargaining power; could withdraw her milk – and love – if that potty wasn't full. Day after day, the grim routine continued. She could feel the horror of it now: the sense of precariousness as she was dangled in mid-air, then plonked fiercely down on that hated, hurting object. Her body lacked the resources required to do what it was ordered, so she was doomed to failure, however hard she tried. And try she did – straining every muscle, tensing every nerve, desperate to obey her parents, who regarded this particular skill as crucial to their peace of mind. The stuff that plopped and spurted out of babies was shameful and disgusting if it soiled clean nappies or – worse – fouled the floor or cot. Indeed, her mother saw it as a personal affront, and would mete out stringent punishment unless the odious mess was channelled into the pot. She, the guilty infant, had grasped that hideous fact at less than eight weeks old, but was powerless to comply.

Before long, she was too scared to sleep. If she closed her eyes, she might have what was called an 'accident', and 'accidents' were unpardonable. She would be snatched up from her bed, slapped on her bare legs, and told she was a dirty, thoughtless, selfish little girl.

'Dirty' meant you'd made your mother suffer; caused her needless work; made her want to leave you at the orphanage, or wish she'd never had you in the first place. Only 'clean' was safe. 'Clean' meant love and praise; 'clean' meant you could stay at home and not be sent away. But 'clean' also proved impossible until she was almost fifteen months – fifteen haunted, nervy months, in which she struggled for her life.

'Excuse me, madam, are you OK?'

Margaret opened her eyes. A salesgirl in a black trouser-suit was standing by her side.

'I'm sorry to intrude, madam, but you looked as if you were going to faint.'

'Oh, did I?' Margaret said, suddenly realizing where she was. 'Gosh! How silly of me! No, I'm perfectly all right. Just a bit … hot, that's all.'

'Yes, it's stifling in here, isn't it? I'm afraid the air-conditioning's on the blink. I reckon this heat-wave was too much for it! Can I get you a glass of water?'

'No, really,' Margaret mumbled, quickly backing off and making her escape.

She stood a moment outside the shop, adjusting to the glare. She had forgotten how sweltering the weather was, enough to trigger another flush. Perhaps it *would* be wise to have a drink before continuing with her shopping, if only to spare herself the embarrassment of collapsing on the pavement. There was a café just a few doors down, so she drifted in, took a seat and ordered an iced tea.

'Anything to eat?' the waitress asked.

'No, thanks.' The display of cakes looked tempting, but she'd been taught early on in life not to eat between meals, and somehow the training had stuck. Everyone around her, though, was tucking in without compunction, and clearly didn't share her qualms about greed and self–indulgence.

She unbuttoned her jacket, wondering why she had worn it on such a blistering day. Most of the women here were dressed in shorts and skimpy tops, whereas *she* was wearing tights, for heaven's sake! Her mother's training again, of course. It had begun so early, lodged so deep that, even after all these years, she still believed it was wrong to expose an inch of naked flesh. She had been born in a heat-wave, similar to this, yet the first photo of her, at three days old, showed her bundled up in layers of clothes and wrapped in a woollen shawl.

Sipping her tea, she enjoyed the feel of the tall, cold glass against her sweaty palms. Stupid to spoil the day by returning to her babyhood. She should feel *pity* for her mother, who'd been extremely young and extremely inexperienced, with little education and no mother of her own to help. It must have been a struggle bringing up two daughters single-handed; her husband not just absent, but squandering most of the money. Blame was out of the question; in fact, she felt a deep compassion for a woman so supremely insecure she'd been forced to impose severe controls on every aspect of her babies' lives.

Best to avoid the subject and concentrate on Clara. She still had to decide on a present, which wasn't easy when the nursery was an Aladdin's cave of toys and clothes and playthings, puppets, mobiles, ornaments. The child even owned a Baby Gym, complete with padded play-mat, breakproof mirror and a complicated electronic device that alternated light effects with bouncy little tunes. And a silvery-pink CD player stood beside her cot, to stimulate her burgeoning brain with tracks of 'Bach for Babies' and 'Mozart for the Under-Twos'.

Margaret drained her tea. How could an average mortal hope to compete in the gift stakes when the bar was set so high? Unless she went for something practical, like that plastic potty she'd seen

– the one in the shape of a car, with big yellow eyes as headlamps and a grinning mouth as bumper. No, Rachael considered potty-training as a form of child abuse, and intended to follow the Californian method, which left children in nappies till the age of three or four. Well, perhaps a box of toiletries: beautifully packaged baby creams and soaps. Except that, too, was bound to meet with disapproval. Her niece was extremely fussy about Clara's delicate skin and tended to buy organic preparations from a special Swedish firm. Indeed, she and Ted had even learned to blend their own essential oils, as part of the baby-massage course.

Fanning herself with the menu, Margaret glanced surreptitiously at the small girl at the next table, who was working her way through a dish of ice-cream in a curious shade of mauve. It reminded her of Clara again, who was regularly indulged with elaborate ices prepared at home from fresh farm eggs and cream, in unheard-of flavours such as boysenberry and nectarine. Rachael refused to buy the commercial ones, loaded with additives and chemicals (not to mention 'lethal' sugar), but would liquidize the sweetest fruits, to provide 'natural' sugar, along with vitamins. In fact, the pampered babe had never touched the normal sort of baby food that came in jars and tins. Her doting parents insisted she experience the variety of tastes and textures that only home-cooked cuisine could provide. Devotedly they laboured in the kitchen, making miniature cheese soufflés to tempt her infant palate, poaching salmon with asparagus, mashing up ripe avocados, or swirling puréed blackcurrants with probiotic yoghurt. Their *pièce de résistance* was what they called Fish Pie Supreme, which included seven different sorts of fish, swathed in saffron-flavoured sauce and with organic mashed potato on the top. Every mouthful swallowed was a triumph for both child and parent. 'Well *done*, my pet!' Ted would coo, spooning in a *soupçon* more of guava sorbet or courgette mousse.

'Pet,' Margaret murmured under her breath – the most bewitching word in the lexicon. It actually had a physical effect on her: made her heart beat faster, brought a flush to her cheek – and nothing to do with the menopause, this time. 'Pet' epitomized the very heights of affection and devotion, the unalloyed approval of a parent for a child. 'Pet' meant your father stayed with you, rather than storming out in fury because under-fives frayed his nerves and drained his cash supplies. There had been no 'pets' in *her* day – the very thought was blasphemous. Even literal pets (cats, dogs, hamsters, budgerigars) were strictly disallowed, as being germy, unhygienic and a source of danger and disease. And as for using terms of endearment to small and self-willed girls, it would only feed their vanity; make them perilously lax. Clara, on the other hand, had been awash in 'pets' since the first moment she drew breath. She was Mummy's pet and Daddy's pet, Granny's pet and Grandpa's pet, and was bound to be Teacher's pet, as well, the minute she started school (still clad, no doubt, in nappies).

Margaret mopped her face with a paper serviette. It was not that she was jealous – she despised jealousy not only as a vice but as a sign of unintelligence. Since equality in fate and fortune was obviously impossible, why waste time and energy deploring a basic fact of life? Politicians might strive to iron out gross discrepancies in healthcare and education, and all power to them – it was an admirable ideal. But no policy on earth could remove the flagrant differences in the upbringing of children, or decree that every baby in the land received its fair ration of 'pets'. And yet those very 'pets' were more crucial for people's future confidence – indeed their very happiness and desire to live at all – than any number of government handouts or social welfare schemes.

A squawk from the child at the adjoining table recalled her to the matter in hand: Clara's birthday present. Perhaps it would make more sense to open an account for her, paying in a substantial sum each year. Already, in her will (which she had drawn up after a cancer scare last summer), she had left most of her money to Rachael, as a way of expressing how much the relationship meant. Having a niece – and a great-niece – made her feel less alone in the world, and helped compensate for the fact that no suitable man had ever come along to give her children of her own.

Yes, the account was the perfect solution and would solve the present problem for many years to come. Although there was still Ted's birthday, just ten days after Clara's, and men were even trickier than babies. She gestured to the waitress, fumbled in her handbag for some change. It was no good sitting here idling her time away, when she should be in a men's-wear shop, choosing a tie or shirt or scarf. She owed a lot to Ted. He could easily have dismissed her as a boring spinster-aunt, instead of welcoming her so warmly; even trusting and respecting her.

She was lucky, extremely lucky in her almost-family.

Easing off her shoes, she rubbed her swollen feet. Despite the pain in her arches, she was glad she'd persevered, traipsing from men's department to men's department until, finally, she'd happened on a most distinctive sweater: softest cashmere in a subtle shade of blue. The cost had been prohibitive, but her 'nephew-in-law' was worth it. Then she had retraced her steps to Debenhams, to buy a silk scarf for Rachael. If Ted deserved a present, then her niece did even more so, despite the fact her actual birthday wasn't till next year. And finally she'd trekked the length of Oxford Street again, in search of a party-favour shop, so she could buy a few unusual trinkets for Clara's special day.

She had to admit she'd probably overdone it, walking so far in such ferocious heat. She did feel almost tearful now, but that was just her hormones playing up. The doctor had warned her that she might get 'weepy' as her oestrogen levels plummeted still further, but it would be criminal to cry when she had so much to be grateful for: a roof over her head, a steady job, and her basic health and strength.

She was also thrilled to be included in the party. Ted could well have put his foot down and told Rachael on the quiet, 'We don't want fossils like Aunt Margaret. Let's restrict it to our friends.' But no – there was her invitation flaunting on the mantelpiece. And the party, by the sounds of it, was going to be sensational. Rachael was making the cake herself, from pulverised almonds and hazelnuts (no 'poisonous' white sugar or unrefined white flour), and decorating it with silver bells and tiny porcelain figurines. And she'd bought everything in Clara's favourite colour – pink figurines, pink streamers, pink helium balloons, a pink fluffy bear for every tiny guest, and bunches of pink rosebuds on order from the florist. She had even hired a bubble machine to create a magical atmosphere: streams of bubbles jetting out in – yes, translucent pink. As for Clara's party frock, that was in a class of its own – a ravishing creation in ruffled silk (pink, of course), interleaved with pink embroidered ribbon, and complete with a pair of matching ruffled pants.

Margaret cast a judgemental eye on her frumpy khaki skirt, only now aware of how unflattering it looked. She would have to make an effort for the party, if only to be worthy of her great-niece, although she had no intention of splashing out on some new, expensive outfit. The less she spent on herself, the more would be left for Rachael, after her demise. Besides, however much she might primp and crimp, who would spare a glance for *her*?

Having put away her purchases, she limped along the passage to the bathroom. A warm bath would help her aching feet and, anyway, she was worried she might smell unpleasant after ten hot flushes in a row, the last exceptionally fierce. In fact, she was perspiring even now, in the small and sweltering bathroom, which often reached a temperature of eighty-five degrees, on account of the hot pipes that couldn't be turned off. She ran the bath, peeled off her sticky clothes, then climbed into the murky brownish water. The landlord had assured her that the peculiar colour was simply due to rust in the pipes, and wouldn't do the slightest harm. Rachael often urged her to find another flat, or at least invest in some bath-salts to turn the water blue, and some soothing plant-oil to moisturize her skin. But whereas Rachael believed in pampering, *she* had been taught it was selfish and remiss, and that baths were strictly functional affairs, whose overriding purpose was to remove basic dirt and grime, not sybaritic experiences that squandered time and money.

She closed her eyes, wincing against the pain in her spine. These sudden stabbing backaches seemed to come on every day now – perhaps another menopausal symptom. She already had most symptoms in the book, including drenching night-sweats that continually disrupted her sleep. The doctor had admitted that her case was extremely severe, yet it would be pointless and self-pitying to make a fuss about a few odd pains and sweats, when poor benighted souls were starving in Malawi or being tortured in Dafur. 'And, for heaven's sake,' she rebuked herself, 'you're only in your fifties. People of *ninety* have to cope, even when they're crippled with arthritis or half-blind from cataracts.'

She let herself drift off. There were chores to do, bills to pay, but they could wait a little longer. Right now she'd snatch a few minutes' peace and quiet before washing the net curtains and cleaning all the windows in the flat. 'Clean' was still her watchword – her long-dead mother saw to that.

'Happy birthday, my little love!' her father cooed, tenderly sponging her legs. The water was a bewitching shade of turquoise and scented with precious oils. She lolled back against his supportive arm as he soaped between her toes. The soap was perfumed too – a luxurious bar, marbled green and white.

'Who's Daddy's little treasure, then? Who's Daddy's favourite girl?'

She crowed in sheer delight. She had his unreserved attention, his undivided love. And Mummy was there, too, hovering beside him, waiting to swathe her in a nice warm fluffy towel. Yes, she could feel the cosy softness of the towel, and then the glorious sensation of warm fingers against her naked skin, as four adoring hands began to massage her whole body with some deliciously fragranced baby-salve. She allowed herself to squirm in sensuous pleasure. How wonderful it was to be free to move her limbs; not bound and shackled in tight, confining clothes.

Even when her parents slipped on the ruffled party frock, she was still perfectly at liberty to roll over on her back, kick her little legs, explore the tiny buttons with her fingers. There were no heavy, hampering fabrics; no hot, imprisoning shawl; no bulky nappies that chafed her tender skin; no jabbing pins or clammy plastic pants. And no one shouted, 'Keep *still*, you wretch!', every time she dared to wriggle or wave her hands about. In fact, the only words were those of approbation.

'You look absolutely enchanting, my sweet. The cutest little baby in the world.'

Praise could make you beautiful. The ugly, stupid baby had entirely disappeared, replaced by a sweet, shining pearl. And when Mummy carried her downstairs to meet the waiting guests, compliments and accolades flowed from every mouth, as all the grownups purred in admiration.

The whole room had been transformed, and solely in her honour, as if she were the most important person in the world. Sparkly pink balloons were suspended from the ceiling; pink and silver streamers looped along the walls, posies of pink rosebuds smiled from every surface, and beguiling pink-pearl bubbles drifted through the air, glinting as they caught the light. And the tablecloth was pink, of course, and all the plates and cups, and pink jellies glowed in pink glass bowls, beside enticing piles of snow-capped Turkish Delight. She didn't even have to sit on an uncomfortable high chair, but stayed safe on Mummy's lap, cradled in her arms; the focus of each doting adult eye. Daddy crouched beside her, feeding her with a silver spoon – not vulgar messes out of tins (boring, tasteless pap), but a host of delicacies. Morsels of choice chicken breast were popped between her lips, followed by slivers of best Dover sole, *soupçons* of Fish Pie Supreme and thimblefuls of asparagus mousse. The puddings were equally delicious: hazelnut pavlova, boysenberry ice-cream, and a blissful swirl of Greek Mountain Honey sorbet, served with damson coulis. Nor were the drinks forgotten. Daddy held her cup for her as she sipped Apricot Nectar and Elderflower Elixir, then Mummy offered her a smoothie made from puréed pawpaw and full-cream Jersey milk.

And now it was time for the birthday cake, which was shaped like a fairy palace and covered with pink roses and tiny silver bells. Daddy lit the big pink candle and helped her blow it out, and everybody clapped and told her she was a clever little girl. And although she ate three helpings, no one called her greedy, or slapped her because she'd made a mess. Even when she sucked her thumb or dribbled down her best pink frock, Mummy didn't raise her voice, let alone lash out.

The best was still to come, though. She had eaten so much, drunk so much, there was a pressing need for all that food and liquid to be voided. Yet the chamber pot, with its obnoxious smell and hard, unyielding rim, was nowhere to be seen. Nor was she being dangled rudely over it, terrified they'd drop her and she'd fall into that gaping, stinking trap. No, she was still snuggled close to Mummy, with Mummy's strong, consoling arms keeping her from harm. But, most wonderful of all – and the bliss of it was beyond the power of words – she was free to *be* a baby, for the first time in her life.

With a smile of total ecstasy, she closed her eyes, let go – allowed mousse and soufflé, pawpaw and pavlova to spurt and spatter out of her, cascading through the ruffles of her flimsy silken knickers, gushing through her flimsy dress, seeping on to Mummy's lap, soiling Mummy's clothes. But Mummy didn't leap up in disgust, or yell those hateful, hurting words that had thundered through her childhood: 'revolting', 'foul', 'repulsive', 'dirty', *'dirty'*.

Only at that very moment did she understand how exquisite 'dirty' was. For fifty-three rule-ridden years, she had been holding on, holding back, stoppered, throttled and bunged up, as she battened down her mind and body in an effort to stay 'clean'. All the pleasures barred to her in those caged and muzzled years were flooding back in torrents as she continued letting go, not just of cake and coulis; sorbet, sole and saffron sauce, but of restrictions and economies, prudery, rigidity, prohibitions, subjugation, penny-pinching, self-denial. Yet there was no punishment, no retribution. Her father hadn't gone storming out in fury, and – miracle of miracles – her mother simply sat and smiled, murmuring, 'Margaret, little Margaret, my own precious, darling pet.'

Paradise Lost

'Excuse me, dear, for bothering you, but I wondered if you were going to the Hackney Empire?'

Harriet looked up in surprise. The old woman sitting opposite looked ordinary enough, yet did she have physic powers?

'I mean, this *is* the train to Hackney, and I couldn't help but notice that you're reading *Paradise Lost*.'

Hardly 'reading', Harriet thought, reluctantly closing the book. All she'd done so far was scan the first page of the introduction. But the bony female was now leaning forward eagerly, obviously keen to engage in conversation.

'Don't you think it's *marvellous* that they're doing it at all? In the normal way, they put on rather low-grade stuff – musicals and comic shows and suchlike.'

'I'm afraid I wouldn't know. This is the first time I've ever been there.'

'Well, it's lucky that we've met then, because I can show you the way to the theatre. Actually, it's not far from the station, but if you don't know where you're going, it's easy to get lost.'

Harriet sat in silence. The way she felt today she didn't want the company of even her closest friends, let alone a stranger tagging on.

'My name's Avril,' the woman continued, reaching out a scrawny hand.

'I'm Harriet.'

'What a lovely name! My father was called Harry and he was a perfect gentleman. I was his favourite, to tell the truth. He never had time for my brother. But then people always say there's this special bond between fathers and daughters.'

A subject Harriet had no wish to explore. Dominic's two daughters had been the decisive factor in ending the relationship; their charm acting like a magnet and yanking him back home.

'And it was certainly true in *my* case. As far as Papa was concerned, I couldn't do a single thing wrong.'

And nor could Kim and Katie, as far as Dominic was concerned. His ten-year-old twins (blue-eyed, blonde-haired and precocious) combined the wisdom of Solomon with the beauty of Venus – in *his* eyes, anyway.

Avril had changed tack, thank God, and was now eyeing the tattered copy of *Paradise Lost*. 'I see you're reading the Penguin edition. I don't rate it quite as highly as the Longman's. The notes are rather sketchy, don't you think?'

'Oh, this is just the one we used at school. I kept all my set texts, even after I'd left. I suppose I hoped I'd read them again, but somehow I never got around to it. We only did Book One, in fact, and I can't remember much of it at all, so when I heard they were putting it on stage …' It was the title that had drawn her, as much as anything else. Having lost her own paradise, she could relate to fallen angels, fallen woman, banishment from Eden. Besides, she couldn't bear being stuck indoors on another lonely Saturday, pining over Dominic.

'You do realize it's an adaptation, don't you?' Avril said, still glancing at the book. 'As far as I remember, there are some ten thousand lines in the original poem, so they couldn't possibly include all that in just a couple of hours. I only hope they haven't truncated it too much. These modern directors are a law unto themselves. Ah, here we are – Hackney Central. Mind how you get out, dear. I missed my footing at Aldgate last week and almost took a tumble. And of course this rain makes things more treacherous.'

Having alighted with some difficulty, the woman spent several moments struggling with her umbrella, a tatty thing with two broken spokes, which looked as ancient as she did. Holding it lopsidedly above her, she glanced to left and right. 'This area's changed enormously, you know. In *my* young days, you'd see children walking barefoot in the street.'

'Look, I'm sorry, Avril,' Harriet said, not wishing to be rude, yet all too aware of the time. 'But it's already ten past two and I haven't got a ticket, so I ought to get my skates on.'

'You haven't got a ticket? Good gracious me! Supposing it's sold out?'

Unlikely, she thought. John Milton was hardly top of the pops, especially here in Hackney.

'Yes, you go on ahead, dear. I'll only hold you up. What you do is walk towards the Town Hall, then turn right into Mare Street. Don't cross the road. It's the same side as the station.'

'Thanks,' said Harriet, jogging briskly down the platform to the exit.

By the time she reached the Empire, she was drenched – although at least tickets weren't a problem. Not a single person was waiting at the box office and, once she entered the huge, ornate auditorium, it looked less than a quarter full. She pitied the poor actors, having to play to a near-empty house, then repeat the performance this evening, maybe again to a tiny audience.

She settled herself in a row towards the rear of the stalls, unoccupied apart from her. Avril was nowhere to be seen – perhaps sitting in the circle or the gods. There was no time to glance at the programme or at her copy of the text, since the house lights were already dimming and some music starting up. The stage looked bare and stark, with no scenery at all and no props except a small wooden chair. And when an actor emerged from the door at the back, he was dressed in tatty jeans and a grey hooded anorak, like some delinquent from a housing estate. She hadn't expected a modern-dress production, but presumably it cost much less and, judging by the tone of things so far, the company seemed severely short of funds.

The actor produced an apple, seemingly from nowhere, and began tossing it around, as if he were a juggler. Next he broke into a dance, his movements becoming faster and more frenzied, until he suddenly stopped dead. After a few minutes' edgy silence, he stepped forward and began to speak, and only at that moment did a frisson of excitement shudder through her body at the sound of his rich, resonant voice.

> Sing, heavenly Muse!
> Of Man's first disobedience, and the fruit
> Of that forbidden tree, whose mortal taste
> Brought death into our world and all our woe …

She recognized the words from school, although when Miss Hethrington recited them in her strangulated whimper, they had sounded different entirely. The actor's perfect modulation was in total contrast to his shabby, casual garb, but thrilling none the less. *Dominic* had a voice like that – velvet steeped in brandy – a voice that made the simplest phrase sound riveting, seductive.

'Concentrate!' she reproved herself. 'You've already missed a chunk.'

Concentration wasn't easy in her present state of mind, although certain words and phrases seemed to pierce her with an anguished personal charge.

No light, but rather darkness visible,
Where peace can never dwell, hope never come ...

Yes, peace and hope were strangers to her now, and there was a continual sense of choking darkness – even in the daytime, even in mid-August. The stage, too, was murky-dark, although all at once a black and scarlet Lake of Fire began flickering across it, engineered by light effects. A figure rose from the lake, clad in a dapper thirties suit in a shade of blatant purple that contrasted with his bottle-blonded curls. Only when he spoke did she realize it was Satan. A blond Satan in a three-piece suit! Shouldn't he be dressed in black, with a scaly tail and horns?

'Oh, how fallen,' he lamented, in a sonorous yet desolate voice. 'How changed ...'

The two words smote her heart. She, too, was changed and fallen. Instead of the bewitching days with Dominic, she now spent her time in tears; lying awake each and every night, aching to feel his warmth beside her. Continually she wondered what he was doing – now, for instance, at quarter to three on a Saturday afternoon. Well, she knew the answer to *that*: he'd be with his wife and daughters, of course, out together as a family. It was impossible to win against a family, or break marriage vows forged from steel. She had succeeded for a few forbidden months, until Dominic's increasing sense of guilt had dragged him back to home and fatherhood.

'Stop it!' she muttered under her breath. 'You're here to watch the play.'

A third actor was speaking now, also dressed in a natty suit – another devil, she gathered from his words.

> Too well I see and rue the dire event,
> That with sad overthrow and foul defeat
> Hath lost us Heaven ...

It *had* been heaven with Dominic. Never before had she met a man with his unusual mix of gifts: seriousness and wit, amazing sensitivity combined with scorching lust. Suddenly she realized she was crying – tears streaming down her face, unchecked. Through a blur and haze, she watched the fallen angels thronging the dark wastes of Hell. How could she not sympathize when she was locked in her own private hell?

At the interval, she escaped into the street outside, anxious to avoid Avril or indeed anyone who might comment on her red eyes and tear-stained face. Wandering up the road, she turned off into a quiet alleyway and stood leaning against a crumbling wall, seeking shelter from the persistent rain. If only Dominic were here, to share the play with her. Creatures like angels and devils, which to her seemed mere delusions – imaginary, fictitious beings – were for him completely real; indeed, part of his world view. Sinner he might be, but he had been brought up as a Catholic to believe in the most extraordinary things, like transubstantiation, resurrection from the dead, Jesus ascending bodily into heaven. Yet that strange and shining faith was part of his attraction, especially to an agnostic like herself. She longed to inhabit his transcendent world, a world in thrall to unseen powers, and pulsing with deep mystery. Even the strong line he took on abortion and euthanasia roused her admiration, despite the fact she didn't share his views. He was never afraid to speak his mind; never cared if he were mocked for believing every person had a soul. She didn't really understand the concept of a soul, but if Dominic had one, then she loved it as much as she loved his mind, his body and his cock.

Keeping her eye on the time, she waited till the very last moment to return to the theatre and slip into her seat, in case Avril was around. The stage was now draped with a peculiar green carpet, with brilliant-coloured flowers and fruits springing lushly out of it. And Adam and Eve were lying on that carpet, both unashamedly naked. She stared in fascination at Adam's penis. Was it semi-erect, or just exceptionally large? Eve's pubic hair also drew her eye: the thickest, darkest, springiest bush imaginable. The pair were utterly at ease – not a trace of embarrassment about their unclothed state. *She* had tried to be an Eve, when first alone with Dominic, desperate to overcome his scruples and her own doubts about her chances of attracting him. She had played the part of a brazen little sexpot, stripping off her clothes and pretending to a confidence she was far from really feeling.

'*No,*' he'd kept repeating, clearly struggling with his conscience. 'We *mustn't*, Harriet. You know I'm married.'

'Sssh,' she'd whispered, pressing her naked body right against his formal navy suit, so he could feel the fullness of her breasts; the pressure of her pubic bone thrust against his groin.

He continued to resist. His wife, she guessed, was prudish – the sort who insisted on undressing in the dark, and hated making love outside. So, the following week, she had lured him to the common, coaxed him to the ground, pushed her skirt up, let her hand stray teasingly down towards his zip.

'We *can't*! It's wrong, my sweet. In fact, as a Catholic, it's a very serious sin for me.'

It took another month – and a long drive to the coast, where they found their own secluded stretch of beach; the waves pounding, crashing, foaming, all around them. After this fall from grace, the former fervent Catholic seemed to lose all trace of conscience and want only to repeat the 'serious sin'. Once, they even made love in his own garden, the week his wife and daughters were away, although at first he objected vehemently.

She shut her eyes, hearing those objections gradually change to cries of pleasure. That day, he'd become a pagan out and out, tickling her nipples with long, soft, feathery grasses, scattering her with petals, passing strawberries from his mouth to hers.

> Besides the Eastern gate of Paradise,
> Betwixt two rocky pillars, Gabriel sat ...

She jumped at a new voice on stage, opening her eyes to see two magnificent angels, dressed in shimmering golden robes and with huge white-feathered wings. Their costumes were so superior to the rest, they had clearly been designed to give these heavenly beings in-built power and majesty, and visibly distinguish them from others in the cast. She continued gazing at the pair, wondering if angels were male or female or something in between. Their voices were deep baritones, their faces strangely androgynous, but their rippling, waist-length, golden locks lent them a distinctly feminine air. It was their wings, however, that intrigued her most of all; wings ethereal and solid both at once, rearing up from their shoulders to form resplendent pinions, poised for flight. If only she and Dominic had wings, so they could soar away together, lift off to a different realm – a realm devoid of obligations, daughters – a shining, selfish Heaven where they could transport themselves eternally.

'Ah, *there* you are!' Avril enthused, bustling over to Harriet as she tried to slip unnoticed from the theatre. 'I searched for you at the interval, but I couldn't see you anywhere. But what a stroke of luck to bump into you again. I presume you're going to the station?'

Harriet nodded, annoyed at being forced to walk at the woman's snail-like pace.

'Well, did you enjoy the play or not, dear?'

Harriet searched for words. 'Enjoy' was too feeble a one for the elation it had roused in her – elation at the brilliant acting and awe-inspiring verse – but elation doused with deep despair. Eve had been banished and left Paradise in tears, but she'd still had Adam with her, to share her future pain. How different from her *own* fate: ejected and excluded from even the smallest scrap of Dominic's life.

'I must admit I had my reservations. And the nudity was shocking! In my opinion, there should have been a warning. I mean, full frontal nudity is offensive to a lot of people, including religious folk. Two Muslims sitting next to me actually walked out in protest.'

'Really?' If Avril objected to simple nakedness, how censorious she would be about a predatory girl like her trying deliberately to wreck a marriage; putting her own base desires above the interests of two ten-year-olds. Any decent person would condemn such callousness. She'd been seriously at fault – there was no escaping the fact – yet only the play had made her see it.

'But I did think it was ingenious when the angel handed Adam and Eve those two suitcases of clothes and they put on modern business suits – shirt and tie for Adam, blouse and skirt for Eve. That made it very relevant to society today, reminding us we can still do wrong, and must take the consequences.'

'Indeed.'

'You're very quiet, dear,' Avril observed. 'Are you feeling all right?'

'Yes, fine,' she muttered tonelessly. She was a shameless, scheming little bitch, who deserved everything she'd got.

She sat on the edge of her bed, clutching her stomach as a wave of nausea shuddered through her body. Her own stupid fault, of course, for using whisky as a sleeping-draught. Normally she never touched the stuff. Scotch was *Dominic's* tipple. It hadn't even worked. Here she was at 2 a.m., still churningly awake, and with a splitting headache on top of everything else.

She stumbled to the bathroom, swallowed a couple of aspirin, took a gulp of Listerine to remove the foul taste in her mouth, then groped her way back to bed. She knew she wouldn't sleep, wrestling as she was with guilt, as well as grief and loss. Her sense of shame had doubled after reading more of *Paradise Lost*, on the long journey home from Hackney. She had gathered from Book IV (which they'd never done at school) that Milton came down really hard on what he termed 'adulterous lust', comparing it with married love, which he saw as 'pure' and 'blessed', and clearly the only type of sex he would ever countenance. At first, she had fumed with indignation. Why should the skewed ideas of a seventeenth-century prig have any credence now? Yet when she closed the book, his words continued to echo in her mind, filling the small flat with reproaches, accusations. She had indeed dragged Dominic from a sacred marriage-bed, to engage in casual couplings in hotel rooms and parks. And, even now, she couldn't accept his return to Faith and family, but kept hoping he'd relent. If she had any sense of decency, she would honour the fact that, as a highly moral man, he had to follow what he saw as right, and not tempt him from that path again.

'It's *over*,' she said out loud, staring into the darkness. 'I give him up. For ever. He belongs at home. With his family.'

Tears sprang into her eyes, but she dashed them angrily away. She had cried enough, for God's sake, and, in any case, the whole thing was her fault. Indeed, if she lay awake tonight, as she had done for the last seven weeks, that was simply her due punishment.

Closing her eyes, she made a conscious effort to distract herself: recited the dates of battles, ran through the names of birds and flowers. Useless. Every battle, every bird and flower began with the word Dominic. Too bad. She would learn, in time, to reprogramme her mind.

All at once, she was aware of a faint rustle in the room. Please God, not mice, she prayed – she was terrified of mice. But surely they wouldn't infest her flat, when she never left food about and kept the place so clean. Nervously she squinted through her eyelids, gasping at what she saw. There, within touching distance, were the two angels from the play – or something remarkably similar – dressed in dazzling silver robes and with long, lustrous, silky hair. One was sitting on her bed, the other hovering over the chest of drawers, their huge white-feathered wings arching up above them, filling all the available space.

She stared in mute astonishment. Was this some sort of hallucination, or was she actually asleep and dreaming? She pinched herself, registered the pain. Of *course* she wasn't asleep. She had been counting every dragging minute since she'd first gone to bed at midnight. Besides, these angels were so tangible – living, breathing presences, as real as any human, yet with some mysterious quality that transcended the material world. Admittedly, the room was dim, with only a soft glow from the bedside lamp, but, even so, she could make out every detail: the diaphanous, glittery fabric of their garments, the golden sheen of their hair, the extraordinary translucence of their faces, which seemed to shine like lamps themselves.

Neither of the angels spoke – there seemed no need for words – and she herself lay silent, astonished by her own composure. Trapped as she was, with angels closing in on her, shouldn't she be rigid with fear and desperate to escape? Yet far from feeling threatened, all her recent agitation (remorse, regret and anguish) had somehow drained away, and she was aware of a deep sense of peace spreading through her body. The sickness in her stomach and jagged pains in her head had both disappeared entirely, as if those powerfully protective wings were healing and consoling her, enfolding her in a sheltering embrace. Her breathing gradually deepened and the feeling of tranquillity began stealing through the room. She could feel her eyelids closing, her body drifting down. These angels had brought the gift of sleep and would watch over her till morning.

She woke with a start, reaching out automatically to switch off the alarm. There *was* no alarm. It was Sunday and singularly quiet – no shrilling clock, no drone of traffic, no sound from the flat above. She peered at the time. Impossible! It *couldn't* be nearly noon. How on earth could she have slept for nine and three-quarter hours, when normally she tossed and turned all night?

Only then did she remember the angels. *Angels*! Was she mad? Now, in the broad light of day, the whole idea of a heavenly visitation seemed utterly absurd. Did she really believe that two supernatural beings would deign to call on her in Muswell Hill? It must have been the whisky, or the effects of drink and aspirin mixed, or perhaps a sort of mental aberration after so long a spell of grief, coupled with the pangs of guilt brought on by the play. Today she must take herself in hand – bin the rest of the whisky, start eating decent food again, go for a run in the park, catch up with her friends.

She swung her legs out of bed, took a decisive step towards the wardrobe to unearth her running shoes, only to stop, astounded, in mid-stride. There, on the bedroom carpet, lay a long white shimmering feather. Unnerved, she picked it up. It was far too large to be a bird's, even a substantial bird like an ostrich or a swan. Never in her life had she seen a feather of that size and shape – except on those angels last night. So *had* they been here, in her room? She'd already dismissed the thought as totally far-fetched; now she was less sure. They had, in fact, seemed extraordinarily authentic – not mere tricks of the light – although with that sublime, unearthly character no words could truly describe. Unearthly or not, one of their feathers had landed on her floor, and that peculiar circumstance required some explanation.

She shook her head, to clear it; ran through her twelve-times-table, to check that her brain was functioning. Yes, everything in perfect working order. She might have been prey to fantasies in the middle of the night, or trapped in some weird dream-state, but now it was midday, for heaven's sake, and she wasn't even tired – instead awake, alert and remarkably refreshed. Nor were her eyes deceiving her. Light was flooding into the room, making every object clear and sharp, including the long, white feather she was holding in her hand.

Totally mystified, she sank down on the bedroom stool, needing time to think. Angels were real for *Dominic*, of course, as real as his wife and children. And she respected his intelligence – indeed, he was one of the cleverest men she'd ever met. So suppose he was right and she wrong? That would mean that angels *could* exist; that Gabriel and Raphael could actually have been here – and been here with a purpose. A jolt of wild elation lasered through her mind. If they had come to comfort her (and there hadn't been a word of rebuke, nor an echo of the punishment meted out to Eve), could she be as rotten as she feared – a marriage-wrecker, child-harmer, a selfish, worthless bitch? Why should she follow Milton's line on adultery and lust? He was a strict, self-righteous Puritan, and so bound to take a jaundiced view of sex. Anyway, it was *Dominic* who mattered, not a patriarchal poet who'd been dead 300 years. And with angels on her side, wasn't there a tiny chance that Dominic would change his mind, see her in a different light, even regard their relationship as blessed?

Racing to the sitting-room, she grabbed the phone and dialled his secret number – the one he kept exclusively for her. She hadn't used it for seven endless weeks, but he was sure to pick her message up within an hour or so. She spoke urgently, triumphantly, the words tumbling over each other, barely making any sense.

Sense would have to wait. All she knew at present was that, with the angels' help, Paradise could be regained.

The Biggest Female in the World

'Edwin!'

He tensed. In his friends' mouths or his parents', his name sounded bland enough – an innocuous, obliging name – so why, when Roza used it, did it become an offensive weapon?

'*Edwin!*'

'No,' he said to no one. 'Not here. Gone away. Missing person. AWOL.'

'Edwin, where in God's name *are* you? Can't you come when I call?'

Reluctantly he dragged himself up to the sickroom. Whereas the majority of invalids shrank and paled and faded, Roza had swollen to twice her normal size, and her usual sallow complexion was now a wrathful shade of red.

Steeling himself, he opened the bedroom door. Yes, there she was, his so-called other half, lolling back imperiously against a pile of crumpled pillows. When they'd first married, it had made some sort of sense to talk in terms of 'halves', since they'd been roughly equal in the roles they played and the space they occupied. But over the last thirty-seven years, she had gradually expanded, in influence as well as size, until she dominated the house and garden (and the entire street, as well, he feared, when she bellowed from her open window, to summon him in from his vegetable patch).

'Edwin, I may be ill, but I'm not actually dead – not yet anyway. Which means I need food and drink at regular intervals throughout the day.'

He cleared his throat. Even his voice had a tendency to dwindle when chivvied by her louder one. 'But I brought you breakfast only an hour ago.'

'Breakfast? Call that breakfast? One piece of toast – and burnt at that!'

'Roza, you asked for toast, and you specifically said you wanted just one slice.'

'I didn't ask for *burnt* toast.'

He sighed. The sigh surprised him by its faintness. The way he felt, it should have been a force-ten gale. 'There's something wrong with the toaster.'

'What d'you mean, "something wrong"? Any normal husband would fix it.'

'Any normal husband would throw it out. It's in terminal decline.'

'Well, go and buy a new one – *now*!'

'But I thought you said you were hungry ...'

'I *am* hungry, Edwin. Which is hardly surprising when you keep me on starvation rations. I'd like a lightly poached egg – *lightly*, did you hear? Not that bullet of a thing you served up yesterday.'

'OK.' He glanced at the flotsam spreading like a dirty tide right across the counterpane: damp tissues, chocolate wrappers, dog-eared magazines, abandoned bits of knitting, a bag of barley sugar. She had long since taken possession of the queen-sized double bed; he banished to the lumpy spare-room couch. And, had he still been sleeping with her, he would be forced, by her colossal size, to lie on the extreme outside edge, in danger of falling off. It was the same with both the wardrobes – crammed and stuffed with *her* clothes, while his hung squashed and gasping at the very end of the rail. And, in the bulging chest of drawers, his puny socks and paltry underpants lay vanquished by her vast pink interlock bloomers, her heavy, clammy nightgowns and fearsome whalebone corsets.

'And a decent cup of tea, mind. Make sure you warm the pot first, and put in three heaped spoonfuls.'

'Roza, I do know how to make tea.'

'Really? I can't say that I've noticed.' She heaved herself up to a sitting position, her pendulous bosom wobbling as she moved.

Deliberately he averted his gaze. On their wedding day, she'd had breasts like little peaches, ripe and full, but small. Now they'd metamorphosed to pumpkins, which, entered for a gardening contest, would have easily won 'Biggest in the Show'. Once, he could hold a whole peach in his mouth. Now, should he try, he'd be instantly asphyxiated.

'Edwin, are you *listening*? When you bring the tray up, could you bring my glasses, too – my second pair, in the navy leather case? And you'd better do the shopping before everything's sold out.'

'It's precisely five past nine, Roza. The shops are hardly open yet.'

'And drop in at Taylor's, will you, so tomorrow's toast isn't cremated like this morning's. I know it's quite a trek, but …'

A good mile, he muttered under his breath, and most of that uphill.

'Oh, and by the way—' Her words were drowned in a protracted fit of coughing.

'What?' he asked, once the chesty, phlegmy, rasping sounds had gradually subsided.

'Are we out of cat-food?'

'Cat-food?' he repeated. They didn't *have* a cat; owned no pets at all. Please God, he prayed, with a sudden sense of dread, let this not be the first sign of dementia. Cancer was one thing, Alzheimer's another. 'Why,' he asked, struggling to stay calm, 'should we want cat-food?'

'Why not?' she said, with an air of such authority he immediately doubted his own mental equilibrium. *Did* they have a cat? And he'd somehow overlooked the fact? Was *he* the one losing his grip on reality? 'OK,' he murmured weakly. 'I'll put it on the shopping list.'

Returning from the village, he took a detour to the churchyard, craving its peace like a tranquillizing drug. In that hallowed spot, his cares seemed left behind – no one complaining save the ghosts and spectres; no one squawking save the crows. He was glad to see his favourite bench was empty, although a man was working just nearby – a gardener, by the looks of it, or perhaps some chappie from the council, sent to tidy up the place.

'Good day,' said Edwin, offloading his piles of shopping on to the bench. Carrying three heavy bags had left red weals on his wrists.

'Good day,' the fellow mumbled.

Edwin sank down on the seat. Few days were good for him, in fact, with Roza in her present state. However, surrounded by these silent graves and quiet, well-mannered yews, he felt his spirits lift. The heat of the sun was tempered here by the shade of kindly trees and by cool, green, soothing, velvety moss embroidering grey stone. The dead were perfect company; made no demands and didn't answer back. Well, he'd better make the most of it. Once he got home, there'd be demands and taunts enough. The new toaster was bound to be wrong, for a start – too small, too big, too shoddy, too expensive, a dreadful colour, a ridiculous shape …

He glanced at the man again: a wiry fellow, with a balding, sunburned pate, and a fuzz of sandy hair glinting on his arms. 'Lovely weather,' he ventured, grateful for some company other than his wife's. She had long since driven all their friends away.

'Bit too hot for this lark,' the chap responded, pausing for a moment and leaning on his spade.

'What is it you're doing?'

'You may well ask! The Reverend gave me orders, but he's expecting the impossible. He might as well have told me to raise these buggers from the dead.'

In his mind, Edwin saw creaky, creepy skeletons start pushing up their headstones and go staggering about. 'Why? What's the problem?' he asked.

'*This* stuff!' The man pointed to a ragged clump of bushes, as tall as he was himself.

'What is it?' Edwin had never been one for Nature Study. Roza invariably mocked him because he couldn't tell a primrose from a celandine.

'Japanese knotweed. Or Big Trouble, as I call it!'

'Oh yes, I've heard of knotweed! In fact, it came up on *Gardeners' Question Time* just the other week. Bit of a bother, they were saying.'

'Bit of a bother? A fucking menace, more like! Pardon my French, but it's nothing but an alien – a sodding great invader that's taking over the country and spreading like wildfire.'

'It looks harmless enough,' Edwin observed, peering more closely at the glossy leaves and delicate clusters of creamy-coloured flowers.

'*Harmless*! We're talking Hitler and Stalin, with Pol Pot thrown in as well. Except all knotweed plants are female, in Europe anyway. So if you can imagine a female Stalin—' He broke off with a humourless laugh, mopping the sweat from his forehead. 'The damned stuff grows so fast, it kills off almost every other plant – not just fragile things like bluebells, but even prickly hawthorns. And the older it gets, the bigger it becomes. In fact, I've heard it called the biggest female in the world, in terms of the total land-mass it takes up.' With a grimace of distaste, he started jabbing with his spade again, trying to dislodge the tangled roots. 'You may find this hard to believe, mate, but if you collected up all the knotweed in one small town like Truro, it would weigh as much as thirty-three Blue Whales! And it's not just England that's affected. The sodding thing has spread all over the world – Canada, the United States, Australia, New Zealand – you name it. They're all fighting back, of course, chucking billions down the drain in an effort to root it out, but they're totally deluded imagining they'll succeed. And the vicar's just as bad. With all due respect to the Reverend, he's talking utter balls. Clear it all out, he tells me. Fine for him – *he* believes in miracles. And you'd need a bloody miracle to get rid of even this amount.'

'You seem to be doing fairly well.'

'Don't kid yourself. I could spend all week here, slashing it to pieces or spraying it with chemicals, and it'll still spring up again. Some people inject pesticides right into the stems, but even that's a waste of time. You see, underneath the soil, is this bloody great rhizome system, which extends sideways twenty feet or more, and goes down really deep. And it keeps throwing up new shoots, so even if I cut it back' – he demonstrated with a swingeing attack – 'and continue every day like this until I'm fucking blue in the face, it'll still defeat me in the end. Nothing seems to stop it, not composting, or burning, or burying it deep underground. It can even regrow, for heaven's sake, if you put it through a shredder!'

'Dear, dear,' said Edwin, sighing on his own account as well as on the gardener's. What he'd hoped would be a pleasant chat had turned into a rant. And the fellow showed no sign of stopping, punctuating his tide of words with further angry lashes at the plant.

'What's absolutely baffling is that it'll put up with conditions that would kill any other species – air pollution, acid soil, contamination with heavy metals – it survives the bloody lot. It can even break through paving stones or tarmac, or between bricks in a ruddy great wall. And, believe it or not, it's been known to pop up in people's living-rooms, having worked its way through the foundations of the house!'

Edwin shook his head, tight-lipped. If *he* kept quiet, perhaps the tirade would abate.

'And that's not all. You can be landed with a dirty great fine if you cause the thing to take root in the wild. Just chuck a bit on a rubbish-tip and you'll be coughing up five grand. And it's no good saying you can't pay, because then they'll bang you up in gaol. Yeah, two fucking years in Wormwood Scrubs, not for rape or murder, but for being a bit careless with a plant!'

'*Shocking*!' Edwin murmured, picking up his shopping bags and beating a hasty retreat. His cemetery-oasis had become a little too like home: a loud, petulant voice haranguing him with a stream of endless complaints.

'But you *told* me to get cat-food!'

'Nonsense! Why should we want cat-food when we don't have a cat?'

Why indeed? He stared down uneasily at the tins of Rabbit Chunks in Jelly. 'Don't worry – I'll give it to the Lloyds at number six.'

'What, waste good money on that flea-ridden creature they have the cheek to call a Persian? Over my dead body! No, you can take it back – this instant.'

'Roza, I'm not going out again. It's boiling hot and I'm deadbeat as it is.'

'Well, tomorrow, then.' She glanced accusingly at the bedside clock. 'It's way past lunchtime, Edwin. Did you get the fish?'

'What fish?'

'I asked for a nice piece of plaice.'

'Roza, I'd swear on the holy Bible that you didn't mention plaice. And anyway the fish-shop closed down months ago. I've told you that enough times.'

In resentful silence, she continued to unpack the shopping, laying out each item on the counterpane. She always insisted that he bring the bags upstairs, along with the receipts, of course, so she could cast her judgemental eye on every purchase, and complain about its price. 'On *no*! Vanilla yoghurt. You know I hate vanilla. I put strawberry on the list.'

'They didn't have the strawberry. In any case, you went berserk when I bought strawberry mousse last week.' He was aware of his stomach rumbling audibly. In his efforts to meet Roza's demands, there was little time to grab a bite himself.

'Edwin, I did *not*! It was the peach I didn't like. It tasted like distemper. *And* it cost a bomb – three times as much as Eden Vale.'

'OK, OK, I'll get the strawberry tomorrow, and I'll make sure it's Eden Vale.'

'And what about today? There's little enough to look forward to, without being deprived of dessert.'

'Maybe I could make a …' He broke off in mid-sentence as the gardener's phrases suddenly re-echoed in his head: a menace, an invader, killing off all other species… the older it gets, the bigger it becomes…. the biggest female in the world … you just can't keep it down … nothing seems to stop it … puts up with things that would destroy any normal plant – chemicals, contamination, burning.

How extraordinarily apt! *Roza* had survived all those grotesque cancer treatments, bouncing boldly back again even after they'd cut her open (twice), poisoned her with chemo, attacked her with radiotherapy, burned her, slashed her, bombarded her with drugs. And she'd had *other* operations; other, previous illnesses, and come through them all unscathed. She even used to smoke, for heaven's sake – sixty a day for over twenty years, and it had done no lasting damage, just left her with a cough. Frailer souls would have withered long ago. *She* was indestructible.

'Make a *what*?' she asked. 'I don't want any more of that disgusting semolina, thank you very much.'

'Well, how about a…?' Yes, that chap on *Gardeners' Question Time* – Bob Flowerdew, wasn't it? – said knotweed, when first introduced, had been highly prized as an ornamental plant. And Roza, too, had been ornamental, way back in her youth – pretty and vivacious, and certainly highly prized. And although she'd been born in England, she came from foreign stock – not Japanese, of course, but definitely exotic, with a Hungarian father and Polish mother, which to him had seemed romantic in the extreme. Even her name intrigued him, with its gypsy ring and that tantalizing 'z'. But what had really clinched it for him was the amazing shoes she wore. Most women in the village clomped about in wellingtons or brogues (and his mother lived in slippers), but Roza owned these sexy scarlet stilettos, with incredible four-inch heels. Once, when they were courting, they'd gone out for a picnic and, jumping up impetuously to brush cake crumbs from her skirt, she had accidentally trodden on his hand. As her stiletto heel jabbed deep into his palm, the thrill of that exquisite pain had made him fall to his knees and propose.

Even as he spoke, he had blushed at his temerity. She'd refuse – of course she would. The fact she had spared so much as a glance for a weedy, red-haired stripling, with a tendency to stammer, was something of a miracle. So why push his luck, for pity's sake?

She *hadn't* refused – which left him lost for words, although so thrilled at his good fortune he'd shot up a good two foot, and spent all day gazing smugly down at smaller, lesser folk. Gradually, however, his trophy had turned tyrant, blighting the land, killing off the native flora, stifling any weaker plants that shared her habitat.

'Edwin, I wish you'd finish your sentences. *What* is it you're planning to make?'

'A ... a ...' He cast about for a suitable dessert. 'A trifle,' he said lamely.

'You've never made a trifle in your life! Besides, we'd need sponge cakes and sherry, and I don't see either here.' With a last poke around the shopping bags, she collapsed back against the pillows in another fit of coughing.

'I could make c...c...custard,' he offered, his teenage stammer suddenly returning as he watched the rampant knotweed work its way through the foundations of the house; emerge through solid concrete, push between the bricks; rampage through every room in a plethora of intransigent shoots and stems. He stood helpless, hapless, as it began colonizing the garden, overrunning his dahlias, swamping his precious marrows and courgettes. Next, it swept on up the street, covering all the village in its tenacious, tangled web, then shooting onwards and upwards as it ravaged the whole country, tunnelling under motorways, resisting any attacker, smothering all native vegetation. Nor did it stop at the British Isles, but stampeded on to Europe, then Canada, the United States,

Australia, New Zealand, until no other living, breathing thing was left in the entire universe.

'Custard!' she mocked, her voice a vast primeval roar, rising from the drowned and stifled planet. 'No *thank* you!'

Blinded by tears, he picked his way between the tombstones, stumbling on the uneven path and all but tripping over tussocks of grass. Stopping by the newest grave (which still looked cruelly raw), he reached out his arms imploringly.

'Roza, *speak* to me, I beg you!'

Silence. Only the mocking crows, cawing in derision.

He glanced behind him at the empty patch where, less than seven months ago, the thicket of knotweed had flourished in defiance. Not a stick of it was left; not so much as a scant twig or fallen leaf. Yet the gardener had insisted that nothing could defeat it; that it invariably sprang up again, surviving all destruction, outwitting even death.

Gazing at the granite headstone, he fixed his full attention on her name: 'Roza, beloved wife of ...' If he willed her return with enough determination, might she not force her way out of the coffin (he'd bought the most expensive in the book: solid oak, with real brass fittings), push up that heavy stone, and stride out in her grave-clothes to rejoin him? She would reproach him, of course, but the sound of her complaining voice would be healing music now.

'Fancy getting solid oak! Just think of the expense! You should have gone for a veneer and saved yourself a fortune. And that appalling wreath, on top of everything else! You know I can't abide carnations. And why *yellow* ones, for pity's sake? And as for ...'

Without her, he was paralysed; the whole house at a standstill. No foodstuffs in the larder, no milk or fruit juice in the fridge, no soap in the bathroom, no toilet-rolls, no Vim. How could he go shopping when no one made the shopping lists; no one gave him orders; no one told him what to wear and when to get his hair cut? It straggled round his shoulders now, its once ardent red faded to a dingy grey. And his shirt was, frankly, filthy. He had always done the washing in obedience to her orders, switching on the machine the minute she decreed. He had washed and ironed, shopped and cooked, scrubbed and scoured – a willing, happy parasite clinging to his host-plant. But now that the host-plant was defunct, *he* had perished with her. For thirty-seven years she had powered him with her energy, swept him along on the tide of her convictions, set the pattern of his days by issuing commands. Without her, there was no reason to get up.

Making one last desperate effort, he crawled on hands and knees right over to the gravestone and beat with anguished fists on the unyielding, callous granite. 'Come back,' he entreated, 'and save me.'

He strained his ears to listen. Not a whisper. Not a sound. Only the church bells tolling forth again – mournfully, regretfully, as they announced yet another death.

Scrambling to his feet, he blundered out of the churchyard. Those specious bells were lying. Death *wasn't* final, *wasn't* irreversible. Some species were so powerful, they could re-emerge from its apparent lethal grip; break through tarmac, break through concrete, break through solid oak, indeed. If he went back home, he'd find her – restored to youth as well as resurrected – his little foreign beauty, his highly prized, exotic bride, with her small, ripe, perfect breasts. And of *course* he'd let her trample him beneath her – she only had to ask – so long as she made sure she did it with those sexy, scarlet, sensational high heels.